# ALSO BY BARBARA MICHAELS . . .

**The Master of Blacktower**: His dark eyes blazed with bitterness, and his mocking laughter echoed across the Scottish estate. Gavin Hamilton terrified young Damaris—but now her very fate lies in his hands . . . "Simply the *best* living writer of ghost stories and thrillers."
—Marion Zimmer Bradley

**The Wizard's Daughter**: In a Victorian mansion filled with haunting secrets, an orphan girl learns the chilling truth about her father—and herself . . . "Barbara Michaels can always be counted on." —*Ocala Star-Banner*

**Houses of Stone**: The lost masterpiece of a long-dead poet leads English professor Karen Halloway into the ghostly thrall of obsession . . . "I wouldn't have missed this for anything . . . Barbara Michaels has surpassed herself."
—Phyllis A. Whitney

**Patriot's Dream**: In Williamsburg, Virginia, Jan Wilde's dreams reveal the fires of war and the fury of passion—and a stranger who calls to her from two centuries past . . . "A tour de force!" —*Oregon Journal*

**Vanish With the Rose**: A lawyer's search for her brother leads to a vast estate—and secrets hidden in the shadows of a rose garden . . . "I loved the book, every page and every character." —Alexandra Ripley

**Greygallows**: Trusting a mysterious Baron, Lucy followed him to his magnificent home—and stepped into a web of betrayal and danger . . . "Masterful and fresh, yet terrifying." —*Gothic Journal*

**The Walker in Shadows**: The house next door stood empty for years. But now it was coming to life—with a haunted love that refused to die . . . "Has a chilling touch of the supernatural." —*Orlando* (FL) *Sentinel*

(continued . . . )

**Into the Darkness**: Inheriting an antique jewelry business brings Meg Venturi closer to a handsome stranger—and to the truth behind a dark legacy. "Barbara Michaels . . . at her best . . . Solid gold with lots of diamonds."
—*Courier-Gazette* (Rockland, ME)

**Black Rainbow**: A young governess is drawn into a world of frightening deception and dark obsession—in a house as mysterious as its master. "Sprightly gothic romance-suspense . . . with an especially dandy final twist."
—*Kirkus Reviews*

**Wait for What Will Come**: A mansion loomed by the stormy seas of Cornwall, waiting for a young woman to claim her inheritance. Waiting to claim her as its own . . . "A master!" —*Library Journal*

**Smoke and Mirrors**: Amidst the world of Washington politics, a campaign worker's enthusiasm turns to dread in a maze of deadly games . . . "Another surefire winner!"
—*Publishers Weekly*

**Witch**: It was the house of her dreams and the start of a new life. But had Ellen buried her past? Or had her nightmare just begun? "This author never fails to entertain."
—*Cleveland Plain Dealer*

**Sons of the Wolf**: Across the misty moors, a heart of darkness is unveiled by the light of the moon . . . "This writer is ingenious." —*Kirkus Reviews*

**Someone in the House**: Historic Grayhaven Manor was the subject of their research, but Anne and Kevin found their work overshadowed—by a compelling force of dark desire . . . "Michaels has a fine sense of atmosphere and story-telling." —*New York Times*

**The Crying Child**: Trapped between madness and danger, a grieving mother hears her child's anguished cries—from somewhere deep within the night . . . "Michaels has a fine, downright way with the supernatural."
—*San Francisco Chronicle*

**The Sea King's Daughter**: By the shore of a Greek island, ancient secrets come to life . . . "[A] master of romantic suspense." —*Mystery Scene*

**Search the Shadows**: An Egyptologist digs into her past and discovers a tainted bloodline within the chilling shadows of a crypt. "**The suspense lingers until the final pages . . .**" —*Booklist*

**Wings of the Falcon**: The ghostly horseman appeared from out of the shadows. He was known only as the Falcon—and Francesca knew he had come for her . . . "**We admit to being hooked!**" —*Denver Post*

**Prince of Darkness**: A mysterious Englishman captures the heart of a small town—and ensnares it in his web of terrifying secrets. "**Gripping.**" —*Boston Herald Traveler*

**Shattered Silk**: The owner of a vintage clothing shop comes face to face with terror—and a killer who would stop at nothing . . . "**Superior . . . *Shattered Silk* glitters!**" —*Kirkus Reviews*

**Ammie, Come Home**: A seance turns from a lighthearted party game into a force of pure terror . . . "**Michaels is a specialist. When the seances get going and the ghosts walk (and talk), even nonbelievers take notice.**" —*New York Times*

**Be Buried in the Rain**: On a decaying family plantation, the dark eyes of the past keep their watch . . . "**An aura of sinister intrigue that will keep the reader spellbound!**" —*Library Journal*

**The Dark on the Other Side**: The house talked: Linda Randolph could hear it. And its insistent whispers told her a story of unimaginable madness . . . "**Spine-tingling.**" —*New Haven Register*

# HOUSE OF
# MANY SHADOWS

# BARBARA
# MICHAELS

**B**
BERKLEY BOOKS, NEW YORK

HOUSE OF MANY SHADOWS

A Berkley Book / published by arrangement with
the author

PRINTING HISTORY
Dodd, Mead edition published 1974
Berkley edition / February 1996

The Putnam Berkley World Wide Web site address is
http://www.berkley.com

ISBN: 0-425-15189-1

BERKLEY®
Berkley Books are published by The Berkley Publishing Group,
200 Madison Avenue, New York, New York 10016.
BERKLEY and the "B" design
are trademarks belonging to Berkley Publishing Corporation.

PRINTED IN THE UNITED STATES OF AMERICA

10  9  8  7  6  5  4  3  2  1

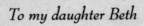

*To my daughter Beth*

# Chapter 1

The sounds bothered Meg most. Calling them auditory hallucinations helped a little—a phenomenon is less alarming when it has a proper, technical name. Meg had always thought of hallucinations as something one saw. She had those too, but for some illogical reason it was easier for her to accept visual illusions as nonreal than to ignore the hallucinatory sounds. When you were concentrating on typing a letter, and a voice said something in your ear, it was impossible not to be distracted.

The problem was hard to explain, and Meg wasn't doing a good job of explaining. But then it had always been difficult to explain anything to Sylvia. Sylvia knew all the answers.

Meg tried again.

"The dictaphone was absolutely impossible. I couldn't hear what Mr. Phillips had said. Voices kept mumbling, drowning out his voice. Once the whole Mormon Tabernacle Choir cut out the second paragraph of a very important memo."

She smiled as she spoke. It sounded funny now, but at the time it had not been at all amusing.

Sylvia didn't smile. "The Mormon Tabernacle Choir? Why them?"

Meg shrugged helplessly. "No reason. That's the point; they are meaningless hallucinations. The doctor says they'll go away eventually, but in the meantime. . . . Mr. Phillips was very nice about it, he said he'd try to find an opening for me when I'm ready to work again, but I couldn't expect him to keep me on. I had to listen to some of those tapes three times before I got the message clear, and there was always the chance I'd miss something important. And I'd already used up all my sick leave. Three weeks in the hospital . . ."

"You should be thankful you weren't killed," said Sylvia. "To think they never caught the man who was driving the car! New York is an absolute jungle. I don't know how you can stand living here. May I have another cup of tea?"

Meg poured, biting back an irritated retort. She couldn't afford to offend Sylvia, especially now, when she was about to ask a favor, but the clichés that were Sylvia's sole means of communication had never annoyed her more. Why should she be thankful she hadn't been killed? She might just as well be thankful she didn't have leprosy, or seven-year itch; or thank God because she had not been born with two heads. It was just as reasonable, and a lot more human, to feel vexation instead of gratitude. Why me, God? The old question, to which there was never any answer. . . . Why did it have to be me in the path of that fool driver; why did I have to land on my head instead of some less vulnerable part of my anatomy; and why, oh, why, God, did I have to have these exotic symptoms instead of a nice simple concussion? Why do I have to be the poor relation, with no savings to fall back on, while Sylvia . . .

Sylvia's close-set gray eyes were intent on the teapot. "Such a nice piece of silver," she murmured.

The tea set was the only valuable thing Meg owned—the only family heirloom her parents had left her. The rest of the apartment was furnished with leftovers and make-shifts—colorful posters instead of paintings, remnants turned into curtains and patchwork cushions, secondhand furniture painted and refinished by Meg herself. It was attractive, because Meg was accustomed to making do, but it was not at all the ambience to which Sylvia was accustomed. And trust Sylvia to pick out the only object of value in the place! She had the old acquisitive gleam in her eyes; it was the only emotion that ever warmed their coldness.

Sylvia's left hand was half buried in the luxurious softness of the sable cape that lay beside her on the couch. She had refused Meg's offer to hang it up; and indeed, the thought of that smoky elegance hanging between Meg's worn trenchcoat and six-year-old fake leopard was rather incongruous.

As she had so often done, Meg studied her second cousin once removed with incredulity. How had Sylvia done it? Three husbands, all wealthy men, one of them a multimillionaire. If Sylvia had been the conventional sexpot, svelte and blond and heavy-eyed, it wouldn't have been so hard to understand. But Sylvia looked like the kind of woman who walked the aisles of the supermarket with a little hand computer, ticking off the prices as she filled her shopping cart. Her hair was nicely tended, but frankly gray; the sables and the expensive suit didn't conceal the dumpiness of her figure. Sylvia wore glasses—pale-blue frames with little rhinestones set in them. As she bent over the plate on which Meg had arranged a few cookies, Meg watched her curiously, seeking something—some warmth of kindness or flicker of wit—and found nothing. With a sigh, she gave it up. Sylvia had her good points, but none of them seemed likely to attract a man, much less a millionaire. They were points that might be useful to an indigent relative, however.

"Manhattan isn't the best place in the world to live in," she said. "In fact, the doctors say it's a bad place for me just now. Apparently this—this condition will clear up more quickly if I have rest and quiet."

"You won't get it here," Sylvia said complacently. "The noise level is enough to send anybody off her rocker."

"I need your help," Meg said abruptly. "I hate to ask you, Sylvia . . ."

"Naturally you do," Sylvia said, looking up. Her plain, lined face was relaxed, and Meg knew her comment referred to the first part of the appeal, not to the second. If Sylvia was without imagination, she was equally without malice.

"I've been thinking what would be best," Sylvia went on. "I don't suppose the doctor gave you any idea how long this will last? No, they never do, do they? Well. . . . Six months, perhaps? Yes, I should think six months would do it."

She reached for another cookie, and then glanced at Meg, as the latter sank back in her chair with an audible gasp.

"You're white as a sheet," she said critically. "You always were too thin; of course you're not tall, but you ought to carry more flesh than you do. I suppose you lost weight while you were in the hospital. Have a cookie. Sugar gives you quick energy."

Meg laughed and obeyed. The laughter was a little shaky, and so was her hand as she reached for the plate. She had known she could count on Sylvia, but. . . . After all, the relationship was a distant one, and Sylvia didn't owe her a thing. It is not pleasant at the age of twenty-three, to find oneself at the end of your rope with nothing to rely on except the charity of a second cousin once removed.

She smiled at Sylvia with genuine gratitude; but she couldn't help thinking that Sylvia's generosity had been qualified. Six months. On what basis, she wondered, had Sylvia decided that six months was long enough for recuperation from her unusual type of injury? But that wasn't the consideration. Six months was Sylvia's usual term. She made a hobby of helping people who were in temporary difficulties; but the key word was "temporary." Sylvia expected her protégés to solve their problems within a reasonable length of time. If they failed to shape up, Sylvia washed her hands of them; and she was the one who decided what was a reasonable length of time.

At this point in her silent soliloquy Meg felt ashamed of herself. Catty and ungrateful, that's what she was. One of the unfortunate by-products of her accident was a newborn cynicism; Meg disliked this trait, and fought it when she could. This was a good place to start—with Sylvia. She gave her cousin such a warm smile that Sylvia blinked behind her thick glasses.

"Let's see," Sylvia said. "You have that little annuity, don't you?"

"It's not really an annuity. Just the interest from the bonds Mother and Dad left me."

"Could you get by on that if you didn't have to pay rent and utilities?"

"Why, I don't know . . ."

"Then let's figure it out." Sylvia extracted a pen from her purse. It was a gold pen, of course. In her diminutive, precise hand, she began to make notes on the back of a napkin. "You won't need to buy any clothes; you won't be doing any entertaining. Food isn't so expensive in the country. . . ."

Meg opened her mouth to ask the obvious question, and then decided to keep quiet. Sylvia had something in mind. There was no point interrupting her, because she wouldn't answer questions till she had finished what she was doing. It did not take her long.

"I think that's it," she announced, studying her list with pleasure. "Medical expenses are the only thing that might get out of hand. If they do, go to Brumbart, he's a local man, but quite good enough; have him send the bills to me. What about drugs? Are you taking tranquilizers? Well, try to cut down. I have no objection to them as temporary help, but you mustn't become dependent on drugs. Otherwise, you should be able to manage. If you can't. . . . Well, let me know."

Love, Meg told herself; think Love. Don't think about Sylvia's millions, and that petty, penny-pinching list she just made. Don't be annoyed because Sylvia knows the exact amount of your tiny income. That's the sort of thing Sylvia would know. And her remarks about tranquilizers are reasonable. . . . It isn't what Sylvia says, it's the way she says it.

"I'm sure I can manage," Meg said, feeling the smile on her lips stiffen. "But where—"

"The Pennsylvania house."

"I don't remember it."

"It's the one George left me. My second."

"Oh, yes." Meg's smile held honest amusement now. "George was the one who died, wasn't he?"

"Two of them died," Sylvia said calmly. "Frederic—my first—was the one who fell off the cliff. Ridiculous, for a man his age to be climbing rocks; but he was trying to show off for that actress. What was her name? Well, I've forgotten, there were so many of them there that weekend. Actors and actresses, I mean. Frederic left me the house in Maine—that was where he fell off the cliff—and the place in the Bahamas and the château. George—my second—left me the Pennsylvania house and the properties in San Francisco and Paris and Rome. He had angina. It was very sudden. They brought him back to life once, but it didn't last."

"It's hard for me to keep your husbands straight," Meg said.

"Well, of course I had a more personal interest. Wilfred, my third, was the one who divorced me. I never could understand what he saw in that woman. Her hair looked like straw, my dear, it had been bleached so often. She didn't last long. He's on his fourth—or is it his fifth?"

"I'm surprised you never married again, Sylvia. It's been five years, hasn't it?"

"Six, next month." Sylvia's voice was expressionless, but for a moment something looked out of her pale-gray eyes—something that made Meg feel peculiar. "I liked Wilfred, you see. Anyway," she added brightly, "he gave me the London house and the one in Palm Beach; and, of course, a very generous settlement."

"I don't know how you keep track of all your property."

"Oh, I haven't much else to do. I never went in for hobbies. Such a waste of time. I'm doing quite well, with my investments and so forth—so well that I've almost decided to sell the Pennsylvania house to the local Historical Association. They won't pay much for it, but I can afford to be generous. George would have liked that; he was always so proud of that house."

"But if you are going to sell it—"

"Oh, I won't sell it for a while. There's a lot that needs to be done first; that's why I thought it would be a good place for you, you know about antiques and that sort of thing. You see, the Culvers have been there for almost a year, and I just gave them their notice."

Meg felt sorry for the just-evicted Culvers. Obviously they had not shaped up. They must be unusually deserving cases to have induced Sylvia to extend her six-month deadline.

"He's an artist," Sylvia went on. "A painter, I should say. Gifted, but hopelessly lazy. He hasn't finished a canvas for eight months. So I told them to leave. You can move into the house. I want you to fix it up—you know what I mean. There was some nice old furniture there, at least I thought it was nice, if old-fashioned. I moved the best of it up into the attic. No point in letting my tenants eat off genuine Chippendale, was there? You'll have to look at it, decide what should stay with the house and what should be sold. Maybe you can pick up a few more pieces at local antique shops; just enough to furnish the place in proper style, you'll know what to do. When I sell it to the Historical Association I want it to be properly fixed up, with the right furniture and pictures and all."

Looking pleased with herself, she reached for the last cookie. Meg stared at her, more than a little confused. She wasn't sure she did know what Sylvia wanted her to do. Her knowledge of antiques was that of an amateur. Then she began to understand. In exchange for her room, she would have to perform some service, even if Sylvia had to invent a job to occupy her.

"I'll do my best," she said. "What period is the house? Colonial?"

"No, it's a perfect monstrosity of a Victorian mansion— Gothic revival, I think they call it, with stained glass and the rest. I think it's perfectly awful, but apparently that sort of thing is now considered amusing, and it's an excellent example of its type."

"Good heavens," Meg said, as the image took shape in her mind. "It sounds overpowering. Are you sure it isn't haunted? I don't think I could stand living with a ghost just now."

"Why should it be haunted?" Sylvia asked reasonably.

"I was joking."

"Oh. Well, I've never heard of any ghosts. It's a huge old place, you'll simply rattle around in it, but the area is quite peaceful. It's in Berks County, out in the country, and there is a caretaker living in the guesthouse. God knows it's quiet. The estate is almost twenty acres."

"Twenty acres!" Meg exclaimed. "That land must be worth quite a bit of money today. Are you going to give all that to the . . ."

Her voice trailed off as she met Sylvia's eyes. Sylvia wasn't looking guilty; no such thought ever disturbed Sylvia's opinion of herself. But there was a certain complacency in Sylvia's look, and Meg understood. Of course Sylvia wasn't going to give away twenty acres of property. The land would be sold to a developer—or perhaps Sylvia planned to develop it herself. The house itself was too valuable to tear down and too big to be marketable. Sylvia would leave it hunched on a half acre of ground and sell it to the only institution that would buy it.

Meg fought another battle with envy and cynicism.

"Sylvia, it's very sweet of you to help me out. I'll do my best with the house. Thank you." On impulse she jumped up and went to Sylvia and kissed her on the cheek.

Sylvia sniffed. "Let's get back to your budget."

By the time Sylvia left, Meg's expenditures were mapped out down to the last stick of chewing gum and emery board. Sylvia had allowed for one cocktail a day— "When you're alone and depressed, you must be careful about drinking too much."

Meg escorted her cousin to the door of the apartment and watched Sylvia march down the hall toward the elevator. She fancied that the aristocratic hairs of Sylvia's cape flattened themselves, shrinking from any possible contact with the peeling, distempered walls. When the elevator door had closed she bolted her own door—an automatic gesture, after two years in Manhattan—and went to the window.

Down in the street Sylvia's long black Fleetwood sedan was drawn up at the curb, in flagrant disregard of the "no parking" sign. Her chauffeur stood beside it, alert for evil small boys. As Sylvia emerged from the building he leaped to attention and opened the car door. Sylvia gathered her cape about her and stooped, preparing to enter; at that moment a daring ray of sunshine penetrated the murk of the city skies and shone full on her hatless head. The gray hair flashed silver.

Watching from above, Meg's lips curved upward, and a dimple, which had not often appeared in the last few months, popped out of hiding. She had a weakness for omens, and this was the first hopeful one she had seen for a long time. Sylvia was a guardian angel, albeit a reluctant one.

Reflected in the grimy windowpane, a dim image of Meg's face stared back at her—a pale, pointed face framed by a fringe of cropped brown hair. Luckily her hair grew fast; she had cut it all short when the shaved portion started to grow out, but it was still lusterless and unbecoming. The reflection didn't flatter her; she looked like a frightened child, her dark eyes too large for the thinness of her face. The eyes seemed to question . . .

I'd better make it, Meg thought, answering the silent query. I've got to make it. Six months. That's all the time I have.

# Chapter 2

From Sylvia's description Meg expected the house to be a monstrosity, with every accouterment of the Victorian Gothic style—wooden gingerbread, pseudo half-timbering, brackets, and stained glass. The first view of the house was a pleasant surprise. It had individuality and a certain dignity.

Standing on a low rise surrounded by trees, it was not as large as she had anticipated. Built of stone—blue marble and limestone—it had three stories, plus an attic level indicated by queer little gabled windows. It reminded her of a small German *Schloss*, the comfortable provincial castle of a petty baron or count. A wide veranda supported by heavy wooden pillars covered the front of the house. Chimneys sprouted over the roof, and at the back was a square stone tower, with balconies and attractive round-arched triple windows. The tower had a gabled roof; the gables ended, as did those of the house itself, in wrought-iron finials. Some of the windows were leaded, others contained the expected stained glass. Even on a bleak winter day it would not have looked forbidding; it was a toy castle, and on that brilliant autumn afternoon, surrounded by copper-shaded trees, it had a distinctly frivolous air.

As the taxi followed the long, curving drive, through wide green lawns, Meg's spirits rose. The lawn needed mowing and the shrubbery was overgrown, but the effect was one of carefree charm rather than neglect. Weeping willows swept green skirts across the grass, and the great oak near the house was a patriarch of its kind.

In her exuberance Meg tipped the taxi driver generously, and he helped her carry her luggage to the veranda. Most of her belongings had been sent ahead. Sylvia had promised the caretaker would see to everything, and sure enough, when Meg peered through the glass panels that flanked the front door she saw that the hall was piled with boxes.

The driver offered to wait while she went through the house, but Meg smilingly refused. For some reason she wanted to be alone when she stepped across the threshold. She could not imagine being afraid here, it was too quiet, too pastoral. She watched the taxi drive off, observing other treasures—a summer house in a clump of beeches, an iron deer peering out from behind an untrimmed mass of spirea. Then she reached into her purse for the keys Sylvia had given her, and with a ceremonious air inserted them into the locks. There was an old, heavy iron key that fitted the original lock, and a Yale key for the new lock. They functioned without a hitch; when she pushed on the door it swung smoothly open. Meg smiled to herself. Not even a creak of Gothic hinges. Another good omen.

She was about to enter the house when a voice hailed her. With an unreasonable feeling of irritation she turned to see a man coming toward her across the lawn. He walked with a slow slouch that increased her annoyance, while it gave her time to pin down the elusive flash of memory his appearance had provoked. It had brought a mélange of impressions: mud and rocks and closed-in dark places. . . .

Although she had never visited this house, Meg had met the man to whom it had belonged—Sylvia's second husband. She had once spent a month with Sylvia in California while her parents were on vacation. She remembered George Brenner vaguely, as a silent, smiling man who seemed unaccountably devoted to his brisk wife. And he had had a son.

Mud and stones and dark, closed-in places. . . . Meg winced as other memories of that horrible month returned. Surely Andy Brenner had been the nastiest, meanest little boy of his generation! Meg had been eight that summer; Andy was a few years older, old enough to be ingenious and young enough to revel in practical jokes perpetrated on the weaker sex. He had locked her in closets and sheds. He had tricked her into bogs that spoiled her shoes and her pretty summer dresses. He had thrown—no, not rocks, one must be fair; but those hard green apples had felt like rocks against her skinny little legs. When she sat down in chairs, hideous noises broke out; when she opened doors, things fell on her head. She had awakened one morning to find herself imprisoned in a cord cage; heavy twine had been wound intricately around the four posters that supported the bed canopy, and she had wailed until Sylvia had freed her. (Sylvia had not cut the cord; that was wasteful.

It had taken fifteen minutes to unwind it, so ingeniously had Andy created his giant cat's cradle.) Sylvia had been annoyed, but her anger had been impartially divided between the two children. "You ask for it," she had told Meg. "He wouldn't pick on you if you'd fight back." Excellent advice, if she had been able to follow it. . . .

Meg's eyes narrowed in nostalgic fury as the ambling figure came close enough to be definitely identified. Andy hadn't changed much, except to add two or three feet to his height. The same shaggy mop of reddish-brown hair, the same snub nose and oversized ears, the same lean, wiry body that had revealed unexpected and painful strength when he practiced jujitsu holds on her. No wonder Sylvia hadn't mentioned the name of her caretaker!

On second thought, Meg decided she was giving Sylvia credit for too much sensitivity. Sylvia hadn't mentioned Andy because she considered his identity unimportant. And as Andy came up the veranda steps, smiling tentatively, Meg felt a twinge of compassion. To give the man a caretaker's job on the estate that had been his father's, and that ought to have been his, was surely rather. . . . It was Sylvia, that was what it was.

So she responded amiably when Andy greeted her, and let him take her hand.

"You're looking well," she said—and realized, as she spoke, that it was untrue. At close range, there were too many lines in Andy's face for a man of twenty-four or -five. He was thin, too.

"You aren't," said Andy. "You're skinny. Those purple bags under your eyes don't go with your complexion, either."

No, Andy hadn't changed a bit.

Meg reached for a suitcase. Andy let her take it; he picked up the other suitcases and carried them into the house. Putting them on the floor, he scratched his head as he looked around at the litter of luggage. "I didn't know where you wanted this stuff. . . ."

"I don't know myself. I haven't seen the house."

"So look at it."

Meg gave him a long look before she turned her attention to the hallway.

A staircase with ornately carved wooden banisters rose to a landing lighted by a round, rose-type stained-glass window. The color of the glass was predominantly crimson; it shed a garish, ghastly glow across the bare boards of the landing. An open archway on the left led to the drawing room—large and well lighted by high windows, but as scantily furnished as was the hall. On the right-hand wall was a closed door; there was a second door farther along, under the curve of the upper stairs. The hall went on back into an area too dark to be visible; either there were no windows in that section, or they were heavily curtained. The wallpaper was old, its once brilliant crimson and gold badly faded. It was also horribly stained with what appeared to be . . .

"Paint," said Andy, as she stepped up to examine the ugly smears. "Just brown paint. I tried to get it off, but that oil-based stuff really hangs on."

"It looks recent. How—"

"Sylvia told you about the last tenant?" Andy sat down on one of her suitcases, which bulged protestingly. He went on before Meg could remonstrate. "Culver thought he had a nice soft setup here; he was mad as hell when Sylvia threw him out. So he left a few little mementos of his displeasure. He calculated Sylvia's aggravation level pretty accurately; I don't think she'll bother suing him, especially since he hasn't got a cent. But there was a certain amount of mess. I cleaned up most of it."

"He didn't calculate Sylvia's character very accurately if he expected to hang on here indefinitely. Would you mind getting up? My suitcases come from Woolworth's; they aren't up to your weight."

"Oh." Andy pulled himself to his feet. "Don't get huffy. I follow the old army rule—never stand when you can sit, never sit when you can—"

"I know the rest of it."

"You ought to follow it. You look like you could use some rest."

"I wish you'd stop harping on how awful I look. You don't look so hot yourself. What was it—pneumonia?"

Andy's face hardened.

"My, my," he said. "The nice little girl I used to harass has grown up. Gotten mean."

"You have to be mean to survive in this world."

"That's a rather cynical attitude for a girl your age."

"Woman, not girl. How would you like people to call you a boy?"

"Damn it," Andy said, "you aren't just mean; you've got as many prickles as a porcupine. Look here, Meg, we're stuck with each other; why don't we try to get along? There's no use kidding you. You know Sylvia as well as I do, and you know she wouldn't hand me two bits for a cup of coffee unless I appealed to that narrow streak of benevolence she's got buried under her fat. Yes, I have been sick. I had to quit grad school last spring, and Sylvia let me come here to recuperate. I understand the same is true of you. And neither one of us is going to give up our sanctuary. So why fight?"

"I'm not fighting."

"Then I'd like to see you when you're belligerent."

"Now who's being provocative?"

"Jee-sus!" said Andy. He picked up two suitcases at random and started up the stairs, flinging a comment over his shoulder.

"Pick out a room and I'll dump your stuff in it. Then I'll get out."

Meg followed. The suitcases were extremely heavy. Watching the movement of muscles across his back, under his cotton shirt, Meg decided to exercise a little tact.

"I'm sorry, Andy, I didn't mean to be nasty. I was ill, and I'm still edgy. Truce?"

"You mean you don't want to have to carry those suitcases yourself," Andy said, without turning around. But his tone was slightly mollified, and when they got upstairs he showed her the second floor without referring to their clash.

"The master bedroom is still in bad shape," he said, opening one of the heavy arched doors than lined the upper hall. "Culver had fun in here."

"His vocabulary was limited, wasn't it?" Meg studied the four-letter words scrawled across the walls in screaming primary colors.

"The wallpaper in here needed replacing anyhow,"

Andy said. "I figured rather than try to get the paint off I'd just strip the walls and get new paper."

"That sounds reasonable. But why should you bother . . . oh. I keep forgetting you used to live here."

"Every summer, till I was eighteen." Andy's tone did not invite further comment. He closed the door of the master suite and went on down the hall.

"This was my mother's room. Sylvia kept it locked, so it's in fairly good condition. I aired it out yesterday and made the bed, but if you prefer another room—"

"I really don't care," Meg said. "Oh, Andy"—as the door swung open— "this is charming. Yes, I like this room."

Wide windows, flung open to the mellow Indian-summer air, showed a vista of green lawns and waving boughs. The faded wallpaper had an old-fashioned pattern of rosebuds enclosed in gilt lozenges. The furniture was simple—white-painted, with gilt trim: a four-poster bed, a dressing table with fluffy pink skirts, the usual chests and dressers and tables. It was more like a child's room than that of a grown woman; and Meg realized that it had probably been Andy's mother's room before she married and moved into the stately master bedroom with her husband. Which meant that the house had belonged to Andy's mother before it came to his father; and that Sylvia's present title to it was even more unfair than Meg had realized.

"Okay," Andy said. "I'll get the rest of your stuff, then."

Meg followed him. Andy was on the landing and she was two steps up when she slipped. Even as she fell she knew she was in no danger; Andy turned, hearing the scrape of her shoe and her stifled cry, and his hands went out, ready to catch her. As his fingers closed over her arms, it happened. Meg recognized the symptoms—the blurring of vision, the moment of disorientation. The stained-glass window darkened and became opaque. The walls lost solidity. Through them she saw, not the green and gold of autumn foliage, but another room—narrow, dark, low-ceilinged. There were dim shapes in the hallucinatory room, but she could not make them out. There was no floor under her feet. The dark walls closed in, but there was no floor. . . .

The vision vanished slowly, almost reluctantly. Blinking in the rainbow-hued light, Meg swayed, and felt Andy's arms go around her.

After a moment she pushed him away.

"Damn," she said, trying to keep her voice steady. "That was a bad one. Damn, damn! It hasn't happened for two days; I hoped . . ."

She could see Andy's face now; it was a caricature of astonishment, pallid and staring.

"What happened?" he asked.

"Sylvia didn't give you the gruesome details? I had an accident—head injuries. Ever since, I've had hallucinations. I hear things—see things—that aren't there. Other places, other people—even animals. Once I saw an elephant on Fifth Avenue, going into Brentano's." She tried to laugh, unsuccessfully.

Andy's face didn't change. "What did you see just now?"

"Another room. Different walls. It's so discouraging. The doctors told me it would gradually go away, but it sure is taking its time. Oh, stop staring as though I were something in a sideshow! Don't tell me you didn't know; Sylvia must have told you."

"She mentioned hallucinations," Andy admitted. The color was slowly returning to his face. "I didn't realize they were so—"

"She had no right to tell you," Meg burst out. "She didn't tell me about you. Now I suppose the whole neighborhood thinks I'm crazy."

Andy's lips parted. There was scarcely a pause before he spoke, but Meg had the feeling his comment was not the one he had originally intended to make.

"Sylvia tells people only what they need to know. She doesn't gossip—thank God. You're planning to live here alone?"

"I'm not sick. I just—"

"See things that aren't there. Rather risky, isn't it? If you walked down a staircase that didn't exist—"

"I tripped. The hallucination started after I fell. Once it begins I can't move at all; I'm paralyzed. Are you suggesting you should move in with me?"

"God forbid," said Andy piously. "I am suggesting I check up on you at frequent intervals. How often does this happen? You have auditory hallucinations too, I gather."

"Listen to the boy's technical vocabulary," Meg exclaimed. She studied Andy with a new suspicion. "What were you majoring in? Not medical school?"

"None of your business," said Andy. "Every well-read layman knows about hallucinations; they are probably behind ninety-nine percent of the so-called occult experiences people have. Damn it, do you think I'm that interested in your goofy problems? Sylvia pays me—not much, but she does pay me—to keep an eye on things around here. That includes you. I'm not going to have you setting fire to the house or breaking your skinny neck in a fit of lunacy."

"Well, that certainly sets things straight. All right; for your information, I have these goofy problems once or twice a day. They only last for a few seconds; once the hallucination has passed, I'm perfectly all right. Sylvia is not paying you to be my keeper, and I'll be damned if I am going to have you sticking your nose in here all the time on the pretense of watching over me. Is that perfectly clear?"

"Perfectly," said Andy.

He walked on down the stairs, leaving Meg holding the breath she had just taken in, preparatory to a further series of critical comments. He crossed the hall, went out the front door, and closed it quietly behind him.

Meg looked down at the boxes of books, clothes, and miscellany littering the hall. Now that, she thought disgustedly, was a stupid thing to do. What's the matter with me? He was trying to be nice—in his own weird way. I didn't have to be so overly sensitive.

She forgot her critical conscience as she began to explore the house. It was a delight. Every room held fresh treasures—window seats whose lids lifted for the storage of toys and blankets; unexpected balconies draped with ivy; fireplaces, and more fireplaces. The tower was the *pièce de résistance;* if the stairs had not been so formidable, Meg would have moved into the topmost room immediately. It had windows on all four sides and balconies all around; a domed ceiling ornamented with plaster bas-reliefs of fruit and flowers and fat cupids; a hooded medieval fireplace tucked into a corner; mahogany paneling that looked as if it must conceal at least two secret passages. . . .

However, there were five flights of stairs from the ground to the topmost tower room. Meg gave the room a last lingering look and retreated. At least she could put some appropriate furniture in the place and use it as a retreat for reading and meditating. Sylvia had given her—well, no, not carte blanche, Sylvia didn't trust anyone that much—but she had implied she might be willing to pay for necessary furnishings. It would be fun to select furniture for this room.

The house wasn't as unmanageably large as Sylvia had implied. The rooms were enormous, but there were only five bedrooms on the second floor, plus a bathroom and a sitting room that formed part of the master suite. The Victorian bathroom filled Meg with joy. It was almost as big as the bedrooms, with a fireplace of its own. The huge marble tub, encased in a mahogany box, was so high she would need a stool to get in and out. The water ran hot when she tried it.

The third floor had more bedrooms, smaller and less elegant. This was children's country. One slightly larger room had served as a nursery, and a cubbyhole next to it had been the cramped bedroom of the nurse or nanny. The central staircase ended on the third floor, but there was another stair at the back of the hall—narrow, steep, enclosed. It went up, presumably to the attic, which Meg decided to leave for another day. She followed the stairs down and found herself in a pantry-service area between the kitchen and dining room. Of course; these were the stairs the servants used—poor devils. Where had they slept? Belowstairs, presumably, with the damp and the black beetles. Meg decided to leave the basement for another day too.

There was a good deal of cleaning to do. Andy's idea of cleaning was typically masculine—perfunctory, in other words. Her own pretty room—she already thought of it as hers—was neat but very dusty, and the bathroom made her hands itch for scrubbing brushes and cleansing powder. Clearly Mrs. Culver hadn't worn herself out cleaning house. Meg wasn't a fanatical housekeeper herself, but as she went through the neglected, grimy rooms, her distaste for both Culvers increased. Maybe Mrs. Culver hadn't felt she was obliged to clean the unused rooms, but how could she live in such a mess? A lawyer might claim that most of it was normal wear and tear—normal for an eccentric painter and a sluttish wife. Only once, in the master bedroom, had Culver's malice gotten out of hand, when he scrawled his Anglo-Saxon expletives. The other damage was subtle but omnipresent—scarred floors, scratched tables, burns and scrapes and layers of greasy dirt.

Meg went through the pantry into the kitchen, expecting the worst. It wasn't as bad as she had feared. The room was a long way from the state of cleanliness she considered minimal, but someone had been at work here.

Originally the kitchen had been one of those vast rooms dating from a period when nobody worried about the cook's fallen arches. It had been subdivided and modernized in the not-too-distant past; as she looked at the attractive breakfast area, Meg wondered whether Andy's mother had done the decorating. Like her bedroom, the breakfast room was delicate and pretty—almost too precious. Walls and appliances were butter yellow, and there were daisies everywhere—on the wallpaper, on the curtains, even on the plate around the light switch. Why not daisy-decorated dishes? Meg thought, smiling.

A search of the kitchen cabinets produced a set of plastic dishes, so new that the labels were still on them. "Dishwasher proof . . ." Meg took the labels at their word and filled the dishwasher. Just like a man, she thought sanctimoniously, as the machine gurgled and wheezed into action. Andy wouldn't think dishes needed to be washed when they were brand new. She was glad she didn't have to use the ones the uncouth Culvers had eaten from. She wondered what had become of their dishes, pots and pans, and so on. Maybe they had belonged to the Culvers and had been removed with their other possessions.

A gleaming new freezer occupied part of the floor space, and Meg investigated it, conscious of a growing emptiness in her interior. It was well stocked; Andy, at Sylvia's request, no doubt. She thought kindly of both of them as she took out steak, worth its weight in silver, and left it to defrost. The refrigerator was just as well stocked. She wouldn't have to shop for several days.

But she had no intention of eating in this room until she had cleaned it thoroughly. She was inclined to give Andy the credit for what had been done; it had the hallmark of his technique. The stove had been wiped, but it was still greasy; the floor had been swept, but the soles of her sandals stuck as she walked. She looked for cleaning supplies, and found them—brand-new bottles and cans, unopened. Part of Sylvia's supplies then, not items left by Mrs. Culver. Meg was not surprised. She peeled the label off the top of a can of cleansing powder and tackled the stove.

Sometime later, while sweeping the floor preliminary to mopping it, she bent to see what she could get out from under the refrigerator: rolls of greasy black dust, a withered olive, peanut shells—and something that chinked musically as it slid across the floor.

Meg picked it up. It was a piece of broken china, thin, with the genuine ring of good ware. She turned it over; and an odd little chill ran through her as she recognized the daisy pattern.

There were more fragments under the refrigerator, and a few others in dark corners that Andy's broom had not reached. All were from the same set—curved shapes that had been part of cups, the sunken well of a saucer, rims of plates. China—not as expensive as Haviland or Wedgwood, but good china.

So Andy's mother had had her daisy-patterned dishes. Sylvia must have left them for the use of her assorted tenants; they were old, no longer in style, not particularly valuable. And someone had smashed the entire set. There was not so much as a fugitive saucer left when Meg searched the shelves. It must have been broken recently or there would not be so many fragments left.

Andy had mentioned cleaning up the house after the Culvers left. He had minimized the extent of the damage. Meg visualized the kitchen as Andy must have found it, with his mother's favorite dishes smashed to bits on the floor. Somehow the wanton, deliberate destruction of the entire set bothered her more than anything the Culvers had done. Anyone might smash a few plates in a fit of anger; she had smashed a few herself, and had found the crash eminently satisfying. But to destroy all of them—every last cup and saucer and platter and bowl—that suggested a degree of malice which was decidedly unnerving.

Meg scrubbed the floor on her hands and knees, using a stiff brush and the strongest disinfectant she could find. She unearthed a few more broken bits of china and deposited them in the trash bag. Then she went to the telephone and invited Andy over for dinner.

## II

Andy's appetite was another thing that hadn't changed over the years. He devoured steak and scalloped potatoes, salad and vegetables and rolls as if he had not eaten for a week, and then leaned back in his chair and regarded Meg approvingly.

"Normally I subsist on hard-boiled eggs and canned soup," he explained. "What other talents do you have besides cooking?"

"Not many. I earn my living as a secretary—when I earn it."

"I thought you were an interior decorator or something. Sylvia said—"

"I took a few courses. But this scheme of Sylvia's, about fixing up the house, is make-work. If she wanted to do the place up properly she'd hire a professional."

"Ah," said Andy, pouring coffee for both of them. "The operative word is 'hire.' Sylvia doesn't pay people to do things if she can help it. I hope you don't mind my criticizing your relative."

"I criticize her myself," Meg admitted. "But I'm ashamed to do it. I'd be in a bad spot if it weren't for Sylvia's help."

"I suppose you could say the same about me."

"I couldn't; I don't know enough about your situation."

Meg hesitated. Normal good manners forbade pointed inquiries into Andy's problems, yet she wanted to indicate sympathy. As so often happens, her tongue rejected the tactful remarks she had considered, and blurted out the question in the bluntest possible form.

"How does Sylvia happen to own this house? Shouldn't it be yours?"

Andy, who had been looking down at his plate, raised his head. Meg had never imagined that freckles and snub nose could shape themselves into so forbidding a mask.

"My father had the right to dispose of his property as he chose," he said coldly. "Let's stay out of each other's personal lives, okay?"

"But you—"

"I stuck my nose into your private affairs this afternoon. True; but only to the extent that your problems affect your present life and, by juxtaposition, mine."

"And none of your problems is going to affect my life?"

Meg was a little surprise at the result of her question. Andy's gaze shifted; the muscles of his face convulsed in a sudden spasm that might have been suppressed laughter—or fear.

"I hope not," he muttered; and then continued, in a voice that was meant to sound affable. "Look, let's forget about this afternoon. There are some practical matters we need to discuss.

"I don't suppose you've ever been a homeowner. All kinds of things go wrong with houses, from the plumbing to the roof. Any problem—call me. I fix leaky taps and nail on new shingles, among other things. There's an extension phone in your room, in case you hear funny noises at night. . . ."

"I hear funny noises all the time," Meg said wryly.

"Call, if you feel the need. I don't sleep much," said Andy expressionlessly. "Next thing is transportation. You can drive, I suppose?"

"I don't have a driver's license. I've lived in Manhattan for two years," Meg added defensively. "I let my Illinois license lapse and never—"

"Why do you have to apologize for everything?"

"I'm not! I only meant—"

"It doesn't matter. My car is undrivable by anyone but me. It has quite a few eccentricities. You'll have to depend on me for transportation," Andy concluded, with obvious satisfaction.

"What about shopping?"

"The nearest town is Wasserburg, about three miles away. The grocer delivers if he feels like it. I can take you there when you want to go. We can go shopping tomorrow, if you like; you may as well see the town and what it has to offer."

"I do need a few things."

"Okay; about ten. I'd better warn you about Wasserburg. Like a lot of towns in the area, it's become a tourist trap and a mecca for antique hunters. This is Pennsylvania

Dutch country, in case you didn't know, and Pennsylvania Dutch is in. There are souvenir joints along all the roads, with wrought-iron trivets and tiles with hex signs all over 'em, not to mention gruesome goodies that purport to be shoofly pie and other genuine ethnic cooking.

"The local merchants despise the city slickers who come up here and gush over the quaint Amish and the handicrafts; but no Dutchman ever turned down a chance to make a buck, so they milk the tourists for all they can get. Watch out for the antique shops in Wasserburg. Unless you know what you're doing, you'll come home in a barrel."

"I don't plan to buy antiques—at least, not many, and not for a while. Sylvia said there was furniture in the attic—"

"Furniture! Wait till you see the place. It hasn't been cleaned out since the house was built, and people in these parts don't throw anything away. I wouldn't be surprised if you found a coffin up there, tucked away by a thrifty ancestor of mine."

"Sounds like fun."

"Wait till you see it," Andy repeated ominously. "That's one project—a big one. We've also got to get the house cleaned up. I'm fairly handy with tools. I run a mean sander, for instance."

"But why should you—"

"Run the sander? Because it would run away with you. Obviously you've never used one."

"I know all about sanders," Meg said. "What I meant was, why should we sand the floors? I know, they are beautiful hardwood floors and they've taken a beating. But I had no idea Sylvia wanted anything as extensive as that done to the house. I was just going to arrange furniture and paint a few things—"

"I don't think Sylvia knows what she wants done," Andy said cheerfully. "Which puts us in an enviable position; we can do pretty much what we like. It's fun, redoing an old house. I helped a buddy of mine restore an eighteenth-century farmhouse in Virginia a couple of years ago; we had a great time."

"But I never did—"

"You're not too old to learn. You know one thing that's wrong with you? You've been sitting around too much, brooding and worrying. Stick with me, kid, and I guarantee you won't have time for hallucinations."

"You sound like one of those popular mental-health books," Meg said coldly. "How to cure yourself of homicidal mania in ten easy lessons."

Andy's smile broadened. "How did you know, darling?"

Meg stared at him as enlightenment dawned.

"I should have known, from the way you talk," she said rudely. "Words like 'subsist'. . . . so that's your gimmick. You're writing a book."

"A novel," Andy said, unruffled. "I did think of a do-it-yourself psychology book; they sell like hot cakes. But feelthy novels sell even better."

"Naturally. Sylvia likes struggling young writers almost as much as she likes struggling young painters. How much have you written? Or shouldn't I ask?"

"I'm revising at the moment," Andy said seriously.

"I'll bet you are."

"You are a cynic, aren't you? I'm not accustomed to that sneering response; ordinarily, when I announce I'm working on a novel, all the sweet young things fall into poses of respectful admiration."

"I worked for a publishing house once."

"Oh."

"Everybody is writing a novel," Meg said cruelly. "Or thinking about writing a novel. About one writer in ten thousand finishes a book. I guess it's more fun to talk about writing than it is to write."

"Much more fun."

"And, of course, if you never finish a book, you never have to submit it for criticism."

"Which could be very bad for one's ego," Andy agreed. "I gather you aren't going to ask me what my book is about?"

"No."

"Well, that ends that conversation."

"You ought to be able to wangle at least a year's lodging out of Sylvia. Even she knows you can't write a book in six months."

"You overestimate Sylvia. Like most people, she thinks you can write a book in six days if you work at it. No, dear, Sylvia lets me stay on because I do twice as much as a paid caretaker for half the pay. It's not a bad relationship— honest, direct, unclouded by sticky emotions like gratitude."

Meg could think of nothing to say. The bitterness with which Andy spoke of Sylvia was not pleasant to hear; it was an ugly reflection of her own feelings.

"Damn," Andy said, after a moment. "Why do we always talk about Sylvia? I think I'll go home and work on the masterpiece. I now have an incentive—to prove I'm not one of the nine hundred thousand odd. Thanks for the meal, Meg."

Meg went to the door with him. The sun had set; twilight dimmed the wide lawns and turned shrubs and trees into amorphous huddled shapes. As Meg glanced around she realized there was not a light visible anywhere. If isolation was what she wanted, she had it here.

"Leave the porch light on all night," Andy said. "And be sure you put the chain up on the door."

"Are you trying to scare me?"

"I'm trying to reassure the poor little city girl on her first night in the country. See you tomorrow."

He crossed the porch and descended the steps; darkness closed over him. As Meg watched she had a curious impression that he was not alone. Another shadow seemed to walk with him, step for step, until he vanished into the night.

# Chapter 3

In an earlier and simpler era, Wasserburg had been a pretty country town whose main street—called Main Street—lined with big old houses, summoned images of turn-of-the-century domesticity—home-baked bread, lilacs in the spring, rows of snowy laundry on Monday morning. The houses were still there, but the air of domesticity was gone. A town of eight thousand, Wasserburg possessed a grocery store, a drugstore–post office combined, and forty-three antique shops.

The antique shops varied considerably. A few, housed in the handsome old mansions, specialized in European imports and contained not a single object that cost less than fifty dollars. Some sold books, others reproductions of Early American furniture, and some were no more than souvenir shops. The Pennsylvania Dutch atmosphere was thick; even the shopkeepers who came from Idaho or Florida tried to speak with an appropriate accent.

To Meg's city-dulled eyes, the town seemed delightful.

She was aware of the artificiality, but was impressed by the neatness and orderliness. Even the pavements looked as if they had been swept that morning by a brigade of industrious housewives.

In the scene of cleanly charm Andy's old car was a profane intrusion. He had not been exaggerating when he said it had its eccentricities. It progressed in a series of jerks, accompanied by frequent backfires and harsh squeals. One door did not open, and the other stayed open unless it was secured by a loop of wire. The color had once been a demure gray, but the vehicle had passed through many vicissitudes since it had emerged from the German factory, and Andy's attempts to remove the appliquéd flowers and slogans had not been completely successful. The car looked leprous. However, as Andy pointed out, it moved. What more could anyone ask of a means of transportation?

Apparently the car was a familiar sight in Wasserburg. Pedestrians looked up and waved as it chugged along. Andy maneuvered the vehicle into a space next to a fireplug and helped Meg slide out under the wheel. The door on the passenger side was the one that didn't open.

"Can we walk around town?" Meg asked. "What a wonderful place!"

"Yes, we'll have a look around. Now, for God's sake, quit enthusing. Every antique dealer in town knows about that attic of Sylvia's; I've been offered bribes by ten different people just for a look at the place. Keep your mouth shut and your eyes open."

Meg thoroughly enjoyed the morning. The casual friendliness of pedestrians and shopkeepers seemed genuine, and very pleasant, after the detachment of the city. She knew she

had to thank Andy for some of the warmth with which she
was greeted; everyone called him by his first name. He was
accepted as "one of us" by the old families, and the
newcomers respected him as a genuine native. Some of the
shops were owned by recent immigrants from other states,
who were cashing in on the lucrative antique craze, but most
of the names were solid Pennsylvania Dutch—Schlegel,
Klees, Konig, Kloof.

With Meg's pleasure went an increasing awareness of
her ignorance. She knew enough about antiques to distinguish Chippendale from Hepplewhite, but that was about
it; she had never realized how complex the field was. The
Pennsylvania Dutch antiques were totally unfamiliar to
her. By following Andy's advice, to keep her mouth shut
and her eyes open, she discovered that sgraffito ware had
designs scratched onto the surface through the coating of
glaze; and that slipware had free-hand patterns of birds and
tulips dripped directly onto the molded clay through a
spout in a pot. She heard about painted dower chests and
bride boxes, toleware and showtowels; and she realized
how much more she needed to know. Her head was
spinning when Andy suggested they stop for lunch. There
was, it seemed, a hotel in town.

"Too damned quaint for words," Andy said. "But it's
good home cooking; almost as good as yours."

Meg thought it was better. The chicken pot pie, followed
by homemade peach ice cream, restored her spirits considerably, and Andy reassured her when she deplored her
lack of knowledge.

"You'll pick it up fast," he said confidently. "Don't flip;

if Sylvia decides to sell the stuff in the attic she'll have to hire an appraiser. It won't be your responsibility."

They had coffee on the veranda of the hotel. After a while Andy excused himself and went inside to talk to the innkeeper, who was an old family friend. Meg sat rocking back and forth, mindlessly content as a cat in the mellow autumn sunlight. Gradually, however, she began to feel a vague uneasiness. Looking around, she saw that one of the pedestrians had stopped and was standing on the sidewalk in front of the hotel. He was staring directly at her.

He was tall and painfully thin. A long cavalry-style moustache drooped disconsolately over his mouth; the ends were ragged and damp, as if he had been chewing on them. His filthy sleeveless shirt displayed long bare arms with stringy muscles. Large holes in his garment framed a set of bony ribs.

As Meg's eyes met his, he stepped back a pace, but instead of retreating he turned toward the steps and mounted them. Meg knew who he was. He was almost a caricature of a Bohemian, and the paint smears on his dirty garments betrayed his profession. She also understood why Sylvia's former protégé had not finished a canvas in eight months. It was one thirty in the afternoon, and the man was so drunk he couldn't walk straight.

Culver came up the stairs in a series of zigzag staggers and advanced on Meg. She was alone on the veranda, and she felt her pulses quicken. There could be no danger, not in broad daylight, not from this scurvy specimen; but his mere presence was unpleasant. He planted himself squarely in front of her, fists on his hipbones, and smiled.

"How nice that we should meet so unexpectedly," he

said, in a high-pitched, surprisingly precise voice. "The old protégé and the new! It helps to be related to the old bitch, doesn't it?"

"She supported you for almost a year," Meg said, rocking.

Culver scowled. "One year! I'd still be there if it wasn't for you."

"I had nothing to do with your being evicted."

"Oh, no?" Culver seemed to think this a devastating retort. He repeated it with relish. "Oh, no?"

Meg continued to rock. She found the movement soothing. It seemed to annoy Culver. He made a grab for the arm of the rocking chair, missed, and almost lost his balance. For a moment Meg was afraid he was going to topple into her lap, but he caught himself and stood swaying. His eyes had gone blank.

"Lousy rotten deal," he mumbled, staring off into space. "Like always. No fair. I always get a lousy, unfair deal. . . . Thanks to you," he added, focusing his eyes on Meg and scowling. "This time I know who's the one. You did it. Told her lies, just so you could get in and get me out."

Meg had to make a conscious effort to keep on rocking. She was beginning to be frightened. The street seemed so deserted. Were small towns as bad as cities in their fear of getting involved? She was only too familiar with Culver's type; he was a city specimen himself. Not drunk; high on some drug, self-pitying and weak, seeking a scapegoat in the manner of all weaklings who refuse to take the responsibility for their own failures. Dangerous, all the same, in the artificially induced courage of drugs.

She was about to abandon dignity and let out a loud yell when the door opened and Andy appeared. He didn't pause; his brows drew together and he started toward Culver. Simultaneously a fourth person made her appearance. Meg didn't see where she came from; she ran to Culver and caught his arm. She was as round as he was thin; rolls of fat wobbled as she moved. She wore shorts and a scarf tied around her heavy breasts like a halter. Her eyes were so heavily made up they looked like the artificial eyes of a doll.

"Come on, Frank," she panted, tugging at him. "Come on, let's go, huh?"

"You took the words right out of my mouth, Mrs. Culver," Andy said.

"You know I'm not Mrs. Culver," said the woman— girl, Meg mentally revised. She couldn't be more than twenty.

"I know, but Sylvia doesn't," Andy said.

The girl giggled. She shifted her weight so that one ample hip protruded, and looked coyly at Andy from under her gummy lashes.

"That old bitch," she said unoriginally. "She wouldn't a let us live there if she knew we wasn't married. I told you before, call me Cherry."

All at once Meg wanted to laugh. Andy's expression, as he studied Cherry and considered her invitation, was one of the funniest things she had ever seen.

"Look, Cherry," Andy said finally. "Why don't you exert your unquestioned charms on handsome here and persuade him to move on? He's gotten all he's going to get out of Wasserburg; the only thing he'll get from now on is trouble."

"You keep out of this," Culver shouted. "We'll stay here as long as we want to. This is a free country!"

Andy sighed. "Okay, I tried. Beat it, Culver. Scram. Leave. Go away. Split." He folded his fingers into a fist and looked at it thoughtfully.

Culver backed away. With Cherry guiding him, he wobbled off down the street.

Meg drew a deep breath. She meant to make a gracious remark about Andy's appearance at the strategic moment, but his smug expression aggravated her.

"Why didn't you tell me that revolting couple was still in town?" she asked. "No wonder you warned me about locking the house! You might have been more definite."

"I knew Culver was hanging around," Andy admitted. "But he's nothing to worry about. All talk and no action."

"That's probably what they used to say about Lizzie Borden."

"Slander, nasty slander. Lizzie was acquitted, free and clear, by the state of Massachusetts."

"What does Lizzie Borden have to do with this?"

"You were the one who brought her up," Andy pointed out. "Forget about the Culvers."

"I found the dishes, Andy."

"What dishes?"

"The ones with the daisy pattern. You missed a few pieces."

"Oh, yeah. They really had a fun time in the kitchen. You should have seen it."

"I didn't have to see it."

Andy looked at her closely. "What bothers you so much about a few pieces of broken china? For God's sake, Meg, don't be so damned oversensitive. That's the sort of feeble malice people like Culver enjoy. Be thankful they smash dishes instead of heads." And then, as Meg stood silent, he took her arm, adding, "Let's go home and get to work. You think too much. As Caesar said of Cassius—"

"'Such men are dangerous.' Men. . . . The trouble with women is they don't think enough."

## II

Andy had tried to prepare Meg for what she would find in the attic, but the reality overwhelmed her; it was beyond anything she could have imagined in her wildest fancies. To begin with, the singular noun was an error. The attic was not a single room but a series of rooms, large and small. Meg had to deal with a large loftlike chamber, as big as the drawing room downstairs, and several smaller areas, some as tiny as closets, others the size of a normal bedroom.

The large room was filled with furniture, not only from wall to wall but from floor to ceiling. Chairs were upended on top of tables, dismantled bed frames lay atop sideboards. Meg removed a few of the smaller pieces but soon realized she could not go any further without some sort of master plan. Some of the objects were too heavy for her to handle alone, and they were so intricately balanced that an injudicious move might bring a heap of wood tumbling down on her. It was also a question as to where she could put the furniture after she moved it. The other rooms were almost as full.

The furniture was only part of the problem. The attics held the accumulated discards of generations, heaped into miniature hills of miscellany. Broken toys and piles of books. Trunks filled with old clothes. Tottering pyramids of magazines, yellowing sheet music, warped records. Household appliances, including two treadle sewing machines, a cherry pitter, and three meat grinders. Meg didn't see any coffins, but she wouldn't have been surprised to find one; every other object the human animal needs or wants between the cradle and the grave was represented. And there were whole sections she couldn't even see, they were so barricaded by piled-up boxes.

Meg spent the first few minutes staring and swearing. Then the place began to cast its insidious spell. She was not immune to the lure of buried treasure, and this was an antique hunter's paradise. The current craze for nostalgia gave value to every article. Meg's interest was not solely commercial. She found it all fascinating, from the moth-eaten cloche hat that came clear down over her eyebrows to the sheet music, which included hits by Victor Herbert and patriotic songs from the First World War. The attic was a pleasant place; it was dusty but dry, and there was plenty of light from the dormer windows. Meg cleared off a rose velvet settee and wasted the first morning reading old *Saturday Evening Post* issues.

On a sunny afternoon several days later, she finished an Edgar Rice Burroughs serial in a crumbling issue of *Argosy* and closed the magazine with a sigh, followed by a long, luxurious stretch. The stuffy warmth of the attic made her sleepy, but as she gazed drowsily around, a faint twinge of conscience pricked through the lazy content that had held her. There *was* quite a bit of furniture in the attic. Maybe it was time she got to work.

Yet Meg knew she hadn't really wasted the time. The leisurely, mindless interlude was just what her nerves needed. She hadn't had a hallucination since the day she arrived. At night she slept soundly and dreamlessly. She had seen nothing of Andy, and she hadn't missed him; the idea of being alone in the big empty house didn't bother her a bit. Now she was beginning to get a little bored with puttering. She was rested and relaxed and ready to work.

A glance at the sunny, dust-streaked window made her decide to put off the work for one more day. It was already late in the afternoon, and the weather appeared to be glorious. She had spent the days inside the house, which was foolish; the fine weather wouldn't last indefinitely.

Meg walked straight down the stairs and out of the house without even stopping to wash her hands. The air had a summer warmth, but the leaves were beginning to turn; scarlet and gold and rust boughs stood out like splashes of paint against the green of the pines. As Meg strolled across the lawn she wondered what Andy was doing. He had called once, to see if she needed any groceries, but she had not felt conversational that day, and Andy had been brief and businesslike. She hadn't even seen his cottage, except as a square of yellow lighted window, visible from her bedroom at night. Now she headed for the row of trees that hid the caretaker's place from the big house.

It was a pretty little house, lacking only a thatched roof to be a perfect replica of an English cottage. Meg didn't go in. The doors and windows were wide open and she could hear the sound of rapid staccato typing. She smiled to herself as she retreated. If Andy wasn't writing a book, he was giving a good imitation of it. His typing sounded like a practiced version of the good old four-finger method rather than the smooth rattle of a professional; in fact, it was almost too fast to be wholly convincing. Even as she thought this, the typing slowed and stopped. Meg's smile broadened. The author's momentary inspiration had run out. It would be followed by a long, desperate silence, as he stared hopefully at his unfinished page and groped for a new idea.

Meg knew better than to intrude. She didn't feel like company, not Andy's, at any rate; his personality was too undependable, abrasive one moment, cheerful the next. She didn't want to risk her gentle, relaxed mood. Slowly she strolled across the lawn toward the summerhouse, which stood in a ring of birches—slim silver-and-gold trees, with their yellowing leaves and white trunks.

She explored the grounds and the nearby woods for another hour and then started back toward the house. It was almost time for the daily cocktail Sylvia had allowed her. She would sit on the veranda and admire the sunset. She opened the front door and had taken two steps across the hall before she heard the sound.

Music. It was a piano, and the tune was familiar—a Mozart minuet, precise and delicate.

Meg's first thought was that someone had entered the house while she was out. She had not locked the door. It had seemed ridiculous to do so on such a bright, peaceful day.

There was a piano in the house—a concert-sized

Bechstein grand. Meg had tried it; it was sadly out of tune. She remembered that, reasoning calmly, and at the same moment she knew that the notes still echoing through the hall were not made by a piano. Like a piano, and yet different . . . less resonant, softer . . .

Meg made a convulsive, groping gesture with both hands. The sounds stopped. They did not end, they were cut off, as if a door had closed.

Meg sat down on the stairs. Her heart was beating too fast, but it slowed after a short time. Rising, she went into the drawing room and approached the piano.

It was a fantastic piece of furniture. The original owner had not been content with the simple elegance of black or brown wood. The piano was gilded. The heavy legs were carved with lions' heads and bunches of fat, aggressive roses, and more roses adorned the music rack. Meg was not much of a pianist; but once, years ago, she had learned that very Mozart minuet. As she struck the yellowed ivory keys, the notes sounded—dissonant, because of the instrument's need of tuning, faulty because of her lack of skill. . . .

No. No piano, not even an instrument in perfect tune, could emit such sounds as the chords she had heard. They must have been made by a smaller, older ancestor of a modern piano—a spinet or harpsichord. There was no need to wonder why an intruder or unexpected guest might entertain himself by playing the harpsichord. There was no such instrument in the house.

Another hallucination.

There was no reason why Meg should be surprised at the idea. The doctors had warned her that the hallucinatory sounds and sights would fade gradually, in intensity as well as in frequency of occurrence. The fact that she hadn't had one for some days didn't mean they were over. Then why couldn't she accept it?

Standing motionless in the silent room, Meg tried to figure it out. The sounds had seemed so real! Never before had she felt the slightest doubt that her senses were tricking her; never had she believed for an instant in the reality of what she saw or heard. Yet on this occasion she had thought, first of all, that a real intruder must be playing a real instrument.

The doctors hadn't warned her about this development. Maybe it didn't mean anything; maybe this was a unique case, If not . . . Meg twisted her hands together. Hallucinations were bad enough when she could recognize them for what they were. If she was unable to distinguish reality from illusion.

A sound from the doorway startled her. Whirling around, she saw Andy.

"How long have you been there?" she gasped.

"I was looking for you. What's the matter?"

"Nothing. I went for a walk and . . ." Meg stopped. "Never mind. Nothing. Would you—would you like a drink? I was about to sit down on the veranda and admire the sunset."

"You never told me you could play the piano," Andy said. "What else do you know besides Mozart?"

Meg felt the color draining from her cheeks. Then she remembered. She had played the minuet—badly, but she had played it—on the Bechstein. With an effort she got control of herself. She was behaving like a fool, and Andy was staring. It would never do to let him realize how badly she was shaken.

"I haven't played for years," she said lightly. "But I'm going to practice some of the music I found upstairs. I can hardly wait to learn 'We're Gonna Kick the Kaiser.' You said you were looking for me; any particular reason?"

"Not really. I owe you a dinner invitation. Haven't seen you for a few days, and thought you might come over and eat a hamburger with me. My cooking doesn't run to anything more exciting."

"Sounds good to me."

If Andy hoped his uninspired menu would prompt Meg to take over the cooking, he was disappointed. She sat on a kitchen stool and watched him broil the hamburgers and cook frozen french fries. After they had eaten he showed her the cottage. It was small, with two tiny bedrooms and a bath filling the upper story, and a kitchen and parlor downstairs. Despite an initial impression of clutter, the place was clean and relatively neat. The greatest disorder was in the parlor, where Andy worked; a long kitchen table, near the window, was completely covered by the typewriter and a scattering of books and papers. Coffee cup in hand, Meg wandered toward the table. Andy got there first. Gathering the typewritten sheets together, he turned the pile face down.

"No fair looking," he said.

"You must become accustomed to criticism. Or is this going to be one of those unpublished works?"

"I'll let you read it when it's done. This is only the third draft."

"Okay, okay."

Meg turned to the bookshelves. There were two of them, tall, homemade structures filled with books. The collection surprised her; it was eclectic, to say the least, ranging from Bartlett and Roget to nineteenth-century poetry. Then she saw the volume that lay face down on a table near a big comfortable chair. She picked it up and looked at the title. It was one of the "true" stories of the occult which had become popular in recent years; Meg replaced it with a fastidious sneer.

"I didn't think you would read such nonsense."

"You think it's nonsense, do you?"

"Worse than nonsense; it's an insult to a normal reader's intelligence."

Andy said nothing, but he looked skeptical, and that was enough to spur Meg on.

"Really, Andy! I've read a couple of these myself— ghost hunters, psychic investigators. The medium goes into the haunted house and gets vague impressions of evil and uneasy spirits; she holds a séance and contacts the spirit of, say, a Revolutionary War captain named John Smith, who tells her all about his military career, and how he was murdered, and like that. Then the ghost hunter checks the records; and lo and behold, he finds that there was a John Smith who fought in the Revolution! Hurray for the medium! Of course the John Smith in the records was a private, not a captain; he served in the Fourteenth Massachusetts, not the Colonial Cavalry; he never lived within a hundred miles of the haunted house, and he died peacefully in his bed at the age of ninety-six. These little discrepancies don't bother the ghost hunter one bit. He chalks up another victory for spiritualism. He ought to award the Pulitzer Prize for fiction to the medium."

"Oh, I agree with you." Andy sat down, and Meg followed suit. "Most people have no conception of what constitutes reasonable proof. But you aren't being fair to the medium. You think she—or he—is always a fraud?"

"What other explanation is there?"

Andy sputtered. "You, of all people, can ask that? Hallucinations like yours are much more common than you realize. They can be caused by lots of things besides a bump on the head, and they probably account for most of the stories of ghosts and haunted houses."

"I hadn't thought of that," Meg admitted. "But my hallucinations have a physical cause, Andy. The parts of the brain that receive sensory impressions react on their own, without an external stimulus."

"Sure, but it doesn't require damage to the brain cells to cause dysfunction of the perception centers. Drugs can do it; the hallucinatory drugs produce visions, sounds, even smells and tactile impressions that are as real to the visionary as impressions that originate in the sensory organs. Psychological stimuli can do the same thing. A person who is bereaved and grief-stricken, possibly guilty, may imagine he sees the spirit of the dead man."

"How do you know all this?" Meg asked suspiciously.

"Oh, I've always been interested in the subject—and very skeptical, let me add." Andy's face was in shadow; the sun had sunk below the treetops and the room swam in a blue haze. "Hell, this is a morbid topic of conversation. Let's talk about me."

"No, I'm interested. I hadn't thought about the ramifications; I've been too worried about my own problems. It makes me feel a little less . . . weird, if you know what I mean. What you're saying is that hallucinations can be caused by physical malfunction, or extreme emotional stress. Like a child afraid of the dark, who thinks he sees a monster, instead of his bathrobe thrown over a chair. . . ."

"No, wait a minute. You're confusing illusions with hallucinations. In the former case, emotional stress causes the brain to misinterpret a genuine sensory impression of something that is really there. A hallucination has no physical reality. It's all in your head—literally."

"I can sympathize with our poor ignorant ancestors, who didn't know about hallucinations. They would think they were seeing ghosts, wouldn't they? No wonder they were terrified. It scares me, even though I know what causes it."

"Yeah. And speaking of roc's eggs," Andy said, "what have you been doing in the attic lately?"

Meg accepted the change of subject. Andy considered it morbid, and perhaps he was right, although she had been speaking the truth when she said it helped her to view her misfortune in a larger perspective.

She stayed late, and Andy offered to walk her home. When they left the cottage Meg saw that the halcyon fall weather had changed. The moon rode high, bright silver on black, but the sky was filled with little clouds that rushed westward, moved by a cool wind. As they walked across the lawn the moonlight flickered on and off, as if someone were manipulating a celestial light switch. Half-clouded moonlight is one of the eeriest of illuminations, summoning and dismissing shadow shapes like the illusions of a master magician. Meg was glad to have human companionship, even though it was silent. Neither of them spoke. The wind whipped Meg's hair into her eyes and Andy seemed intent on the gathering clouds.

When the front door swung slowly open, neither of them moved for a moment. The darkened hall was pierced by a long ray of moonlight; it seemed to dart past them, into the house, as the opening door allowed it entry. Then Andy spoke. His voice sounded strange, as if he stood in a vast wall-less space that swallowed up human speech.

> " 'Is there anybody there?' said the Traveller,
> Knocking on the moonlit door. . . ."

Meg had to make a conscience effort to speak lightly. She felt as though she must counter the growing spell of witchery before it engulfed her.

> "And his horse in the silence champed the grasses
> Of the forest's ferny floor,"

"I learned that in high school too," she added. "Look, no horse. Cut it out, Andy. It's a spooky night, without de la Mare."

"Too true," Andy said, in his normal voice. "And a perfect example of what we were talking about earlier. Illusions of shadows and moonlit. . . . Another minute, and we'd be seeing phantom listeners like crazy. Come on in."

But before he entered the house he reached a long arm around the doorframe and pressed the light switch. The chandelier came to life, reducing the hallway from a place of magic and moonlight to its normal barrenness. He went into the house without letting Meg precede him—a casual thing, which she wouldn't have noticed ordinarily. Yet the impression still lingered—the feeling of expectation, of something waiting.

With a silent reprimand to her overactive imagination she followed Andy and closed the door behind her. The windy night was shut out.

Andy had gone into the drawing room, switching on lights as he went. He stood in the middle of the room, gazing around.

"Want to search the house?" Meg asked, half joking.

"Maybe I should."

"Oh, for heaven's sake! What are you afraid of?"

"Me, afraid?" Andy put a casual hand on her shoulder. "I'm not the one who sees things that aren't there."

The words were like a summoning, an invocation. The thing that had been waiting in the room swooped down. Meg's hands moved; but no physical rejection could ward off the unreal. She stood among shadows, struggling for breath. Reality was slow in returning. Andy was shaking her. His distorted face was close to hers.

"Twice in one day," she moaned. "It's getting worse. Since I came here. . . ."

"Meg!" Andy shook her again. "Stop yelling! Listen to me. It was not a hallucination. Don't you understand? I saw it too."

# Chapter 4

Meg wasn't sure which of them had led the retreat. The cool night air brought her back to her senses; she stopped at the bottom of the veranda stairs. Andy stopped too. He was holding her hand. The last one out, whoever it was, had left the front door open, and yellow light spilled out across the porch and onto the drive. For a few seconds neither of them spoke.

"Let's go to my place," Andy said finally.

"No. I've got to go back in there."

"You're crazy. There's something there. Something waiting."

"I don't care. Don't you understand? If I can't stay in that house, I'm sunk. I have nowhere else to go."

"Wait a minute. Let me think."

Meg was shivering. She pulled her hand from Andy's and wrapped her arms around her body.

"Running away won't help," she said. "I can't run away from my own brain. Only this was different . . . Andy. You said you saw it too. What did you see?"

"Another room."

"Collective hallucination?" Meg suggested.

Andy shrugged—or perhaps he shivered. "Words. What do they mean?"

"They must mean something, or you wouldn't be using them to write a book," Meg snapped. "You were glib enough about hallucinations and related phenomena a few hours ago. It isn't so easy to be academic when it happens to you, is it?"

Andy didn't answer. His hands in his pockets, his shoulders hunched, he might have been shivering from cold; but he looked like a dog that expects to be kicked, and Meg relented.

"Maybe it is a shock, when you're not used to it," she said more gently. "Go on home and get some sleep."

"While you march back into the house and play heroine?" Andy straightened. "Thanks. I guess I deserved that. All right, I'll come with you; but I'm not buying the hallucination theory."

"What do you mean?"

"We'll talk inside. Might as well be scared to death as freeze."

By unspoken consent they avoided the brightly lighted drawing room and headed for the kitchen. Its utilitarian cheer seemed to deny the extraordinary. Meg sat down at the table while Andy roamed around the room, putting on water for coffee and then searching through drawers.

Now that she was calmer, Meg felt sure the panic that had sent her flying out of the house had been contagious, sparked by Andy's fright; and she watched him curiously. The hallucinations were disturbing, no one knew that better than she; but surely Andy's reaction was strange. Beneath the veneer of sophisticated skepticism he was as superstitious as a peasant. It wasn't difficult to figure out what he was thinking, and she decided she had better play along with him, for a while at least.

"Shall we compare notes?" she asked. "You said you saw—"

"Quiet." Andy came to the table carrying pencils and a pad of paper. "Comparing notes is precisely what I intend to do, but we'll go about it scientifically instead of feeding one another verbal clues to build on. Here. Write down exactly what you saw. I'll stand at the counter with my back to you and do the same thing."

"Oh, this is ridiculous!"

"No, by God, it isn't." He was still pale, but there was a gleam of amusement in his eyes as he regarded her. "You were griping a while back about the sloppy methods of the ghost-hunter types. Okay. Here's our chance to go about it properly. This is a classic case—the typical visions and emotional impressions. Neither of us is consciously faking. At least I'm willing to admit you're honest, and I trust you'll do the same for me."

"I guess so. You have no reason. . . ." Meg stopped. To cover her confusion, she reached for the pencil. "Okay, we'll do it your way."

"Wait a minute. Don't start writing till I've turned my back. Write down the date and the time, and then go to it."

For a while there was no sound except the scratch of the pencils and the mindless whir of the refrigerator turning itself on and off. When Meg had finished, she looked at Andy.

"I'm through," she said.

"Okay." Andy turned. "We'll swap papers, then."

Meg had not read more than a few words before she knew she was in trouble. The terse descriptive phrases had a cumulative weight that was difficult to resist.

"Another room. Three walls, a low ceiling with dark beams. A picture, or something, in a frame on the wall to the left. Wide, dark frame; couldn't make out what was inside. Not a portrait, the shapes were geometric, brightly colored. Window on right-hand wall. Daylight. Table and two chairs near the window. A figure standing in front of the table. Couldn't see details, but was a man's figure— wore pants, not skirts. Impression of facial hair—white, gray, possibly blond. Dark coat, something shiny on it—buttons, medals, braid?"

Meg looked up. Andy was a quick reader; her account had been longer than his, but he had already finished. Their eyes met, and his lips curved in a wry grimace.

"Interesting, isn't it? We'll have to discount the initial coincidence—that we both saw another room. I told you, when we were outside, that that was what I saw, and I seem to remember your mentioning something of the sort once before, the day you arrived. So we could have suggested that to one another."

"Aren't you being too persnickety?"

"Persnickety is what we have to be. Even so, making all possible allowance for coincidence, suggestion, and other rational explanations, the details match up. You saw more than I did, but you saw the same things. You say the picture was a sampler. That's one of those embroidered things, isn't it—the ones little girls used to make to show off their skill in sewing, and keep their idle hands out of mischief? I couldn't make out what the thing was, but I did see bright colors and a formal pattern. You saw a house and trees and an embroidered motto—though you couldn't read the words.

"You saw the table and the chairs and the window, in the same locations I saw. You saw an elderly man with a long white beard. His coat had silver buttons.

"You mentioned collective hallucinations. Sure, I believe in them; I've seen the mass emotion of a crowd and the way people reinforce one another's vague impressions till they build up a picture of something that never happened. But I don't see how that can apply here. The details are too exact to be coincidental."

"It needn't be a coincidence. It was a spooky night, and we are both too suggestible. You knew I have hallucinations—"

"But Meg, a collective hallucination doesn't work this way. When you investigate closely, you find that people did not, in fact, see the same thing—unless it was a phenomenon they all expected to see beforehand. Like, you know, the stories about holy images. People come to the church on the saint's day expecting to see the miraculous statue weep, because the legend says it weeps. And sure enough, they see it. One hysteric yells, 'There—look at the tears flowing down the face!' His neighbor chimes in, 'Yes, yes, the saint is weeping!' And before long, half the crowd is caught up in the delusion. But that's not what happened tonight."

Meg shook her head speechlessly. She didn't know what she believed, or what she wanted to believe; she was still dazed by the parallels in the two accounts. Andy sat down across the table.

"Look at it this way," he said patiently. "Collective hallucination accounts for the majority of the stories of visions and ghosts. But that doesn't mean all the stories can be explained that way. Suppose you walk out of the house one morning and see a puddle of water on the porch. You know there is usually a puddle in that spot after it rains. But you can't assume that it rained because you find a puddle! See what I mean? We can't scribble "Q.E.D.," collective hallucination, at the bottom of these papers and forget them. We can look for another cause."

"What other cause?" Meg's voice was shrill. "Are you seriously suggesting that we both saw—well—ghosts? I'd rather have my hallucinations."

"There are other explanations."

"Such as?"

"Mental telepathy. I got the picture from your mind; that's why the details are the same, and why your picture was more distinct than mine. Your transmission, or my reception, was faulty. If we practiced—"

"For God's sake, who wants to practice? Even if I believed in ESP, I wouldn't have it as a gift. I can't imagine anything nastier than being able to read someone else's mind."

"Especially mine, you mean. I wasn't suggesting we practice. I only mentioned ESP as one possibility." Andy leaned forward, his arms resting on the table, his eyes intent. "You've accepted your hallucinations as inevitable— just another of life's dirty tricks. Maybe they were, at first. But what we saw tonight is not in the same category as . . . as elephants on Fifth Avenue. Doesn't it make sense to fight this thing—study it, as you would any other unexplained phenomenon—instead of sitting back with folded hands and waiting for it to hit you again? Who knows, we may be on the threshold of a great discovery."

"I don't know, Andy. I'm too tired to think. I'm going to bed."

"Okay, we'll talk about it in the morning. I'm going to sleep here tonight." He sounded tentative, as if he expected her to object.

Meg shrugged, "I don't know what you think you're protecting me from, but suit yourself."

"I'll take the master bedroom. And I'll leave the door open. Don't be shy about yelling if anything bugs you."

"I won't. And the same to you."

Andy grinned. "You can't insult me that way, love. I'll scream my head off if my nerves get out of hand."

For some time after she had gotten into bed Meg could hear Andy moving around the house. She didn't know what he was doing, and she didn't care. Maybe he was making the bed. It was his problem; sleeping in the house had been his idea.

She was inclined to believe Andy's statement that he would yell for help if he got nervous. In fact, she wasn't at all sure who was protecting whom. Andy's behavior had not been notably courageous. He was the first to run, and he had to be shamed into reentering the house.

Meg wasn't particularly vain, but she knew she was a reasonably attractive woman, and she was accustomed to fending off—or not fending off—interested males. She didn't expect every man she met to make a pass, but Andy's fraternal attitude was a little suspicious.

Meg smiled wryly. It was really the height of conceit to assume that because a man wasn't interested in her, he wasn't interested in any woman. Besides, Andy's habits were his own affair. What was more important was his intense reaction to her—their—hallucination. If he hadn't been terrified, he had given a good imitation of it. Maybe he had won a place as one of Sylvia's lame dogs not by virtue of his aspirations as a writer but because he had been temporarily crippled by mental illness. That was his affair too. Except, Meg added to herself, it was a little unfair of Andy to insinuate that the mental instability was hers alone. He could at least share the responsibility.

It was another thought that kept Meg awake, however. Earlier in the evening she had started to say that Andy had no motive for wanting to trick her. And that wasn't true. He might have a very solid motive for wanting her to leave the house.

Andy hated Sylvia. He didn't bother to hide his dislike, and he had ample cause for it. The house, and the entire valuable estate, ought to have been his. Meg couldn't imagine how Sylvia had conned Andy's father into leaving the estate to her, especially if it had come to him through his first wife, Andy's mother. Sylvia had been amply endowed by her first husband; there was no excuse for her snatching all of Andy's inheritance. But there was no use wondering how she had done it; whatever her methods, they were obviously effective. Andy had every reason to resent them.

In their discussion that evening Andy had pretended to

be dispassionate, but it was clear what he believed—what he was trying to make her believe. "Something is in there," he had said. "Something is waiting." By sharing Meg's hallucination, or pretending to do so, he had changed its nature. He wanted her to think the house was haunted.

But, Meg argued silently, what could Andy hope to gain by this maneuver? He might frighten her away from the house, but that wouldn't affect Sylvia's control of the property. Sylvia wouldn't believe in ghosts if a regiment of them rattled chains at her nightly, and if her property contained anything undesirable she would simply unload it as fast as she could, to the highest bidder. And caveat emptor.

## II

Meg overslept the next morning, lulled by the drip of rain at the windows. When she opened her eyes her room looked dreary in the gray light, and it felt chilly and damp. As she came down the stairs, wearing jeans and a red flannel shirt, she heard thumps and groans from the nether regions, and went to find out what they meant. The noises increased in volume when she opened the cellar door, and she followed them through dingy empty rooms to find Andy, grease encrusted, struggling with a behemoth of a furnace.

"I've got it," he announced, without so much as a "hello." "Should have checked the thing before, but I didn't get around to it. Let's see."

He replaced a plate, tightened a few screws, and pressed a button. The furnace went on with a breathy roar.

"I'm glad I didn't have to do that," Meg admitted. "Is there anything else of interest down here?"

"Servants' rooms. They didn't store anything good down here; it's too damp."

"Too damp for furniture, but not for servants," Meg said.

"What are you, some kind of radical hippy do-gooder?" Andy demanded, grinning.

They went back upstairs. Andy said he had had breakfast, so Meg made herself toast and coffee while Andy continued to exude good cheer and feeble witticisms. He made no reference to their experience the night before, except to announce that he had moved into the master bedroom.

"I'm going to start stripping the wallpaper," he explained. "It'll have to be done eventually, and Culver's comments are beginning to grate on me already."

"Have fun," Meg said cheerfully. She had decided on the line she meant to take: bland acceptance of anything Andy proposed. To express suspicion of his motives would be dangerous, if he was up to no good, and pointless if he was innocent. It was worth some effort to keep him in an affable mood; the monstrous old furnace had reminded her of what she would be up against if Andy walked out in a huff.

"What are you going to do today?" Andy asked.

"Today is D-day. I'm going to start inventorying the attic."

"Rather you than me. I'd just soon tackle the Augean stables."

"It's not filthy, just dusty and jumbled."

"I commend your energy. Well, guess I'd better get moving."

But he continued to sit, watching her as she rinsed off her dishes and put them in the dishwasher.

"Listen," he said after a while, "don't worry about extra work with me here. We'll get our own meals, keep our own schedules."

"We could take turns getting dinner."

Andy brightened.

"I did it last night."

"So it's my turn tonight. The only thing is . . ."

"What?"

"Well, obviously I'm not worried about what the neighbors will say. But if Sylvia dislikes having an unmarried couple in her house—"

"Sylvia is a pain, but she's not stupid," Andy said. "If you and I were engaged in what Sylvia would probably call hanky-panky, or something equally nauseous, a distance of a few hundred feet wouldn't slow us down. She knew I was here when she sent you. She also knows that I know I'll lose my soft job if you complain about me."

Meg retreated in some confusion. She had not expected such a direct answer to her doubts about Andy. His attitude wasn't very flattering to her; he had made it clear that her questionable charms weren't worth risking his job for. Well, she thought, climbing the steep attic stairs, it was an acceptable explanation, whether it was true or not.

On a wet, gloomy day the vast attic loft was an eerie place. Fortunately it had been electrified, and the upper regions of the house were warm, compared to the lower floors. Meg expected to work up a good healthy sweat. She would have to shift several tons of furniture before she finished the job. It would take weeks—possibly months.

Expecting that an inventory would be needed, she had bought a loose-leaf notebook and a fat sheaf of lined paper. By using a separate sheet for each object, she could rearrange and classify them at a later time. Now she would have to list them as they came to light, more or less at random. The descriptions would have to be detailed, amplified with sketches and measurements, for Meg was uncomfortably aware of her inability to identify all the objects by type and date. Filled with virtuous determination, she rolled up her flannel sleeves and began.

It was slow, hard work, unbelievably complicated by the crowded state of the rooms. The only empty space was in the narrow corridor at the top of the attic stairs. Before long Meg realized she would need some system of labeling the objects as she listed them—a number, corresponding to the number in the inventory. She didn't want to write on the furniture, not even in pencil. What she needed were gummed labels, the kind that stuck without water and could be peeled right off. Why hadn't she thought of that? Maybe Andy had some. She would ask him later.

Meanwhile, as she scrambled under tables and over dressers, she noticed something that ought to have occurred to her before. The farther she penetrated into the interior of the big room, the older was the furniture. The occupants of the house who had carried their discards up to be stored, had started at the back of the room and gradually filled it up, generation by generation, layer by layer. It was the older period that interested Meg; the florid, heavy carved Victorian furniture attracted her less than the earlier, simpler styles. But there was no way of getting at such hypothetical treasures unless she moved a vanload of heavy furniture first.

Frustrated and perspiring, she decided to postpone the furniture inventory until she could get some labels. A heavy glass-front bookcase was accessible; it was filled with leather-bound volumes. Meg sat down on the floor in front of the bookcase. She was quite ready to sit for a while, and anyway the books would have to be listed sooner or later—by author, title, date of publication. There might be a valuable first edition among them.

The books were disappointing. Pretentiously bound, they were not as old as Meg had hoped. One of them caught her interest, though not for its antiquarian value. It was a genealogy of the Emig family, privately printed in 1933. Andy's last name was Brenner; Meg wondered if the Emigs were his mother's family. Surely the book wouldn't interest anyone who wasn't an Emig. It was written in a turgid, labored style, and the organization of the material was poor.

The family had not been particularly distinguished, but if the author's research was accurate, it was a very old one. Of course, Meg reflected, the same could be said of any family. Every human being has prehistoric ancestors. The Emigs had come to America not on the *Mayflower* but on the very next boat; they had fought bravely in the Revolution—on the Patriot side, of course—and had produced men of honor and women of integrity, with never a black sheep in the lot.

Meg began to yawn. The Emigs couldn't have been as dull as their biographer implied. She glanced at the title page. Her suspicion was correct; the author's name was

Emig. That would account not only for the pious bias of the entries but also for the awkward literary style. She skipped the earlier chapters and began searching for a reference to the house in which she was living. It was an impressive mansion and undoubtedly represented a period of relative prosperity for the family.

Sure enough, the building of Trail's End had inspired several pages of fulsome description. The builder, one Benjamin Emig, had invested in steel mills. His epitaph, quoted by his admiring descendant, was an excellent example of sanctimonious pomposity—and, Meg suspected, a tissue of lies from beginning to end. Men who built fortunes in those days often built them on the bodies of their workers. And the bearded, buttoned-up patriarch whose portrait was reproduced had the cold, unwinking stare of a snake and a mouth like a paper cut. Meg felt a stir of pity for the meek little wife who stood by him, her hand on his shoulder in proper wifely humility. Any man who would name his house Trail's End had a negative attitude toward life.

She read on, with growing interest. The text was fun if you interpreted it with a liberal quantity of salt and deduced the truth under the formal phrases. Benjamin Emig had left a large progeny—no doubt that fact accounted, in part, for his wife's worn look. But the family had dwindled as the twentieth century succeeded the nineteenth. Alexander Emig, born in 1895, inherited his father's money and Trail's End, but by 1933, when the book was written, he had produced only two offspring, and one of them had not survived infancy. The other child—Beverly—must be Andy's mother. The date was right. . . .

A hand touched her shoulder, startling her so that she

dropped the book. She had been so absorbed in the fortunes of the obscure Emigs that she had not heard Andy's approach.

"It's one o'clock," he said. "What's so fascinating about that book?"

Meg handed him the volume.

"I'm investigating your ghost theory," she said maliciously. "I thought I'd see whether any of your ancestors had a reason to haunt the house."

Andy's eyebrows shot up. He looked curiously at the book.

"I don't think I ever saw this."

"It is your mother's family, I take it."

"Yes." Andy turned to the back of the book. "Here she is—Beverly Emig. Anything in here I ought to know about?"

"Your ancestors were a singularly virtuous crowd. Not that I believe a word of it."

"No, I wouldn't. Wow." Flipping through the pages, Andy stopped at the picture of Benjamin Emig. "Here's a face that might haunt a house."

"He built it. But if anybody had a reason for revenge, it would be his wife. I bet he beat her."

"You said the man had a beard." Andy's eyes were fixed on the picture, but a muscle near his mouth was twitching oddly.

"The man? Oh. That man. No, it wasn't Benjamin."

"How can you be sure?"

"The beard was white," Meg said positively. "Oh, I see; it could be Benjamin when he was older. But the other man's clothes didn't look like clothes of this period. Oh, blast it, I'm not sure. I don't think so, though."

"I hope not. If we must be haunted, I'd prefer a more benevolent-looking ghost."

"So you admit it." Meg straightened her bent knees and stretched. "You are trying to find a ghost."

"Why not? Think of the book I could write. I could make a fortune."

"We," Meg corrected, matching his frivolous tone. "It would have to be a collaborative effort. Didn't Bridey Murphy make a few bucks out of that book? Like me, she was the goat—or the guinea pig."

"You're all mixed up. Bridey Murphy was the original personality reincarnated in the modern housewife, whose name I forget."

"So do I. And what's more, I don't believe in Bridey." Meg rose stiffly to her feet. "I guess I could do with some lunch."

"And a bath," Andy said critically.

While Meg showered, Andy made sandwiches and opened a can of soup. They had almost finished the makeshift meal when Meg returned to the attack.

"I didn't hear you scream last night. Didn't you see anything frightening?"

"Obviously not, or I would have screamed. How about you? No visions up there in the gray solitude of the attic?"

"Not a thing. But cheer up; the day isn't over yet."

"Damn it, what makes you think I'm looking for trouble? I'd be delighted if you never had any more fits."

"Thanks for putting it so tactfully."

They glared at one another across the table. Then Andy's scowl smoothed out.

"Sorry," he muttered. "What's the matter with us? Is it the house? The unholy aura of—"

"Oh, stop it. It's not the house, it's us. We always fought. If there is an aura in the house, it's . . ."

"What?"

"I wish you hadn't quoted that damned poem," Meg burst out. "I can't get it out of my mind."

Andy leaned back in his chair.

> *"But only a host of phantom listeners*
> *That dwell in the lone house then*
> *Stood listening in the quiet of the moonlight*
> *To that voice from the world of men:*
>
> *Stood thronging the faint moonbeams*
> *on the dark stair,*
> *That goes down to the empty hall. . . .*

"What comes next?"

"If I knew, I wouldn't tell you," Meg muttered.

"Wait a minute, I'll get it. . . . The Traveller banged on the door again; you'd think he'd have caught on by then, wouldn't you?

> *" 'Tell them I came, and no one answered,*
> *That I kept my word,' he said.*

"But they never did answer. And

> *"The silence surged softly backward,*
> *When the plunging hoofs were gone.*

"Slick, sentimental stuff," he concluded, and popped the rest of his ham sandwich into his mouth.

"It may be sentimental and old-fashioned, but it packs a wallop. When that door opened last night and the moonlight slid into the hall, I could almost see Them, waiting on the stair. Oh, it was sheer imagination—illusion—not one of my hallucinations, if I may still be allowed to call them that. But it was shivery, all the same."

"I know. It's the vagueness of the poem that gets to you. Who was the Traveller? Who sent him? Why didn't anyone answer?"

"They were dead," Meg said. "All dead, long before he came. He came too late."

"That's stupid?" Andy said angrily. "As a literary critic you make a good furniture mover."

"There you go again, losing your temper over nothing."

"I am not losing my temper! I am perfectly calm. I—" Andy stopped speaking. His mouth hung open. His eyes were focused on some invisible object in the near distance. Meg was about to remonstrate when he brought his fist down on the table with an impact that rattled the dishes.

"Stupid!" he exclaimed. "My God, are we stupid!"

"Thanks for including yourself," Meg snapped. "What are you mad about now?"

"Our stupidity. Here we are looking for ghosts among my ancestors, when it is perfectly obvious that we didn't see this house, or anyone who ever lived in it. The old man with the white beard brought his ambience with him. Another room. A room with different walls, a lower ceiling. . . . Meg, there must have been a house on this site before this one. That's the house we saw. That house, and one of the people who lived in it. None of my relatives."

This new idea made him look years younger, brought

color to his cheeks and a genuine smile to his eyes. He really believes it, Meg thought incredulously; he was honestly afraid . . . of what? Of seeing his dead mother sharing the ghostly vigil of her grim old grandfather?

Meg was touched; sympathy made her reply less emphatic than it might otherwise have been.

"I hate to discourage you, Andy, but aren't you jumping to conclusions?"

"That's how scientific discoveries are made—by researchers jumping to conclusions and then checking them out. The difference between a scientist and a fanatic is that the scientist discards his theory if the evidence doesn't confirm it. The fanatic twists the evidence to fit the theory."

"What kind of evidence do you think you can find?"

"First, I'll try to learn whether there was another house here. There probably was. This one is only a hundred-odd years old, and the area was settled in the late seventeenth century. I've got some books on early Pennsylvania history, and there may be more in the library."

Andy's eyes were shining with enthusiasm. He ran his fingers through his mop of reddish hair, disturbing a collection of colored scraps that floated down onto the table.

"Wallpaper," he explained, brushing at them. "It's a messy job, getting that stuff off."

"But it's a job that has to be finished, now you've begun. I've got a job to do too; I hope you don't expect me to help you hunt for your ghosts."

"Stop talking about my ghosts. If they belong to anybody, they belong to you. You brought 'em here."

"Of all the rotten things to say!" Meg jumped to her feet. "You're contradicting your own dumb theory. If there are ghosts, they've been here all along. If they belong to me, they aren't ghosts; they're scars on the brain."

"What are you getting so excited about?"

"Oh, you're impossible. I'm going back to work. You can scrape wallpaper or invent ghosts or do whatever you like. Good-bye!"

Andy followed her out, leaving the dirty dishes on the table.

"Come along and see what I've done," he said placatingly. "Don't worry, I'll finish the job; Sylvia's paying me, and I'll give her eight honest hours of my precious time before I start ghost hunting."

Meg shrugged, and let him lead the way to the master bedroom. She stopped on the threshold with an exclamation of dismay. To call this a messy job was the understatement of the year. Andy had finished one wall. The floor was covered with scraps, some damp and sticky, some dry and flaky. The fragments were a rainbow confetti of colors—red, white, green, gold, flowery blue. He had moved the big bed into the middle of the room and covered it with newspapers; there were scraps of paper even on that protective surface.

"Three layers," Andy explained. "The lowest was that green stuff with gold patterns. Too bad I couldn't save it, but the layer above was practically fused with it. At least this is honest-to-God plaster, not plasterboard, which softens and peels when it's wet."

"Fascinating," Meg said drily; but she felt a ridiculous urge to pick up the nearest tool and start scraping. She suppressed her instinct and turned to the door.

When she got upstairs she realized she had forgotten to ask Andy about the labels. Standing on the threshold of the vast chamber, Meg felt her spirits sink. The room was so big and so full. . . . The inventory was impossible without labels; the furniture was too heavy to move; even the books had been a disappointment. She decided to abandon this room for a while and tackle one of the smaller chambers.

At the risk of life and limb and antiques, Meg began dragging things out into the corridor. Sylvia hadn't been kidding when she mentioned Chippendale; Meg found two chairs that had that maker's distinctive hallmarks, and she thought she saw others farther back in the room. The attic windows were darkening with a rainy twilight when she caught sight of the door in the wall.

She was kneeling on top of a massive dining room table from whose surface she had removed four chairs, two end tables, and the pieces of a broken bookcase. She had taken her shoes off, although the precaution was probably useless; the top of the once shining mahogany was badly scratched, as were most of the other wooden surfaces in the room.

Meg sat back, crossed her legs, and contemplated the door. It was only a rough square cut into the unfinished wall of the room and furnished with hinges and a catch. It probably opened into a space under the eaves of the roof, and the possibility of anything valuable being stored there was remote indeed. Yet, Meg argued with herself, why should the door have been cut unless there was something beyond it? Something old.

She knew then that her decision to abandon the inventory had been motivated by something more positive than frustration. She had been guided, all afternoon, by an unconscious urge that had only now come to the surface of her mind.

Andy's ghost theory had gotten to her. He had played brilliantly on her situation and her state of mind; she admitted to herself, although she would never have admitted it to him, that she would almost prefer ghosts to mental illness. The idea had its own macabre fascination. Who can resist a ghost story? And in her cynical theorizing about Andy's possible guilt she had forgotten one thing: there was no way she could think of in which he could have produced a description of the visionary room that agreed so devastatingly with her account.

If the room they had both seen was in an earlier house, now destroyed—and Andy's comments on that subject made sense—that house must have existed in the early nineteenth, or even the eighteenth, century. Was that what she was searching for—relics, mementos, of the house that had once stood on the site of Trail's End?

Meg frowned. Hunches are supposed to be the result of the subconscious reasoning; but in this case her subconscious was reasoning like a three-year-old. Even if there had been an earlier house, there was nothing to suggest that any of its furnishings had been moved to the newly built mansion, or that the same family had owned both houses. Certainly there was no reason to suppose that the surviving relics, if any, would be concealed behind that particular door.

Brushing the hair from her face with a very dirty hand, Meg crawled forward.

A wilderness of table legs and bedposts still lay between her and her goal. She moved only those objects over which she could not crawl or through which she could not squeeze, and before long she had lowered herself into the tiny space before the door. If it opened outward, she was out of luck. There was barely room for her own slim body, and a slate-topped chiffonier stood squarely in front of the door. But if it opened inward . . .

It did not. The catch moved readily enough. The door opened, with a squeak of rusty hinges, and then caught against the chiffonier, leaving a dark opening barely large enough for Meg's arm.

By dint of movement which would have strained a contortionist, Meg got herself around the chiffonier and squatted down, with a slate corner denting her arm and a brass bedpost poking a hole in her back. She put her face up to the opening and peered in. The darkness was absolute; there was no window in the area under the eaves, and the solid old house had no cracks in its structure.

The dark, long-enclosed space smelled musty and strange, but there was no stench of decay. There would be cobwebs, of course, but no rats; she would have heard them by now, scuttling away from intrusion. Meg gritted her teeth, and delicately inserted her hand.

She felt dust—not ordinary dust, but the accumulation of decades, soft and thick as old velvet. Under the dust was a hard surface.

The odd compulsion that had brought her this far was very strong now, strong enough to overcome her fear of touching something nasty. Meg's fingers groped exploringly, and then closed around the curved sides of what seemed to be an oval box, about a foot long and six inches high. She forgot about mice, rats, dusts, and cobwebs. She knew she had to have that box.

The opening was too narrow. Meg let go of the box and

stood up. Bracing her feet, she shoved at the chiffonier. Perspiration streaked her face and the muscles in her back protested, but inch by inch she edged the chiffonier away, careless of what damage it might be inflicting on the furniture behind it. Then she squatted down and tried again. Big enough—just barely. Without waiting to examine her prize, Meg crawled back through the maze of furniture and settled herself on the top of the dining room table from which she had started out on her bizarre quest.

Her intelligent fingers had recognized the object even before she saw it; there was no mistaking the precise, meticulous handwork of early American craftsmanship. This box was no factory product. The neatly matched tenons, where the ends of the curved wood met, reminded her of Shaker work. Unlike the simple Shaker boxes, this seemed to be painted. She could see dim shadows of color under the muffling dust.

Using the tail of her shirt, which was already filthy, Meg wiped the dust from the top of the box. The pattern emerged, like a garden from which fog is driven by the wind—stiff bright tulip shapes, scarlet and blue, with green leaves; red hearts, sulfurous-yellow birds with green and blue feathers.

Meg thanked whatever gods may be for that morning in the antique shops of Wasserburg. She knew the designs— hearts, parrots, and tulips were typical Pennsylvania Dutch decoration. The authenticity of the piece was beyond question. Not only did the pattern have a primitive vigor and force that was impossible to imitate, but the box had lain in darkness for more years than Meg could imagine. Reproductions of Pennsylvania Dutch work had not become popular until recently. Was this what she had been seeking all afternoon? It was old enough—eighteenth century, almost certainly.

The top fitted so snugly that Meg broke a fingernail prying at it. When it came off she saw a crumpled layer of what appeared to be heavy paper—a protective wrapping, for it bore no trace of writing, and Meg could feel something beneath it.

The windows were squares of deep gray, now, and the single bulb hanging from the ceiling gave poor light. Meg tore at the paper, knowing that she was breaking all the rules of the antique trade. The object under the paper had the softness of cloth. Sudden exposure to air and rough handling could damage fabric. But urgency made Meg ruthless; she dragged the thing out, spreading it across her knees and smoothing out the creases of centuries.

Centuries . . . more than two of them. The first thing she saw was a date, not printed or drawn in pen and ink, but rendered in exquisitely minute cross-stitch. A row of neat little trees hung with rosy fruit; a white house, done in the same precise stitching. Animals. A black-and-white cat, a fuzzy white dog with a blue bow in its topknot. A pony, stiff and angular, with legs no healthy equine ever possessed.

The colors were faded into pastel beauty—rose, pale blue, soft green, cream, buff. The design had the stiff charm of a primitive painting. But it was not a painting. It was a sampler—the same sampler she had seen in her vision of the shadowy room, hanging on an unreal wall in a house that no longer existed.

# Chapter 5

The implications of what she had found whirled around in Meg's brain, unsorted and incompletely realized; but one thing was clear. Under no circumstances could she have seen this sampler before it appeared in the vision. It had been packed away behind a wall of stored furniture for at least a hundred years. The violence with which she attempted to reject this unpalatable fact told her she was still a long way from accepting Andy's ghosts. But it was hard to find a rational explanation for this.

Andy's voice made her jump.

"Have you taken up mysticism? You look like a flower child—stringy hair, dirty jeans, torn shirt—squatting cross-legged on a tabletop. I'll bet you can't get out of that position without breaking a leg."

Meg turned her head. Her neck felt rusty; she expected to hear it creak like an antique spring.

In spite of Andy's sarcastic comments he seemed to like what he saw; he was smiling, and as her dust-smeared face came into view the smile broadened into a laugh.

"Talk about dedication to duty! Come out of there, Meg, and let me restore you with flagons. Or is it apples? I'd come after you, but I don't trust my weight on those priceless antiques. How the hell did you get there? And why?"

Meg looked at the sampler, still spread across her lap. Her body shielded it from Andy's sight; the light was too dim for him to see clearly. Suddenly she knew she didn't want him to see the sampler. It was too much for her to take in all at once, she had to have time to consider the possibilities—time to invent an explanation that would quiet her reeling senses—before she exposed the sampler to Andy's too-susceptible mind. With the same rough disregard with which she had ripped the sampler from its box, she folded it and thrust it down the front of her shirt, jamming the tails of that garment into her jeans in order to hold her prize in place.

"What's the matter, are you too stiff to move?" Andy's voice had a note of suspicion. "What have you got there?"

"A box," Meg said. Her coolness surprised her; it was as if a battery of unsuspected defenses were snapping automatically into place. "Look, Andy; I think it's a bride box. They put these things in museums."

She crawled across the table, carrying the box under one arm. When she reached the top of the sideboard, near the door, Andy caught her by the wrist and swung her lightly down. Still holding her, he smiled down into her upturned face.

"Dirt becomes you," he said softly. "You look about fifteen, Meg. Or are you too young to be flattered by that?"

His hazel eyes were flecked with gold that danced

dangerously. For a moment Meg forgot her worry and confusion; she even forgot the sampler, hidden in her shirt. Her lips parted. Andy's hands tightened, pulling her closer to him.

The box, which she was clutching to her bosom, lay between them as effectively as a chastity belt. Andy's expression altered as the hard surface pressed into his chest.

"Hey. That's old, Meg. How old?"

"Eighteenth century, probably."

Andy released her and Meg wondered, disgustedly, how she could have forgotten herself even for a second. She didn't even like Andy much. The brief interlude had settled one question, though; Andy's reactions were one hundred percent heterosexual, even if he was easily distracted.

"Lord, I'm tired," she said, and yawned widely.

"And dirty."

"You've mentioned that several times," Meg snapped. "If you'll get out of the way, I'll take my offensive body to the bathtub."

A spark shone in Andy's brown eyes, and was quickly quenched. "Make it fast, and I'll have a drink ready," he offered, stepping back. "I'll take the box—"

"I'll take the box. I found it."

"Oh, all right. But no fair looking till we're together."

Meg had replaced the top. It looked as if it had never been removed.

"Of course not," she said smoothly. "Andy, get some meat out of the freezer, okay? I'm in no shape to do gourmet cooking tonight, so make it something simple."

"Want me to get dinner?"

"No, it's my turn. I'm just warning you that it won't be *paté de la maison* tonight."

When they met later, in the kitchen, Meg saw that Andy had changed his shirt; but his hair was still speckled with confetti chips of wallpaper. He looked at her long blue robe with raised eyebrows. Flushing, she pulled the belt tighter.

"It's cold in here," she said defensively. "Can't you turn up the heat?"

"What, and waste fuel? Sylvia anticipated the national crisis by ten years; if the temperature of this house goes over sixty-five, she knows about it, by some tingle of the subconscious, and writes me a nasty note."

"You can't even mention her name without a dirty crack, can you?"

It was Andy's turn to flush—with anger. "You aren't especially charitable yourself."

"All right, all right. Drop it."

Meg put the box on the table. It distracted Andy; he reached for it eagerly.

"Careful," she warned hypocritically, as he wrenched at the lid. "The wood is dried out. You don't want to break it."

The lid was as hard to remove as it had been the first time, but Andy got it off without doing any damage. He lifted out the scraps of wrapping paper.

"This looks as if something has been removed," he announced, eyeing Meg suspiciously.

"Maybe they put in scrap paper to keep the contents from rattling."

"Maybe."

But he seemed to accept the suggestion, all the more readily because the objects he removed from the box were small and hard.

The first was a small disk, black with tarnish. It was attached to a ribbon that had once been blue; the color was now visible only in the folds. Meg picked it up from the table.

"It's a medal," she said, answering Andy's inquiring look. "Or would you call it an order?"

"Let's see." Andy snatched it and held it up to the light.

"Can't make out the design," he said, after a moment. "A bird, maybe, like an eagle with outstretched wings. And there's a motto, but it's too tarnished to read. These things around the edge. . . ."

He moved the metal shape, and sparks of brilliance leaped.

"Diamonds?" Meg asked uncertainly.

"I wouldn't know. They're too small to be worth much, anyhow."

Andy discarded the medal and picked up another piece.

"The jewels around this aren't diamonds," he announced. "Not even dirty diamonds."

"Garnets?" Meg suggested, trying to peer over his shoulder. "Rubies?"

"They don't sparkle. And they aren't red. They look black. What's this in the middle?" He held it close to his eyes and then withdrew it, with a disgusted noise.

"Hair. Dusty, dried-up hair."

He handed it to Meg.

"It's part of a locket," she said slowly. "There's a ring on top, where the chain went through, and the broken halves of hinges and catch. The stones could be jet. Later—I mean, at some period, they used to make mourning brooches like this, with a lock of the dead person's hair."

Andy didn't appear to notice her slip of the tongue. "White hair," he said.

Meg nodded and put the locket aside. Time yellowed many things, including white hair, but she had a feeling there were two different tresses inside the glass frame. One white, one silver blond.

Andy's next discovery was a collection of small round objects wrapped in a fragment of rusty black velvet.

"Buttons," Meg said, as he spilled them out onto the table. "Silver buttons; see how badly they're tarnished?" She went on resolutely, banishing the memory that widened Andy's eyes and confirmed her own growing unease. "There's a design or something on them. What else, Andy?"

The last object was also wrapped in cloth. As Andy shook it out onto the table, Meg gasped. It lay in a jumble of glowing color—blue and fiery crimson and pearly white, amid a tangle of gold. Gently Meg lifted it.

The object was a necklace of opals set in gold. It was a massive thing, too heavy for modern taste—a collar rather than a necklace. But the stones were glorious, fire opals, all of them splendidly colored. The blue depths shone as if sparks of flame were imprisoned within.

"Well, now," Andy said appreciatively. "That's better. What is there about gold that gets to you?"

"It doesn't get to me. The value of this rests in its age. The setting is old-fashioned, and although the stones are good ones, opals are not all that precious. Not like diamonds or sapphires."

"Yes, but it has some value. Why would it be packed away, instead of being part of the family jewels?"

"I don't know. Maybe all these things form a sort of collection. I mean, they belong together. And opals are considered unlucky."

Andy was fascinated by the necklace. He dangled it from his fingers, watching the glow of light on gems and gold.

"How much *is* it worth?"

"I haven't the faintest idea," Meg said warily. "A few thousand, maybe? Peanuts, to our rich relative."

"Have you ever known Sylvia to be indifferent to any amount of money? She'd strain her back picking up a quarter from the gutter."

Meg stood up. She was more tired than she had realized, and the rest had stiffened her muscles.

She put together a quick meal while Andy brooded over the treasure trove. Meg watched him out of the corner of her eye. His interest in the necklace, the only object of monetary value, aroused her worst suspicions. He was the one who had suggested they investigate the past in search of clues; didn't he grasp the implications of what she had found? But then, Meg reminded herself, Andy hadn't seen the sampler. That item would have aroused his ghost-hunting instincts with a vengeance. If the curious little collection of objects did belong together, it could be dated by the sampler, and that date, well before the building of the present house, could hardly fail to arouse his interest.

They ate quickly, without conversation. Andy only

spoke once, but the question indicated that she had underestimated his intellectual curiosity.

"How do you clean silver?"

"I thought you claimed to be the little handyman," Meg snapped.

"I'm not the butler," Andy replied coolly. "But I've seen my share of TV commercials. Maybe Sylvia has some of that metal-cleaning gunk."

"You'd better take it easy with that stuff. If it's too strong it could damage the metal."

"I'll be careful."

"You're on your own." Meg stood up. "I'm bushed. I think I'll go to bed."

"It's early."

"I'm going to read for a while."

"Likewise. I'll be in the library if you want me."

He didn't look up; he was pushing the buttons around with his fingertip, arranging them into patterns.

When Meg got upstairs she went straight to the bureau drawer where she had hidden the sampler. Kneeling, she spread it out on the floor. She meant to examine it in detail, calmly and dispassionately. Her familiarity with this form of folk art was of the slightest, but since needlepoint and crewel embroidery were back in style, she had acquired some information from enthusiastic friends who carried embroidery to work, to restaurants, and Meg suspected, to bed with them.

The making of an embroidered sampler was part of the education of a young girl during the eighteenth and nineteenth centuries. The ones that had survived were now collector's items, and moderns marveled at the proficiency attained by children of ten or twelve; for the young ladies usually signed their work and stated their age. As its name suggests, the sampler employed a variety of different embroidery stitches and patterns; thus the girls learned the tricks of the trade, and they used the stitches to decorate bed hangings, cushions, and clothing for themselves and their equally fashion-conscious husbands. Probably a hard-working colonial housewife looked forward to the hours she spent upon embroidery as a pleasant change from the other backbreaking chores that filled most of her eighteen-hour day.

But after the first moment Meg forgot analysis in sheer delight. Around the edges of the sampler a scrollwork of flowers and fruit wove a bright border; acorns, strawber-ries, carnations, wild roses. The picture inside the border showed a small house, rather out of perspective, but quaint and pretty; in the front yard, before a picket fence, stood a little lady with a high white wig and full skirts. Her dog lay at her feet; cat and pony attended her. There were stiff green trees and vines, and scattered decorative motifs had been added with a cheerful disregard for perspective. Several lines of text included the embroidered alphabet, which was an essential feature of a sampler.

More and more fascinated, Meg leaned forward to examine the details of the work. It was done in silk on linen; the seamstress had fashioned her cross-stitch design by counting the threads of the ground fabric instead of following a pattern printed on the cloth—or, as would have been the case in her day, a pattern painted or drawn by her own hand.

Carefully lifting the sampler, Meg sat down on the bed

and spread the cloth out so that she could see it in a better light. Its beauty and charm had made her forget momentarily her real reason for wanting to examine it more closely. She had hoped to find a discrepancy between the reality and the vision. If her battered brain had chosen to present her with a hallucination that included a sampler, it was no more, and no less, unreasonable than an elephant or the Mormon Tabernacle Choir. Given the initial insanity, the discovery of a real sampler could be a wild coincidence; for all samplers were more or less alike.

But as she admired the delicacy and the fine stitches, a cold certainty continued to grow. This was the sampler she had seen in the visionary room. She had not discerned the details, but the shape of the pattern was unmistakable—the solid form of the house, the flowery border, the shapes of the animals and trees.

Or was she backtracking—readjusting the vision in terms of what she now saw?

Meg groaned. She began to sympathize with the psychic researchers she had criticized in her discussion with Andy. Was it possible to keep the layers of memory distinct and separate? How could she possibly remember a momentary impression seen some days before?

Sitting quietly, in the glow of light cast by the bedside lamp, Meg folded her hands in her lap and did something she would never have considered a week ago. Deliberately she made her muscles go limp and cleared her mind of thought. She invited the intrusion of what might be waiting to come.

Nothing happened. She felt the effects of this form of self-hypnotism—a soft ringing in her ears as she strained to hear unreal sounds, a flicker of shadow movement beyond the bounds of actual vision—but she was wise enough to recognize these things for what they were. They were in no way akin to the hallucinations she had experienced.

The knock on the door broke through the shell of silence. Her hands went out, snatching at the sampler, but she was too late. The door opened and Andy looked in.

"I forgot to ask you—"

He stopped speaking as he saw what she was holding. It lay exposed, under the light. A hiss of indrawn breath told Meg that he was as quick mentally as he was in other ways. He crossed the room in a series of acrobatic leaps and grabbed. Meg relinquished her hold at once; the fabric was old, so old; she didn't want to risk tearing it.

After one quick comprehensive glance at the sampler Andy looked at Meg.

"I thought you were acting funny," he said. "This was in the box, wasn't it?"

Meg nodded dumbly. She didn't know what an appealing picture she made as she knelt on the bed amid the folds of her soft blue robe, her hands clasped on her lap, her eyes wide with apprehension: Andy's angry face relaxed as he looked at her. He sat down on the edge of the bed.

"Why didn't you show it to me?"

Meg lifted her hands and let them fall; it was a gesture of bewilderment which Andy understood.

"This is what you saw the other day—framed, on the wall of that room. . . ." It was not a question. After a brief pause Andy went on. "Are you sure?"

"I'm not sure of anything."

"I know what you mean." Andy smiled mirthlessly. "Meg. Are you scared?"

"Yes. No. . . ." Meg thought about it. "I don't know. Andy, what made you suppose that what we saw might be a genuine psychic intrusion? No, don't look away, I'm serious. Why did you think of ghosts when there was a perfectly good medical explanation?"

"It isn't good enough." Andy was staring at the sampler. "Good God, how can you talk about medical explanations with this in front of you? This is evidence, Meg. Don't you think this business is worth investigating?"

"How?"

"We've got a whole list of data. I cleaned one of the buttons; that's what I came up to show you. Look."

It lay in the palm of his hand, shining dully. Andy had not overdone the cleaning process; dark tarnish still lay in the sunken lines of the design, making the pattern easy to distinguish.

"It looks like a crest," Meg said. "A diagonal line, with three round balls on one side and—what is it, a bird?—on the other."

"It's not my family crest. Cousin Emig, the one who wrote the book you found upstairs, managed to dream up a family crest for the Emigs; it's quartered with the fleur-de-lis, of all things. Probably a fake. It certainly doesn't resemble this. We can look it up, Meg. There are books."

Meg nodded speechlessly.

"Then there's the sampler," Andy went on. "It's almost as good as a diary. We've got a date and a name. Do you think this could be a picture of the kid's house? Maybe the same house that once stood here?"

"You're getting carried away. They copied patterns for needlework in those days; ships brought pattern books to the colonies, and the women exchanged them among themselves. I've seen houses on other samplers."

"Well, how about the text?" Andy held the sampler up to the light and read aloud: "Lord Give Me Wisdom to Direct My Ways I Ask Not Riches Nor Yet Length Of Days, My Life's a Flower the Time Is Morn To Last Is Mixt, With Frost and Snow with Every Blast. This work in hand my friends may have when I am dead and laid in grave. Anna Maria Huber, her work in ye year 1734, Aged eleven years.' Morbid little creature, wasn't she?"

"It was a morbid age—if you want to call it that. Life spans were short, infant mortality was high; many of the Protestant sects were fundamentalist and grim. It's fairer to say that they were realists, about the difficulty of life and the certainty of damnation."

"That sounds impressive. You seem to know quite a bit of history."

"I read a lot." But Meg was beginning to share Andy's curiosity. "I wonder who she was—Anna Maria. Not one of your ancestors?"

"I don't think so. Let's check. The genealogy book is downstairs in the library."

"Okay." Meg scrambled down off the bed. "Be careful with that, Andy. I saw a sampler that was no nicer, and not nearly as old, selling for two hundred and fifty dollars in an antique shop in Connecticut."

"Maybe we ought to do something with it—to keep it from getting damaged," Andy said vaguely.

"We should do something about lots of things. After working in that attic, I'm beginning to feel overwhelmed."

"I can imagine." Together they walked down the hall and descended the stairs. "I think I'll go to Philadelphia tomorrow." Andy went on.

"What for?"

"I want to look up the crest on that button. Some genealogical research is also in order. Maybe we can find Anna Maria. I don't trust cousin Emig's scholarship. I'll bet he made up half his information, especially the earlier part."

"That's a good idea." Meg's enthusiasm was growing. There was something to be said for Andy's approach; the prospect of ordinary, everyday library work lessened the supernatural awe of the coincidence. "I think I'll go to Wasserburg and take the sampler with me. One of the antique dealers ought to be able to tell me what to do with it, and maybe I can get some free lectures on old furniture while I'm at it."

Andy looked dubious. "None of that crowd would give you a free 'Good Morning.' They'll steal the clothes off your back."

"Some of them must be honest."

"Oh, they're all honest. . . ."

Andy opened the library door and followed her in. The room was cozy and warm, despite its vast size and high ceiling; the worn velvet draperies had been drawn to shut out the rainy night, and Andy had kindled a fire on the hearth. Meg sat down in one of the leather chairs before the fireplace and held out her hands to the blaze.

Andy stood beside her. He was pulling at his lower lip and frowning, as if puzzling out some problem. Finally he said reluctantly, "If you want advice, you might try Georgia Wilkes. Her place is called the Antique Market."

"I remember; we passed it the other day. Why didn't we go in?"

"She's a friend of Sylvia's," Andy said. "We're not exactly buddies, Georgia and I. But she's honest and knowledgeable. Just don't sell her anything—especially the sampler."

"I can't sell anything. None of it belongs to me. Where's the book, Andy?"

Andy produced the volume and sat down on the hearthrug so Meg could look over his shoulder as he leafed through the pages. There was no Anna Maria Huber. An Anne Hofstetter, whose birth was given only as a question mark, had married Amos Emig in 1774.

"The dates would be about right," Andy muttered.

"No, they wouldn't. Girls married young; your ancestress Anne must have been born in the 1750's. If Anna Maria was eleven in 1734, she was born in 1723. Anyhow, why should she change her name?"

"I guess you're right. But if she wasn't related to the family, what was her sampler doing up in the attic?"

"I don't know." Meg leaned back in the chair and closed her eyes. The drizzle of rain and the hiss of the fire made her sleepy after her day of hard work. "I suppose you've looked at the books in here. Anything we can use?"

"They're all recent, and mostly fiction. Apparently none

of my recent relatives were interested in antiques or in family history."

"Uh-huh," Meg said agreeably.

She was roused from a doze by Andy's hand on her shoulder. "You had better go to bed. Can you walk, or shall I carry you?"

"All the way up those stairs?" Meg rubbed her eyes. "I'd like to see you try."

"That sounds like a dare."

Andy put his arms around her. Laughing, Meg slipped out of his grasp. He caught her wrist. He was smiling too, but there was a familiar gleam in his eyes, and Meg was in no mood for wresting or romance. She tried to free her arm.

The light began to fade, like the dimming of electric bulbs when the current is failing. A queer brownish haze spread over the room. Then Meg saw the girl. She was small and slim, with an absurdly tiny waist above her spreading peacock-blue skirts. A white apron emphasized the slimness of her waist, and there were other touches of white at wrists and throat. Her hair was yellow, falling in curls to her shoulders and held back from her face by a blue ribbon. But her face was only a shadowy blur. It seemed vitally important to Meg that she should see the face clearly. Unaware of Andy's tightening grip, she strained to see. She was only vaguely aware of the fact that the part of the library where the blue-clad figure stood had also altered. Alien walls had replaced the velvet draperies of the library, but she could still see the draperies behind them, like a photographic double exposure.

The vision faded as it had come, with a slow vanishing; and Meg cried out at the pain of Andy's taut fingers.

"Sorry," he mumbled, dropping her hand. "I didn't mean to."

"Did you see her?"

"Yes."

"Let's write it down, the way we did before."

"Why bother?"

Andy looked as if he were going to be sick. Meg felt abnormally clear headed. She studied her companion critically.

"Wow, it really bugs you, doesn't it? Come on, you were the one who said we had to be persnickety."

It was Meg who found paper and pencils, and who forced Andy into a chair. When they exchanged papers, Meg found his writing almost indecipherable.

" 'Girl in blue dress,' " she read aloud. " 'Blond hair.' You'll never make a living as a writer, Andy, if that's the best you can do. Didn't you see any background?"

Andy's blank stare focused. Annoyance countered shock, as Meg had hoped it would.

"God, you're a cold-blooded specimen, Meg. Give me a minute to catch my breath. I'm not used to this, even if you are."

He took the paper back and added a few more lines.

"That's better," Meg said. " 'She was standing by a fireplace. Benches or settles beside the hearth. Round rug. Things on the mantel.' The things were pots and crocks and dishes, don't you suppose? The rug was braided. . . ."

"Wait a minute. Are you describing what you saw, or

what you think you ought to see? You didn't write any of that down."

"I didn't see much of the room," Meg admitted. "I was so intent on trying to see her face. The features were blurred, but I felt that if I concentrated, in another second or two I would see them plainly."

"You saw the rest of the figure pretty clearly. 'White apron, collar, and cuffs; blond hair in ringlets, blue ribbon.' How could you see all that and fail to see the face?"

"All of a sudden you're a skeptic," Meg said. "I thought you believed . . ."

Andy's expression and voice were normal now—normally exasperated. "Of course I'm a skeptic. What I believe or disbelieve is absolutely irrelevant. We have to have a devil's advocate."

"Seems to me we keep switching roles."

"Yes, we do, don't we? But this—illusion, whatever you call it—is singularly unconvincing. If it hadn't been for the first one, I'd write this off as suggestion."

Meg started to object, but Andy raised his voice and continued, over her mutterings:

"We were talking about a girl, the one who made a sampler in 1734. A girl of German origin, from her name. And you proceed to conjure up a blond damsel in an old-fashioned costume. That's just what the professional mediums do—they see what they expect to see, and then they project the image to the receptive minds of the people near them, who are—"

"Feebleminded and weird," Meg finished. "Like you. All right, I see your point. I see all your points. Scratch Anna Maria."

"No, we don't scratch her. We merely surround her with question marks. Ironically—the room was not the same one we saw the first time, was it?"

"No. At least, it wasn't the same part of the room. Maybe we were seeing it from a different angle."

"Maybe."

They stared at one another across the library table.

"That's it for tonight," Meg said flippantly. "The show seems to be over. I think I'll have a second try at getting to bed."

"You aren't afraid?"

"It's funny, but I'm not."

"No auras?" Andy persisted. "No feeling of impending doom, no sense of imminent evil?"

"I'm looking forward to reading your book," Meg said. "You are a master of clichés."

She rose. The first step wasn't easy; she half expected another illusion to halt her progress. But nothing happened, so she continued to the door. Andy followed. He reminded her of a nervous puppy, crowding close on her heels but never actually touching her.

"Maybe I shouldn't go tomorrow," he said.

"Why not?"

"You aren't—no, I asked you that before. I may have to be away for a couple of days, you know. Are you sure you aren't going to be nervous?"

"You're not much help with the ghosts," Meg pointed out unkindly. "Don't worry; if I see anything, I'll record it in the proper fashion."

"I may not be much help with ghosts, but I could be useful if Culver shows up."

Meg was halfway up the stairs, with Andy close on her heels. She stopped. "Culver? I thought he and his charming lover were gone."

"No such luck. They're camping out in the state park."

"Serves them right," Meg said, with a glance at the rain-streaked window. "Maybe they'll both catch pneumonia. Stop fussing, Andy. Culver won't bother me."

In spite of her bravado, Meg was disturbed by this piece of news. She didn't really think Culver would threaten her physically; but why was he hanging around the area unless he had something in mind? Culver was weak and unstable, but he was not stupid; if he wanted to revenge himself for the fancied injury she had done him, his plan might take on strange forms. Even . . .

Even the creation of a haunted house.

Meg was no longer sleepy, although the slow drip of the rain was as soothing as a lullaby. Lying straight and stiff under the blankets, she considered an idea that was by no means new to her. Could the manifestations have been produced by a human agent, using ordinary physical means?

The answer, of course, was yes. Meg was sufficiently familiar with stage magic to know that professionals can produce very convincing allusions. She was no professional, but even she could think of several methods of creating ghosts. The ethereal music was simple: a tape recorder or other portable recording device. As for the optical illusions, equally portable devices could produce them. A color projector would give an effect similar to what she had seen, with background objects showing through the image.

Culver had had time, after receiving his eviction notice, to concoct such a scheme, and it was the sort of thing an imaginative man might think of as an alternative to physical violence. That the illusions happened to fit Meg's specific disability was pure luck—or maybe Culver knew what her ailment was. Gossip spreads in small towns.

An equally convincing case could have been made out for another suspect; but for some reason she preferred not to analyze, Meg did not consider it—at least not consciously.

## II

Next morning the rain had stopped, but the ground was soggy, and the trees looked desolate with their drooping branches. Andy dropped Meg in Wasserburg before he started on his trip to Philadelphia. The car drove away in a cloud of exhaust smoke, and Meg watched it go with mixed feelings.

The Antique Market, a handsome old stone house, was on a side street. A sign on the gate said forbiddingly, "Admittance by Appointment Only." Meg walked up the path and rang the bell.

After a while she rang the bell again. Finally she heard footsteps inside, and the door was flung open. The woman who confronted her with an inimical stare had obviously just woken up, and resented the fact. Her rusty-gray-and-red-streaked hair stood up in little wisps. She had a long, squared-off face with strong features that had started to sag; the lines in cheeks and forehead looked as if they had been cut with a chisel. She wore a pair of ragged jeans and a floppy, once-white man's shirt with the tails out.

"Well?" said this apparition, in a growl.

I wonder how she makes a living, if this is the way she greets customers, Meg thought. Aloud she said,

"Good morning. I'm so sorry to have disturbed you. I'm Meg Rittenhouse, Sylvia's cousin."

"Oh." Georgia Wilkes blinked. She rubbed her face vigorously with her hand. "What time is it?"

"Ten o'clock. But I can come back another—"

"No, you might as well come in." Georgia stepped back and gestured Meg across the threshold. "I'm a wee teensy bit hung over, to tell the truth. Can you make decent coffee?"

"Why, yes, I think—"

"This way."

Georgia closed the door very gently, and then pattered on ahead of Meg. She was barefoot. The front room had been the parlor of the house; it was now a sales room, crammed with objects that ranged from secretaries to snuffboxes. Meg had no time to examine them; Georgia led her through a door at the back, which had a "Private—No Admittance" sign tacked to its panels. They went down a dark, narrow hall and emerged into a kitchen. It was also dark and rather shabby, but somewhat to Meg's surprise, it was in perfect order. The only discordant note was an empty bottle of bourbon that stood in the exact center of the kitchen table.

Georgia picked this up and deposited it in a bag under the sink. She then collapsed into a chair.

"Make instant; the other takes too long," she ordered. "It's on the third shelf to the left. Cups in the second. Water in the tap, teakettle on the stove, stove in the corner."

Amused, Meg followed directions. Georgia said no

more until the coffee was on the table. She picked up the cup and swallowed most of the contents, gasped, rubbed her eyes, and smiled.

"That's better. I may live another day after all. Let's have some breakfast."

"Thank you, but I already had—"

"Sit down, sit down. I'm beginning to function. Another cup of coffee and I'll be running on all four cylinders."

"I really should apologize again for waking—"

"No, I should thank you. I've got a sucker coming at noon. Snuffbox collector. If you hadn't waked me up, I wouldn't have made it."

She was already moving around the kitchen, with a speed and efficiency that astonished Meg. Before long, Georgia was engulfing cereal and eggs, and Meg was nibbling at a slice of coffee-cake—rich and delicious and obviously homemade.

"Yes, I made it," Georgia said, in answer to Meg's question. "I'm a good cook. Good at a lot of other things, too."

She laughed. The teacups on the shelf rattled.

"Now," Georgia went on, pushing her empty plate away and lighting a cigarette. "Let's have the amenities— belated, but sincere. I believe in the amenities; I'm simply unable to comply with them early in the morning. I'm Georgia Wilkes. What a pleasure to meet you, my dear. Sylvia has spoken of you so often. I was sorry to hear you had been ill. How do you like our little town? I do hope you're not lonely out there in that big old house. Is there anything I can do to make you feel at home here? Do feel free to call on me at any time."

Meg began to laugh. Georgia grinned at her and lighted another cigarette with the stub of the first; she smoked in great gulps that burned down half an inch of cigarette at a breath.

"Good, you've got a sense of humor. Those big solemn eyes in that little pale face made me wonder. That, and the fact that you're related to Sylvia, who has no sense of humor whatever."

Meg could think of nothing to say to this, except things that should not be said. It seemed incredible that this woman could be a close friend of Sylvia's.

Georgia needed no response. She rattled on.

"Poor old Sylvia. We were at school together, in case you were wondering how we happen to be friends. Not that that answers the question. We were just as unlike each other then as we are now. Sylvia was a fussy old maid when she was born, and I've always been sloppy, promiscuous, and profane. I don't recommend my life-style; it has certain shortcomings. But when I compare my life with Sylvia's . . ."

She shook her head. Her smile had faded; she looked sad, rather like a shabby old lion, with her mane of rusty hair and her long jowls. Meg felt a surge of liking for Georgia, who could pity a woman who had all the worldly luxuries.

"I wish I could say Sylvia has spoken of you," she said. Georgia's candor was contagious. "But she hardly ever mentions her friends."

"She doesn't have friends—except me. Only business acquaintances."

"Do you know her stepson?"

"Andy? Sure. I visited Sylvia here when she was married to—what was the poor devil's name? Never could remember it. Never could remember what he looked like five minutes after I'd left him. Nice guy, though. He was always nice to me. It was when I was visiting Sylvia that I fell in love with the town and decided to open a shop. I was here for a couple of years before what's-his-name died and Sylvia went looking for the next victim. Haven't seen much of her since, but we exchange Christmas cards."

Meg had found that she could get out a complete sentence, before Georgia interrupted, if she kept it short.

"Wasn't she here recently?"

"Yep. She came down to evict the bloody painter and his girl friend. I wrote her about him a couple of months ago. Never did approve of Sylvia's letting the house to ne'er-do-well bums, but most of 'em were harmless enough. Not this guy, though. The little bastard was selling off Sylvia's antiques. Had the gall to come here with what he thought was a Windsor chair. I played it cool. Told him it was a late-nineteenth-century copy—which it was—and then wrote Syl. She was down here like a shot; she never can stand being taken for a sucker. She stopped in for a drink—pardon me, a cup of tea—and told me about you. I've been meaning to call you, but never got around to it. You know how it is."

"Yes," Meg said, slightly dazed. "I know how—"

"Culver's still around," Georgia said. "Give you any trouble?"

"Not really. I met him—"

"Oh, sure, the whole town knows about that. Town knows all about everything, honey; keep that in mind in case you have any low-down schemes in mind. You and Andy sleeping together? Oh, come on, you don't have to look so indignant; you might as well have the game as the name, the whole damn town assumes you're shacking up. They don't mind. Young Andy seems to be pretty popular. Don't know why."

"I'm not that crazy about him myself. And contrary to what this town may think of city slickers, I'm not in the habit of popping into bed with any man who happens to be—"

"Okay, okay, don't get mad at me. I *was* in the habit; fun while it lasted; but I don't expect everybody to share my tastes. That makes me a rare bird in this conformist world. Most people would rather kill you than see you differ from them, and I am not talking about this generation or this country only. It's human nature. Look at the religious wars."

"Some other time," Meg said, taking advantage of Georgia's pause to light a cigarette. "Right now there is something I want to consult you about. And if you have an appointment at noon—"

"Right, right. Go on. I'm listening."

And listen she did; she was as good a listener as she was a talker, when the other party had something pertinent to say. Leaning back in her chair, arms folded, she did not interrupt once while Meg poured forth a description of the job Sylvia had set for her, and her feeling that she was incompetent to do it.

"I think I could furnish the house properly," Meg concluded. "I mean, I could pick out the right furniture and ornaments; it would be fun. But I don't know enough about value. All that stuff in the attic—I'm afraid to touch it for fear I'll damage a valuable item."

"There isn't much you can damage," Georgia said. "Unless you've got an Aztec feather cloak or something in the bag you've been hugging to your chest ever since you came in."

Meg didn't answer; she opened the bag and took out the sampler.

Georgia leaned across the table, her shirt front almost in her coffee cup.

"Where the hell did you get that?"

"In the attic. In a box under the eaves." Meg held the sampler up so Georgia could examine it. The older woman didn't touch it, but she studied it for a long time in silence. Then she glanced at Meg.

"If I didn't know better, I'd say it was a fake."

"Why?"

"Samplers of this early date are fairly rare, for one thing. Especially samplers of this type. The early-eighteenth-century examples usually have alphabets and random motifs, not a scene; that type is commoner during the nineteenth century. Another thing—the girl has a German name, but the sampler is of the English type and the motto is in English. At this early period you'd expect an immigrant to use her own language. But it's genuine. Look at the needlework. Very few people can do work of that caliber today, and they are making fortunes running needlework boutiques and giving lessons to fat bored housewives. The colors, the fabric—all correct. I could get you—oh, seven fifty, a thousand, maybe. . . ."

"But that's an awful lot of money," Meg exclaimed.

Georgia shook her head pityingly.

"You are an amateur, aren't you, honey? Are you ready for Georgia's quicky lecture on the antique biz? Point one—there is no such thing as absolute value in this trade.

An object is worth what you can get for it—no less and no more. Right now you can get quite a bit. People are opulent and antiques are in style. Which brings me to point two: what is an antique? The purists will raise their noses and tell you nothing after about 1840 is an antique; Victorian furniture is nasty pop stuff. But I can sell Victorian like crazy. In fact, I can sell the suckers anything that's more than twenty years old. You should see some of the crap I've got out in the barn.

"One of the reasons why your sampler surprised me is that I've never seen anything near that old in that house. Sylvia let me take a quick peek around the attic after Culver played his games. I've got a pretty good idea what's there. It's junk. Good, solid, well-made junk, which I could sell in a minute; but there are no Jacobean chests or Queen Anne chairs, baby."

"Then those are not Chippendale chairs? I thought—" Georgia grinned nastily.

"You spotted those, did you? Copies, my dearie. There was a revival of Chippendale style cabinetmaking in the 1850s. Takes an expert to see the difference in some cases. Incidentally, you had better get your terminology straight. A Chippendale chair is one made in Thomas's own London workshop, and there aren't many of those around. Other cabinetmakers of the same period used his designs, which he published in a book of patterns in 1754. 'Chippendale style' furniture was made, in England and in this country, between 1750 and 1785, approximately. Imitations of Chippendale style come back at various periods, but the most valuable pieces are the ones that date from the time when Chippendale was working. The same can be said of Hepplewhite, Sheraton, and other big names.

"Now you get to somebody like Duncan Phyfe—you have heard of him? Well, thank God for that. Phyfe was a cabinet-maker, an American; and although he originated some of his own designs, he was much influenced by other great designers, especially Sheraton. You can talk about Duncan Phyfe chairs, not Duncan Phyfe style chairs. He made 'em, they have his label or else a well-authenticated pedigree proving they were built in his workshops. As a matter of fact . . ." She hesitated, eyeing Meg with a comical mixture of doubt and defiance; then she shrugged. "Oh, hell, some people even I can't cheat. I suspect Sylvia's got a Duncan Phyfe dining-room suite up there. There are a few other goodies among the junk. I didn't say anything to Sylvia; I mean, why the hell should I give my expertise away for free?"

Meg waved this question away; Georgia sounded a lot tougher than she was, and Meg knew she had never had any intention of cheating Sylvia.

"Why didn't Sylvia ask you to do this job?" she demanded. "You make me feel even more ignorant than I did when I walked in here, and God knows I was humble enough then."

"You don't get it?" Georgia raised shaggy red eyebrows. "Sylvia doesn't care a rap about selling that stuff. She's a pack rat. She doesn't need the money; she loves owning things, lots of things. It may sound funny, but I think Sylvia gave you the job out of kindness. Her philosophy of life is half-baked, but it makes some sense; it wouldn't be good for you to sit around that house with nothing to do.

Sylvia doesn't come across as especially bighearted, but that's just her manner. Because she doesn't express emotions well doesn't mean she has none."

"Sylvia?" Meg smiled faintly. "Don't get the wrong idea, Georgia. I'm grateful to Sylvia. I'm even fond of her, in the same wishy-washy way she's fond of me. You're a warmhearted person yourself, that's why you attribute better motives to other people than they deserve."

"Well, well, you're young," said Georgia maddeningly. "You'll learn. You'd better scram, kiddo. I've got to work on my face or my buyer will scream and run at the sight of it. Let me give you one piece of free advice—don't do anything to that stuff upstairs. Put what you want downstairs, inventory the rest—with photos, if possible—and forget it. If you have any specific problems, call me. Your sampler, for instance. You can't leave it like that. Want me to frame it for you? Don't worry, I'll bill Sylvia."

It was a reasonable suggestion, and Meg had every confidence in her new acquaintance. But she was oddly reluctant to let the sampler out of her hands, even for a few days. Georgia read her expression correctly, but misinterpreted the reason for her hesitation.

"I know; it's exciting when you find something really good. Okay; just be careful with it. You might get a couple pieces of glass and put it between them. Tape down the edges. Of the glass, I mean, not the sampler. And for God's sake, don't iron it or wash it."

"I know better than that," Meg rose. "Thanks, Georgia. I do appreciate—"

"We've had the amenities, honey. Once a day is enough."

As Meg walked along the flagstone path under the

dripping trees she realized that she would have to walk all
the way home. She was not anxious to return to the empty
house, so she had lunch in town, at an overly quaint tea
shoppe where the prices were outrageous and the food
mediocre. Then she explored the shops for a while. The
local bookstore held her for some time; she squandered a
part of Sylvia's small allowance on some reference books.
They cost the moon and weighed a ton.

Several people stopped and offered her rides as she
slogged along the gravel shoulder of the highway. By the
time she had walked a mile the offers were exceedingly
tempting. Her shoulders ached and her load felt like lead
instead of books. But although she told herself that
hitchhiking was probably safe out here in the country, she
was too wary to succumb, and when she finally turned into
the long driveway leading to the house she was dragging
both feet. The house had never looked more welcoming.

She had to put the books down in order to find her key
and unlock the door; and when the portal stood open she
fell back a step, peering into the hall, for fatigue forgotten
in a surging wave of. . . . What was the feeling that
moved out of the house to engulf her? Not fear. Expectation. As in childhood, when she had come back from
school, entering a house where she was welcomed and
wanted and awaited. . . .

Abandoning her parcels for the moment, Meg walked
slowly into the house. But if something waited there, it did
not wait for her. She was not the one it welcomed; nor
even the Traveller, bringing news.

# Chapter 6

Meg had expected to miss Andy—not because he was so charming, but because the house was rather large for a single occupant. The time passed quickly, however. Two heavy volumes on antique American furniture kept her occupied for hours. She worked in the attic, moving furniture and carrying some of the smaller pieces downstairs. Having purchased labels the day she visited Georgia, she was able to start the inventory.

Georgia called the following day. Meg had almost forgotten there was a telephone in the house, and the shrill ring, after so many hours of silence, startled her so that she dropped her notebook.

"Figured I'd better check, make sure you hadn't broken your hip or something," Georgia said cheerfully.

"That's a happy thought," Meg said, remembering the way she had raced down the narrow attic stairs. It would be ironic to break a leg running to answer a call inquiring after her welfare.

"Those things do happen, even to the young and spry. How long is Andy going to be gone?"

Meg said she didn't know. They chatted for a few minutes, and then George rang off. Meg was left with a feeling of mingled appreciation and annoyance. It was nice to know that someone was interested in her welfare, but she wished the town were not so well informed about everyone's comings and goings.

After looking over one of the books she had bought, on American samplers, Meg was inspired to start another project. It was a crazy project for someone who had never been able to sew on a button without stabbing herself in the thumb, but Meg was determined to reproduce Anna Maria's sampler. Georgia had not underestimated its value. According to the book's register of samplers, the one Meg had found was among the earliest, and certainly one of the prettiest. It would probably end up in a collection, and yet Meg yearned to own it. A copy would be the next-best thing. Embroidery, she reminded herself, was considered excellent occupational therapy.

She went to town next morning to buy graph paper and paints. These were obtainable at the general store, which stocked arts-and-crafts items not normally found in such establishments. Meg also bought eggs and milk and a few other perishable food items. When she came out of the store, her arms were full. It was then that she saw a familiar and unwelcome form across the street.

Meg hesitated in the doorway. She was tempted to duck back inside before Culver saw her. It was too late. Indeed, as she learned later, he had been waiting for her to come out.

He started across the street, an ingratiating smile on his face; the expression was even less attractive than his scowl. He was still wearing his torn, short-sleeved T-shirt, and Meg felt a stir of pity at the sight of the bare arms patterned with goose bumps and blue veins.

She nodded at him and began walking, but escape was not so easy. Culver fell in step beside her.

"Where you going?"

"Home," Meg said shortly.

"Buy you a cup of coffee."

Meg looked at him in amazement. Really, the man was too much. He might have apologized for his behavior on the occasion of their first meeting. Apparently he considered his present amiability sufficient cause for rejoicing.

"No, thanks," she said. "I haven't got time."

"I wanna talk," Culver insisted. "Got a business proposition for you."

Meg stopped and turned to face him. He had not shaved for a week, nor bathed for at least that length of time. As he stood posturing, one hand on his hip, Meg knew he considered himself quite seductive.

"Go ahead and talk," she said. "I haven't time to stop for coffee, and anyhow, I can't imagine what sort of business we could transact."

"It's cold out here," Culver whined. "How about if I walk home with you?"

"I'm meeting Andy."

"Oh, yeah? I thought he was in Philadelphia."

Meg was both angry and alarmed. Damn these people, she thought; don't they realize it's dangerous for me when they spread this kind of information?

"He's coming back today," she said coolly. "I really am in a hurry, so—"

"Okay, okay." Culver scowled, and then forced his features into a less threatening aspect. "Look—uh—you could use some bread, right? I mean, like, we're both in the same spot. Broke."

"No. I've got a job waiting for me as soon as I get over my—my illness."

"Me too, sure. I've had a run of bad luck. You know, a creative person can't just produce on demand, like an assembly line. That old—I mean, your cousin—doesn't dig that. She doesn't understand the artistic temperament. Pretty soon I'll be painting again. Any day now. I'm waiting for inspiration, you dig? And when I do . . . Christ, will I make some people crawl! I'll be famous and rich and people will be standing in line for my paintings. She'll come around then, and brag about how she helped me when I was down and out, and, man, will I tell the world about her! I'll fix her. . . ."

His voice trailed off into silence, but his lips kept moving; his eyes, staring, were focused on a vision of success that blotted out the real world of cold and hunger and contempt. Meg shivered. He was a pitiable character. Perhaps he had had talent once; he must have had, to attract Sylvia's patronage. But there was no hope for him now, barring a miracle. He was trapped in a spiraling circle of self-pity and drugs, and the spiral could only lead down.

"Mr. Culver," Meg said loudly.

Culver started. His eyes focused on Meg, but dazedly, as if he had never seen her before and were wondering who she was.

"You ought to get away from this town," Meg said. "There's nothing for you here. You need a big city—the stimulation, the inspiration of crowds and other creative people."

"Yeah," Culver mumbled. "Yeah. I'm going to split. Get out of this stinking hick town. No wonder I can't paint here. No stimulation."

"Good," Meg said heartily. "I wish you luck."

She turned away. Culver hopped in front of her.

"I can't split till I get some bread," he said.

Meg glanced around. Once again the streets had emptied themselves; Culver had that effect on the townspeople. Meg wondered what this prolonged interview was doing to her reputation. No doubt the town would add Culver to the list of her hypothetical lovers.

"I can't give you any money," she said crisply. "I'm not rich. Good-bye, Mr. Culver."

"No, wait, dammit." He reached out as if to touch her. Meg stepped back. She could not have concealed her revulsion even if she had wanted to. Culver's face darkened.

"Okay, I'll spell it out, since you don't seem to like my company," he said with a sneer. "You need bread, so do I. That place is loaded with antiques. She'll never notice if something is missing. I'll split with you, fifty-fifty—and I'll do the dirty work, marketing the stuff."

They were standing in front of a private house, one of the few on Main Street that had not been converted into a shop. Meg saw a shade move in the front window. Even if she had been tempted by the petty larceny Culver proposed, common sense would have warned her; the whole town had seen her and Culver talking together, and now she would be suspected if any of Sylvia's property came onto the market. The only thing she could do was express her anger, and let the town see that, too. Anyway, there was no point in being tactful with Culver. He would keep on hassling her unless she gave him a flat refusal.

"No deal," she said. "And don't try anything on your own, Mr. Culver. I'm going to tell Andy about your proposition. In fact, I think I'll call the police and mention it to them. If anything is stolen, they'll know whom to look for."

She got the reaction she expected, and more. Culver's face turned purple. He raised his arm, and Meg retreated hastily.

"You touch me and I'll have you arrested," she said, not troubling to lower her voice. "You've got a lot of gall making me a proposition like that!"

Culver's eyes left her face; she deduced, from his expression, that he saw someone coming. There were also two pedestrians at the far end of the street, behind Culver. Meg felt a surge of gratitude and relief; the town was not so indifferent as it appeared.

Culver cursed her under his breath and walked away. Meg turned—she had not dared turn her back on Culver—and saw a tall, gray-haired man approaching. She remembered his name—Stoltzfuss. It was a memorable name. He owned the Antique Barn at the far end of town.

"Everything all right?" he asked.

"It is now. Thank you."

"Just happened to be passing by," Stoltzfuss said.

"And those two gentlemen too?" Meg indicated the

other pedestrians, who had stopped several hundred feet away, as if in conversation.

"We didn't want to butt in if you were having a nice private talk."

"Oh, wow," Meg said, with feeling.

Stoltzfuss grinned. He had a craggy, attractive face and the ruddy complexion of a man who spends a good deal of time outdoors. He was probably in his late fifties, but Meg could see why Culver wouldn't choose to tangle with him. But then she imagined Culver would avoid an encounter with anyone over twelve.

"Wonder if you'd like a ride home," Stoltzfuss said. "I'm going to Cartersville, right past the house, if you're ready."

"You're a liar," Meg said, smiling. "But I'll accept, with thanks."

A few minutes later they were on their way out of town in Stoltzfuss's truck. He kept insisting he really did have to go to Cartersville, to pick up some antiques. Meg decided she had handled Culver correctly; she had aroused his animosity, but she had gained the goodwill of the town, and that was worth quite a lot. She told Stoltzfuss what Culver had suggested. He shook his head.

"Doesn't surprise me. Tell you what, I'll just telephone Fred Zook over at the state police barracks. He knows about Culver, but I'll ask him to keep close tabs on the fellow."

"Can't they arrest him or evict him or something? I'd feel a lot better if he were someplace else."

"You and a lot of other people. But you can't run people out of town unless they break the law. Some folks would say that was a shame," he added, with his slow smile. "Me, I'm an old-fashioned Jeffersonian democrat. Freedom is darned inconvenient at times, but it's worth it."

"Right on," Meg said.

Stoltzfuss insisted on coming in with her and checking the house. He asked when Andy was due back. Meg said she didn't know, and Stoltzfuss looked concerned.

"Tell you what, if he doesn't get back today, give me a call."

"I don't want to bother anyone—"

"It makes for no trouble," Stoltzfuss said cheerfully. "We Dutch gotta stick together, ain't? Don't tell me you're not one of us, with a name like Rittenhouse. We'll just keep an eye on Culver, make sure he doesn't hike out this way. He's the only one you have to worry about. The rest of us are honest—except when it comes to buying antiques."

## II

After a quick lunch Meg started on her sampler. Copying the pattern was easier than she expected, thanks to the precision of the stitches. She made a pencil copy first and then went over it in colored ink, indicating the colors. Matching the lovely, time-faded shades would be the most difficult part, Meg knew; she meant to mix paints until she got a close approximation, and then try to find equivalents in embroidery silk. That would probably mean a trip to a large town, so she wouldn't be able to start embroidering right away, but in any case she would have to practice before she started the actual sampler. She covered scraps of cloth with crooked stitches, cursed her clumsy fingers, and tried again. The project became increasingly absorbing; she could hardly bear to tear herself away from it long enough to eat.

Andy returned that evening. Meg thought she heard the characteristic sound of the car, but although she waited for a knock or a hail, none followed, and she concluded she had been mistaken. Then, when she was getting ready for bed, Meg saw the light in the caretaker's cottage.

She thought immediately of Culver; but after she had watched the light for some minutes she decided he wouldn't be so careless or so indirect. The antiques in the house were what he wanted. Andy must have returned, then.

Meg reached for the phone and then changed her mind. Andy had a lot of nerve; he might at least have called to make sure she was still alive and undamaged. The more she thought about it, the madder she got; and although she slept soundly, undisturbed by dreams or premonitions, she was still angry when she woke up in the morning.

The wall of white fog that enveloped the house didn't improve her mood, but by ten o'clock the sun was out and the puddles in the yard were steaming energetically. Meg was still annoyed, but she was beginning to get worried, and when she heard footsteps on the porch she ran to the door and flung it open before Andy could knock.

He looked terrible—sunken eyes, bristly chin, and a general air of exhaustion. Meg's relief was so great she started to scold him.

"Where have you been? Why didn't you tell me you were back? What did you find out?"

"Not much." Andy headed like a homing pigeon for the kitchen. "But I have a new respect for genealogists. It's the most frustrating damned pursuit. I didn't come over last night because I—because I didn't want to wake you up."

Meg decided not to challenge this statement. It was a lie, of course. Andy must have seen her lighted window, as she had seen his. But she was learning how to handle Andy. A direct accusation would only infuriate him. If she kept quiet he would break down eventually and tell her what was bugging him.

Silently she poured coffee, which Andy accepted with a nod of thanks.

"I'm about ready to call it quits," he muttered. "Two days wasted. . . . I didn't find Anna Maria. There are plenty of women with the same or similar names; but none the right age."

"And the crest on the button? You were going to look for that, too."

"Same damned thing. The design is worn down; details are hard to make out. There were hundreds of petty little dukes and counts in eighteenth-century Europe. I found some possibles, one from France and three from Germany— or rather, from the mess of little countries that later became Germany."

"The majority of the settlers in this area were German or Scotch-Irish," Meg said.

"That's no help. I could go on guessing for months. I'm ready to call a halt."

"You really mean it? What happened, Andy? Something is bothering you."

"Well . . ." Andy gloomily contemplated his coffee.

"Hell, I might as well come clean. I didn't exactly tell the truth. I did come to the house last night."

"I didn't hear you knock. Did you lose your key or something?"

"I never got that far. I was ambling along, battered but not bowed; temporarily discouraged, but not disheartened, when all of a sudden. . . . It was like running into a wall. I couldn't go any farther. I felt sick. Literally sick; the sweat was pouring off me, I was shaking, and my heart was beating so hard it felt as if it were going to pound a hole in my chest. I had a roommate in college who had severe anxiety attacks. He said it was like walking along and suddenly coming face to face with a monster—the worst monster you can imagine, slimy and fanged and dripping venom—ready to attack you. Only there wasn't any monster. There wasn't any cause for him to be afraid; and that was the most terrifying thing of all. Now I have a faint idea of what he was talking about."

If he was acting, he was doing a magnificent job. Even the memory of the sensation dilated his eyes and brought a sheen of perspiration to his face. Meg was shaken.

"Fear?" she asked.

"That's too simple. Believe me, I was in no mood to analyze what I was feeling, but it was more than fear. I did not want to go into that house. It was as if I knew there was something in there that I couldn't stand seeing, something that would drive me right off my rocker."

"Something in there. . . . I've had that feeling too. But it wasn't frightening, not to me."

Andy leaned back with a sigh and mopped his face with his sleeve.

"I meant to ask if you've had any more visions. Sorry I got preoccupied with my own miseries."

"Nothing happened. Except the day you left . . ."

Meg described the feeling of anticipation that had greeted her when she returned from town.

"I wasn't afraid," she concluded. "I felt more—well, more regretful. Sorry it wasn't me They were waiting for."

"I hope it isn't me," Andy muttered. "Oh, hell, Meg, don't you see how crazy this is? There's no pattern to it."

"But that is what convinces me," Meg said earnestly. "If we saw a pattern at this point, I'd suspect we were making it ourselves—twisting the evidence to fit the theory. The fact that we don't understand these experiences proves they're genuine!"

Andy smiled faintly. "I don't know what fascinates me more, the illogic of your reasoning or the inconsistency of your attitude. You switch sides so often it makes me dizzy."

"You're not exactly the soul of consistency yourself. Whose idea was this anyway?"

"You've got me there. Okay; we'll go on with it. But not right this minute. I need therapy. I'm going to eschew psychic research and go back to scraping walls. See you later."

"Okay. Did you find out anything about another house on this site?"

"I didn't have time."

Meg decided it was better to leave him alone. As she passed the master bedroom on her way to the attic she saw that he was scraping so vigorously that scraps flew like snow. She did not stop or speak, although she was tempted to join him; there was something therapeutic about controlled destruction of that sort.

Meg poked around in the attic for a while. In the back of her mind was the hope that she would find another windfall like the chest—another clue to the time of Anna Maria Huber; but she knew the futility of the hope. Few of the objects in the attic seemed to be older than the mid-nineteenth century. Meg's reading was beginning to help; she recognized some of the pieces as similar to illustrations in certain of her books, though she was far from being certain of their value or authenticity. Finally she gave up all pretense at work and settled down in a warm corner with a pile of old magazines.

Meg skipped lunch, as she often did, but by late afternoon her stomach was growling and she had had enough nostalgia. She glanced in the bedroom on her way downstairs. Andy wasn't there. He was not in the kitchen either. Meg finally found him in the library. He was so absorbed in the book he was reading that he didn't hear her, and at the sight of the lurid orange cover on the paperback she let out an exclamation of disgust.

"You do read the most awful tripe, Andy! Where did you get that?"

Unabashed, Andy leaned back in his chair and smiled at her.

"Some former tenant must have been a mystery fan. There's a whole shelf of old paperbacks. Great stuff. Nonfiction and the occult, as well as the masters of detective fiction. This one is about a real case—a Pennsylvania murder, in fact. The killer was a poor feebleminded neurotic who thought the victim had hexed him. That's one way to take off the curse—kill the witch."

"I'll bear that in mind." Meg sat down. "Maybe I owe you an apology. You're doing background reading on the eighteenth century?"

"This happened in 1923." At the sight of her astonished face Andy's grin widened. "Amazing, isn't it? Yet I don't know why we should be surprised. Look at the nuts who believe in Black Magic today."

"Including present company."

"Now, now, let's not be too hard on ourselves. Serious scholars are interested in the occult as a manifestation of unknown scientific principles. Nobody but an egomaniac would claim we know everything about the universe. There's a difference between that approach and the contortions of neurotics who paint themselves red and try to raise the devil in a suburban basement."

"They get more results than we do, though." Meg leaned back in her chair. The afternoon sunlight was warm and she felt pleasantly tired. "Maybe we aren't going about it the right way."

"We're doing all we can."

"Are we? I was thinking, Andy. Practically all the manifestations have occurred when we were together. You've felt things, and so have I; but I haven't seen anything except when you were with me."

"What's that supposed to mean?" Andy dropped his book and sat up straight.

"Well, maybe it takes both of us. Not just together, but actually touching. Wasn't there some kind of physical contact whenever we've seen one of the visions?"

"Hmmm." Andy scratched his chin. Though light in color, his beard was heavy. He looked thoroughly disreputable. "I guess you're right. So what are you proposing? Not a séance, I hope."

"No, not exactly. Just—well, just open our minds and try to see what we get. And if something comes, don't panic, keep cool, and see if we can't control it."

"I don't know. . . ."

"I don't blame you for having cold feet, after your experience last night," Meg said persuasively. "But is there any reason to believe we're dealing with something evil or dangerous? I don't believe in the devil or in Black Magic. Neither do you. If these things are not illusions, they are only pictures—pictures out of the past. Maybe something more than pictures—a lingering trace of personality, spirit—call it a ghost, if you like. But I don't feel any evil. The old man, the girl—they don't threaten us. I know they don't."

Slowly Andy shook his head. "Your feelings aren't evidence, Meg. Why make such a big thing of this? Is it that important to you?"

The question hit Meg like the shock of an electric current, focusing her unconsidered motives. It *was* important to her; she had not realized how important until this moment. Not only did she believe wholeheartedly in the visions, but she wanted to see more of them. It was the girl, of course—the slender blurred figure in blue, and the gay, precise pattern of her sampler—that had caught at Meg's imagination. The sampler was a physical link, stretching across two and a half centuries; the fabric her fingers touched had been held by hands long since dissolved into dust.

She had no intention of telling this to Andy. He would either laugh or express disgust.

"Please, Andy," she said softly. "Please? It can't do any harm to try."

She put her hand on the table, like a propitiatory offering—palm up, fingers gently curved in appeal. Andy eyed it with all the enthusiasm he might have shown a dead fish. But the mute challenge was too much for him. Probably, too, his curiosity was aroused. Slowly his hand slid across the table till his fingers touched Meg's.

Although she had suggested the experiment, Meg was the one who almost lost her cool when the image came. She had not expected such a quick response. Perhaps she had really not expected any response. But the shapes began to form only seconds after their hands were joined.

The distortion was disturbing enough to make her feel physically queasy. The shadow room was just a little askew in all dimensions, and the overlapping of illusion and reality made it difficult to distinguish the two. Meg forced herself to concentrate. The image shifted and wavered, and then took on a distinctness far superior to anything she had yet seen.

The room was the same one they had seen before, with a fireplace flanked by settles, and a braided rug on the hearth. This time Meg could make out the objects on the mantel. They were an odd combination of elegance and crude simplicity. A brown pottery jug stood next to a figurine that could only be Meissen—a shepherdess, delicately pastel, with two white lambs at her feet. A silver bowl with a finely chased design rubbed elbows with a copper kettle.

There was a fire in the fireplace. Above the flames hung a large black pot, suspended on iron rods. An animal—a small dog or a large cat—lay curled up on the rug. Its plushy black form was rolled into such a tight ball that she couldn't tell exactly what it was.

Only then did Meg allow herself to look at the human figures. The girl was sitting on one of the benches by the fire, her golden head bent over her sewing. . . . Or was it sewing? It was hard to tell exactly what she was doing, for she wasn't moving. She was frozen, like a still picture projected onto the air.

There was no sign of the old man, but a third personage had entered the scene. It was bent over the fire, as if in the act of stirring the contents of the kettle. The face was hidden, but from the costume—a long dark dress and white cap—and the shape of the bowed back, Meg thought it must be an elderly woman, a servant, probably.

There wasn't much else to be seen. A window in the wall to the left—small, narrow-paned, and dark, as if it were night outside—a tall cupboard on the right, the shelves filled with dishes. Yes, Meg thought, it must be night in that other place—that other time. The only light in the room came from the fire. That was why she couldn't see more; the corners of the room away from the fire were obscured by shadows. And it was utterly still. Even the flames were as motionless as if they had been carved out of glowing red stone.

Like a flick of a switch, the image was gone. Pale

sunlight dazzled Meg's eyes, and she was aware of her aching fingers, squeezed by Andy's hand.

"Let go," she gasped. "It's over. You're hurting me, Andy."

Andy obeyed. His upper lip was beaded with perspiration.

"I need a drink," he said.

While he collected bottles and glasses, Meg found writing materials, and they sat down at the kitchen table to record their impressions. Andy emptied his glass as he wrote, and mixed a second drink while Meg read his description.

It agreed with hers. She was used to that now, it no longer shocked her as it had done at first. He had seen one thing she had not seen—the face of the old woman bending over the fire. "The Witch of Endor in person," he had written. "Wrinkled and toothless and a thousand years old."

She waited for Andy to read her paper before she spoke, although she was bursting with eagerness.

"Andy, it is beginning to make sense. Everything in that room fits a date in the early eighteenth century—the architecture, the costumes, the objects in the room. The same room, Andy! I'll bet if we tried it in the drawing room, we'd see the room with the sampler. That must have been their parlor. What is now the library was their kitchen."

Andy's eyes flickered with reviving interest. "That makes some sense," he admitted. "Another house, on the same site. We see it as it once looked, occupying the same space. Only it is askew; the ground level wasn't quite the same a hundred years before this house was built."

"The house and the people who lived in it," Meg said. "An old man, a girl—his daughter?—and a servant, an old woman. My gosh, Andy, if we can't track them down, we flunk as historians. We even know the name."

"You're assuming the girl is Anna Maria. We've no proof of that."

"But we have to make some assumptions," Meg argued. "Didn't you say scientists start out with a hypothesis and discard it only after it has been proved incorrect? What we need are some histories of the area back in Colonial times. Not general histories—books that tell about the old families and their names and all."

"The county Historical Association," Andy said. He was as enthusiastic as Meg now. "Damn, I should have tried them instead of going to Philadelphia. It's local trivia we need, not constitutional history."

"Where is the Historical Association?"

"Reading, I think. I'll find out for sure. We may need tax and land transfer records too. I don't know whether they would have copies of those at the Historical Association. Maybe we'll have to go to Harrisburg."

He looked like the old Andy—the freckles, the smile, and the wide hazel eyes reminded her of the boy she had known, in his more agreeable moods. Meg hadn't realized how much his depression had affected her until she felt it lighten. When he reached for her glass she let him refill it, and they drank a toast to their mutual intelligence. Then Andy tore a sheet off the pad they had been using and started to make notes, mumbling to himself.

"I'll get something to eat," Meg said, rising. "What would you like?"

"Anything. Richard is himself again. Full of beans and champing at the bit." Andy looked up at her. "I'm sorry I flipped this morning."

"That's okay. I get moods myself."

"Wait a minute. This morning. What was it I—oh, I remember. You got some mail. I left it on the hall table. Forgot to tell you about it."

"Mail?" Meg paused, a package of frozen vegetables in her hand. "Isn't that funny? I never thought about getting mail here, even though I did give the address to my friends. To me, this is Sylvia's house. I walked right past that mailbox on the road the other day and didn't even look in it."

"I could see you hadn't. There was quite a stack of mail there today—most circulars, but I do have a few friends who can read and write. Apparently you do too. Go ahead and get the letters. I'll get dinner. I've lost track, but it's probably my turn."

Meg sat down at the table to inspect her mail while Andy fried chops. There were three letters, in addition to the inevitable junk addressed to "Occupant." Two were from friends in New York. The third was from Sylvia.

Holding the letter, she looked at Andy, who had given up all pretense of watching the chops.

"I saw it," he said. "What did you expect? Sylvia doesn't make phone calls unless someone has died, but she isn't about to let you off the hook. You'll have to keep her informed of your hourly progress, or she'll be on your back like a leopard."

"Your similes are so charming," Meg grumbled.

She opened the letter with a mixture of trepidation and guilt. Come to think of it, she had promised to write Sylvia at regular intervals.

She had not intended to read the letter to Andy, although he was watching her hopefully; but the first paragraph was too much.

"Listen to this! 'I have received a telephone call from Georgia Wilkes; where she gets the money to make long-distance calls I can't imagine, but I suppose she thought she was doing both of us a favor by informing me that you feel at a loss with the job I gave you. Obviously I don't expect you to perform the services of a trained decorator or antique dealer. You must learn to control these anxieties, Meg, they are symptoms of your illness and can be eliminated if you are firm.'

"She underlined 'firm,'" Meg added.

"She would. It's just about what I'd expect Sylvia to write. Georgia has a hell of a nerve, calling her."

"Oh, I think she was trying to help me. Let me read you the rest. The worst is yet to come. 'In order to relieve your anxieties I told Georgia to look over the things in the attic. She's as honest as these people ever are, and I hope the many favors she has received from me will make her treat me with the gratitude I deserve. Write down her evaluations and estimates, but don't sell her anything. You haven't the legal right to do so, of course, but I repeat the obvious so you won't let Georgia bully or pressure you. You have a weak and yielding character, Meg. I may pay a quick visit toward the end of the month and will then settle any matters that demand my attention. I haven't heard from you, as I expected to do long before this. I must insist that you keep me informed as to your progress. I refer to your state of health as well as the condition of my property. . . .' "

"And on and on and on," Andy said, as Meg's voice died away. "Hell, I'd say that was a pretty affable letter, for Sylvia. Just a couple of cracks about your feeble character."

"Yes, she sounds positively mellow, doesn't she? I'm surprised she warned us she might be coming; I'd expect her to drop in to see what we're up to. Blast it. I don't want Georgia around here all the time."

"Me neither."

"Why don't you like her? I think she's funny and kind of nice."

"She's entertaining, in small doses. But that hearty manner wears thin pretty quick. I don't like her because she has no use for me. I suppose she told you what a rat I was—and am?"

"She didn't say much. Just a crack about how popular you are around town, and how that surprises her. And she said the whole town thinks we—"

Meg stopped. The statement she had been about to make could be considered provocative. She was too late; Andy's lips curved in an unamused smile.

"I know what they think. Leers and winks and nudges follow me as I progress innocently down Main Street. They don't think anything of it; bundling is an old Pennsylvania custom. It doesn't bother you, does it? Except, of course, for wondering what's wrong with you, or with me, that I haven't tried to lay you."

"Talk about male ego," Meg said angrily. "I never—"

"Sure you did. Sometimes I wonder myself. . . . Hell and damnation, the beans are burning."

They were not only burning, they were charred. Meg dumped the vegetables into the sink, pan and all, and turned on the water. The hiss of rising steam echoed her sentiments admirably.

"Actually, we've got the worst of it, the way we're living," Andy said pensively. "All the irritations of a permanent relationship without any of the compensations. Look at the way we snipe at each other. Do you suppose that's an inevitable consequence of the failure or absence of sexual activity?"

Meg couldn't help being amused. "I don't think they're mutually exclusive. You're crazy, Andy, and you're not a very good cook, either. Put on another pot of beans."

### III

Georgia came by next morning. She had called to announce her imminent arrival; and Meg, watching from the window in the drawing room, was delighted to see that she was riding a bicycle, which she handled with the panache that characterized her personality. She flung the battered bike on the ground and climbed the porch stairs. Meg went to the door and admitted her.

She was wearing the same jeans she had worn before, with a turtleneck sweater of a bilious green. Her hair, blown about by the wind, looked like a rusty kitchen scraper. But Meg's welcome was genuine; she was glad to see Georgia after all. She didn't even mind the darting inquisitive glances Georgia cast around the house.

Georgia accepted the offer of a cup of coffee before they started work.

"I drink coffee all day," she said. "Up to two in the afternoon, when I begin drinking seriously. Hey, you really have cleaned the place up. It looked absolute hell while the Culvers were here. I came out with Sylvia when she called on them to deliver her eviction notice. Figured she might need some moral support."

"Did she?"

"Hell, no, not Sylvia. She had that little louse cowering by the time she got through. And she never raised her voice or used a dirty word. I don't know how she does it. It's more effective than my cussing, though. I tell you, she can flay a victim and make him bleed. I'm surprised Culver didn't set fire to the house when he left. If I ever saw hate and frustrated malice in a man's face . . ."

"He did considerable damage," Meg said. "I found scraps of broken dishes in the kitchen, and that was after Andy had cleaned most of them up. He's stripping the wallpaper in the master bedroom now; Culver had covered it with comments in acrylic paint."

"Oh, yeah?" Georgia put down her empty cup. "I'd better have a look. You kids shouldn't mess around with stuff like that, you might destroy something valuable."

Meg led the way upstairs. Andy was ostentatiously hard at work; he was on the last wall now, and the floor was ankle-deep in scraps. He glanced up as they entered and greeted Georgia correctly, if unenthusiastically.

"First time I ever saw you working," she said rudely. "Hold it, pal; let's see what you're ripping off that wall."

Lips tight, Andy stepped back.

George peered nearsightedly at the wall and examined some of the scraps. Finally she said gruffly, "Right. No use trying to save this. You planning to repaper yourself or get someone to do it?"

"That's up to Sylvia. I can do it, but I don't know if she's willing to trust me with the job."

During the tour of the house that followed, Andy and Georgia did most of the talking. Meg listened meekly while they discussed the treatment of the floors and the patching of stair rails and mantelpieces. Georgia seemed to be impressed by Andy's knowledge; she became quite affable as the morning wore on, and once, when Meg returned from making fresh coffee, she found the two of them doubled up over a joke Georgia had told. Georgia refused to tell it to her.

"You're too nice a girl," she said, grinning, while Andy continued to whoop with rude laughter. "What—lunch? Is it that late already? No, thanks, honey, I've got my own work to do, and I'm not going to heckle you kids all the time. That's what you were thinking, wasn't it?" She winked at Andy, who grinned back at her. "Forget it, buster. I've got better things to do than spy on you two. I do want to look over the stuff in the attic. Monday be okay? I'm closed that day."

Meg and Andy stood in the doorway watching as she rode away. Midway along the drive she took both hands off the handlebars and wrung them over her head in the old victory gesture. The bike wobbled but remained upright, and Georgia vanished around the curve in the driveway, still riding "no hands."

"That wasn't so bad, was it?" Meg demanded, as they went back into the house. "I thought you two got along fine."

"Listen, I was on my best behavior. If we hadn't gotten along, it would have been Georgia's fault."

"You were nice," Meg said soothingly. "You even laughed at her jokes."

Andy grinned reminiscently. "It was pretty funny."

"Tell me."

Andy looked her over, from the top of her head to her scuffed sneakers. "Some other day. Today you don't look old enough. I'll tell you what, I'll take you on a picnic. It's too nice to work."

It was an idyllic afternoon—the last they were to have, although neither of them knew it. Yet perhaps a premonition of coming trouble gave the day its special quality. They ate their lunch in a glade in the woods, where sunlight sifted down through the leaves and a heap of rocks provided a rough dining table and chairs. There was a constant rustle of shy movement in the leaves beyond the clearing; Andy scattered crumbs and they both sat motionless until, after an interval, a squirrel gained courage enough to creep up to the food. Before they left there were several squirrels and a flock of scolding sparrows snapping up their leftovers.

"If you sit long enough you can see rabbits and foxes and raccoons," Andy said. "Not to mention birds; it's a paradise for bird watchers. One thing I'll say for Sylvia; she never would allow hunting, not even the ritzy red-coated kind."

They wandered on, finding little streams and butternut and black-walnut trees, and multitudes of brambles. Meg began to realize the extent of the place. What a pity it would be if it were sacrificed to subdivisions and shopping centers! Glancing at Andy, who was stalking along in silence beside her, she wondered if he was thinking the same thing. He looked grim.

They returned homeward at last as the sun was setting, tired and scratched and muddy, but enjoying the most amicable feelings toward each other and the world in general. As they crossed the lawn toward the house, Andy came to a sudden stop.

"What . . . oh. Is this where it hit you, the other night?"

"About here. Don't look so worried, I didn't feel anything just now. I was—remembering. Let's go in."

They spent the evening in the library. Meg was inspired by Georgia's visit, and determined to learn as much as possible about antiques before she came back Monday. She sat with her head braced on her hands, determinedly absorbing names and details from a book on Victorian furniture. Spool beds, finger moldings, spandrels and skirts swam around in her brain and, one by one, were nailed down in some sort of order. When she looked up to rest her eyes she saw that Andy was making no pretense at doing anything useful. He had a pile of bright-jacketed paperbacks at his elbow and was deep in a volume whose cover displayed a bloody ax and a dripping knife.

Once, when she glanced up, she found him looking at her.

"You don't want to try anything, do you?" he asked, with the air of a man performing an unpleasant duty.

Meg started to laugh.

"I don't see what's so funny," said Andy, and returned to his book.

"Maybe 'funny' is not quite the word," Meg admitted.

# Chapter 7

They had planned to investigate the Historical Association collection in Reading next day, but when Andy went out to start the car, that monstrosity refused to respond. Returning, grease-smeared and infuriated, to the front hall where Meg waited, Andy called his vehicle bad names.

"It's the damned battery," he grumbled. "I knew the thing was just about to go."

"Can't you call the garage in town and get it recharged?"

"That thing has been recharged so many times it can find its way to the garage alone. I'll have to get a new battery. Might as well walk into town right now and get the job over with. I can bum a lift back. And don't suggest calling the garage. That's for rich people and incompetent females. If I install the battery myself I'll save enough money to take us out to dinner some fine night. Sorry about Reading, Meg; it'll be too late to go by the time I get through."

"Tomorrow, then."

Meg walked him down the driveway, his hands in his jacket pockets, kicking viciously at loose pebbles as he went. She felt frustrated too. She had been in a ghost-hunting mood that morning; it was maddening to be prevented from checking out some of the information they had gathered. But perhaps there was something she could do. The records at the Historical Association might give them what they needed, but that source might fail; and in the meantime, they had left several loose ends dangling. The buttons, with their obscure crest, were one such loose end. Andy had shown her his notes, and Meg had to agree that the rubbed design on the button he had cleaned might be any one of the crests he had copied in Philadelphia. But there were several other buttons. One of them might be less worn.

The liquid metal-cleaning solution she found in the back of one of the cupboards did an excellent job, far better than the paste Andy had used. The buttons emerged bright and shiny, and, as she had hoped, two of them were in much better condition than Andy's. The details were as sharp as if they had been cut the week before. Tense with excitement, Meg ran into the library and got Andy's notes out of the desk drawer. She spread the designs out on the table and compared them. They were similar in general design, but after a few seconds Meg was certain that she had found the original of the crest on the buttons. The diagonal bar, the rounded objects that turned out to be a fat five-pointed stars, and the bird—a hawk or eagle. . . . It was the crest of the von Friedland family, of Brunswick-Wolfenbüttel.

Wherever that is, Meg thought. The discovery really

didn't tell her anything; in fact, it contradicted the assumption she had been making all along, that the house had belonged to a family named Huber. Had Anna Maria married a von Friedland? On the face of it, it did not seem likely. The latter family bore arms and possessed the significant "von" prefix which commonly, if not always, indicated noble blood. Yet the alliance wasn't impossible; in the freedom of a new land, noble and commoner met on equal ground, and perhaps marriages had taken place in the colonies that would have been socially unacceptable in the German principalities.

That seemed the obvious solution, and yet Meg wasn't satisfied with it. She couldn't forget the image of an old man in a blue coat with silver buttons. The image was a long way from being evidence, of course; and even if it was legitimate, Anna Maria's father wasn't the only man in Pennsylvania to boast of silver buttons on his coat. And yet. . . . Without realizing it, Meg had already put some of the pieces of the puzzle together. The buttons from the old man's coat and the military decoration—both suited the straight, soldierly bearing of the figure whose pose she had seen, although she had not been able to distinguish his features. The locket, perhaps, held a lock of his hair and a lock from the head of Anna Maria's mother, who had passed on her coloring to her fair-haired daughter. The necklace had to be the heirloom of a once-wealthy family; no peasant would own such a thing. All had belonged to Anna Maria and, with her sampler, had been cherished by her as the last mementos of a family whose name had died out with the sole surviving daughter.

It was so real in her mind, so strangely structured, that

when Meg began to think of confirmatory evidence she couldn't believe she had based her reconstruction on such insubstantial proof. Of nothing, in fact. Why was she so sure Anna Maria's mother had died when she was small? The fact that they had not yet seen a woman who might fill that position didn't mean anything; they hadn't seen the servant until the day before. The old house might have held a swarm of people who were yet to become visible. And why, against the single solid fact they knew, did she continue to feel that the family was of higher social standing than the simple name Huber would suggest? The silver and the crest, the medal—these things fit the von Friedlands. But the von Friedlands and the Hubers didn't go together.

With an exclamation of disgust Meg jumbled the papers together. She could sit here all day speculating. There was something else she could do; she couldn't imagine why she had not thought of it before. The cubbyhole in the attic that had yielded the sampler and the box might hold other objects. She hadn't even looked inside, she had simply pulled out the first thing her groping fingers had touched.

Equipped with a flashlight and dressed in her oldest pants, Meg went upstairs. It did not take her long to realize that she was about to encounter her second frustration of the day. Squirming and wriggling, she retraced her former route, over tables and under chair legs, but when she had inserted herself into the narrow space in front of the door, she found that the slate-topped chest had moved as far as it was going to move. It was blocked by a dining-room table, and even if her muscles had been up to shifting that massive object, it was jammed up against an even heavier sideboard. She would have to start at the far end of the room and move practically every object in it.

Well, then, Meg decided, she would move them. They would have to be inventoried eventually; she would ask Andy to help with the heavier pieces. But she would not be able to get into her cubbyhole that day, or for several days to come. In the meantime, she might at least have a look. Thank goodness she had had sense enough to bring a flashlight.

She squatted down, adding another bruise to the one on her hip as she did so, and opened the door as far as it would go. A cloud of dust billowed up. Meg sneezed. She waited for the dust to settle and then shone the flashlight into the opening and applied her right eye to the crack.

Dust and cobwebs. Bare, rough board planks. Beyond, the roof sloped abruptly down; she saw where it met the wall at an acute angle. Under the muffling blanket of dust there were several shapes, shrouded as if in gray velvet.

Meg put the flashlight down and reached in through the crack. She strained till her shoulder ached, but was unable to touch anything except dust. It was a futile exercise; even if she had been able to reach any of the mysterious objects she could not have gotten them out. It was maddening to be so near her goal and so far from attaining it. Panting, she scrambled back across the table and began to move furniture.

She had not made any discernible progress when she heard a faint hail from below. She went to the attic door.

"Andy?"

He was no more anxious to come up than she was ready to go down. Both of them had to bellow at the top of their lungs in order to be heard, and the ensuing conversation was carried on at top pitch.

"How about lunch?"

"Get your own," Meg screamed. "I'm busy."

Andy replied with a single word. It came through loud and clear, being a one-syllable noun.

Meg grinned. "Did you get the battery?"

"What?"

"DID YOU GET THE BATTERY?"

"Yes. I left my right arm and a pint of blood."

"I'm sorry."

So that was the cause of his ill humor. Meg sympathized; she was a member of the underpaid classes herself.

"Come help me," she yelled.

"I'm busy too."

After a few hours Meg went down in search of sustenance. She had moved an étagère, a cast-iron settee and two matching armchairs, a brass bed, and a transitional writing desk; the only consolation she could offer her aching muscles was six feet of empty space and the undeniably consoling fact that she had been able to identify all the furniture she had moved. Her reading was beginning to pay off.

Andy was nowhere to be seen, but he had left his dirty dishes, in a gesture whose childish spite amused Meg. She went to the kitchen door. A distant, hollow clanging indicated that Andy was working on the car. It sounded as if he were rhythmically kicking the fender, but Meg's knowledge of auto repairs was slight. Perhaps the installation of a battery demanded such a technique.

Cheered by the sounds of struggle and alarm, she ate her

lunch and forced herself back to the attic. Only grim determination kept her working; she had never put in such continuously strenuous effort, and when she stopped she could have fallen flat on the dusty floor and gone to sleep. She had to stop. The next object to be moved was a square piano with legs as thick as a baby elephant's. She had shoved on this with her full weight and hadn't even heard it squeak. Andy would have to help with this little number. He was in no mood to be helpful today. By tomorrow he might have cooled off.

A shower restored her, and she started for the kitchen with the virtuous determination to cook a nice dinner and demonstrate her maturity by overlooking Andy's bad humor. But she had not gone far before a spicy smell reached her nostrils—something with tomatoes and basil and garlic. It smelled wonderful; she was ravenously hungry.

Andy was stirring something on the stove when she came into the kitchen. He turned to greet her with an angelic smile. Meg's answering smile was as warm as appetite could make it. Men were such volatile creatures; cheerful one minute, sulking the next. Andy's good moods were nice while they lasted, though; and he certainly made excellent spaghetti sauce. Meg scraped her plate under Andy's benevolent gaze.

"Your hands don't fool me into thinking you are eighteen," he commented. "What have you been doing up there, sawing up the furniture to get firewood?"

"Moving things. I'm just about beat. One thing I'll say for the Victorians—they built ugly, but they built solid."

"Why didn't you call me?"

Meg looked at him. After a minute Andy burst out laughing.

"You're right. I'd have bitten you. I seem to be always apologizing for my rotten moods."

"You get over them in a hurry, anyhow. I would like some help, maybe tomorrow. I'm clearing out that room, Andy—the one where I found the box with the sampler. I can't get into that cubbyhole under the eaves without moving all the damned furniture. There's something else in that space."

"Where you found the box? Don't get your hopes up."

"I have to clear out some of the furniture anyhow, if I'm going to inventory it. I found a darling cast-iron couch and chairs. I'm going to paint them white and put them on the lawn, under that big oak."

"White's kind of dull, isn't it? Why not pink or puce? You're getting all fired up about this job."

"I guess the more you learn about something, the more interesting it is. You know the tower room? The minute I saw it I thought of Sir Walter Scott—"

"Abbotsford," Andy said, nodding. "I fell for that study of him myself."

"You've seen it? I've just seen pictures. When were you abroad?"

"A couple of years ago."

"Are you lucky. I've never been able to afford it. But I'd love to furnish that tower room like Scott's study. According to the books I've been reading, it's Elizabethan—not genuine Elizabethan, you know, the style that was revived in Scott's time—but it's an English style and I don't suppose you could find much of it in this country. So then I thought Victorian Gothic—"

"What's the difference?"

"It's sort of hard to describe—especially for me. I'm still an amateur. But I'm learning. Andy, Georgia was right. There is a Duncan Phyfe dining set up there!"

"Imagine that!" Andy's eyes narrowed with laughter. "You could tell me it was a Herman Pifflesnoot and I'd be equally impressed."

"I thought you knew about old furniture. That house you helped fix up—"

"The old furniture I refinished came out of junk shops, sis. None of my friends have enough bread to play around with antiques."

"Me neither. The stuff in my apartment is strictly board and brick. But I wish I could afford some good antiques. This job is spoiling me."

They went on talking antiques as they cleared away the dishes. The days were taking on a routine. When the chores were done they headed automatically for the library. It was beginning to feel like their room, with their books scattered over the long library table, and the chairs they always sat in.

Tonight, though, the massive tomes on American furniture did not attract Meg. The very sight of them made her shoulders ache reminiscently. Andy, settling down in the big leather chair by the fire, glanced up at her as she wandered around the room.

"Bored by antiques? Have a nice soothing murder."

"What are you reading?"

"It's not exactly soothing. Historic American murder

cases. I don't know why it is, but American murders lack the charm of the English equivalents. There's a certain *je ne sais quoi*, a recondite mustiness. . . ."

"What about Lizzie Borden?"

"That's an exception. The most mystifying damned thing! If she did it, how did she do it without getting blood on her clothes? It was a particularly gory ax murder—double murder, in fact. But if she didn't do it, who did? And how do you account for Lizzie's peculiar activities in the boiling-hot barn loft? Yes, it's a lovely murder. But the English have got Burke and Hare, Constance Kent, and dozens more."

"You can keep them. I'll see if I can find a nice book like *Little Women*. Unless you feel in the mood for—"

Andy chuckled. "What a weird life we're leading. If you had said that under any circumstances but these. . . . However, knowing what you mean—the answer is no, I do not feel in the mood for summoning spooks. Let's have a quiet evening, okay? We'll hit the Historical Association tomorrow and get back on the track."

"All right."

Meg finally found a copy of *The Sheikh*, which she had heard about but had never read, and was soon absorbed in the struggles of Diana Mayo. It was too good to keep to herself.

" 'She fought against the fascination with which his passionate eyes dominated her, resisting him dumbly with tight-locked lips still he held her palpitating in his arms . . .' "

"What?" Andy exclaimed, looking up from his book.

" 'She writhed in his arms as he crushed her to him,' "

Meg went on. " 'Numbly she felt him gather her high up into his arms, his lips still clinging closely, and carry her across the tent through curtains into an adjoining room. He laid her down on soft cushions. . . .' "

"You've got a lot of nerve criticizing my literary tastes."

"Men don't act like that anymore," Meg said sadly.

"If I tried anything like that on a woman she'd either laugh in my face or break my jaw."

He returned to his murders, and Meg read on. She had put in a hard day, and the sexy sensation of the twenties began to read rather tamely after a while; she was beginning to yawn when a sudden movement from Andy distracted her.

She looked up. Andy was staring at her. His expression was one of pure horror. The white of his eyes showed all around the dilated pupils; if she had not known it to be impossible, she would have sworn his hair was standing up on end. With a muffled exclamation he leaped to his feet and ran out of the room.

Meg felt her spine crawling. Fearfully she turned her head and glanced over her shoulder. But there was no monster in the shadows; there was not even the shimmering glow of a fading vision. Utterly bewildered, she closed her book and stared at the dying fire. Perhaps she should go after Andy. He might be ill. She almost hoped he was; that explanation would be less disturbing than any other that occurred to her.

Deliberately Meg moved around the room, turning off lights, making sure the windows were locked, checking the screen in front of the fire. Then she went upstairs.

She listened, unashamed, at Andy's closed door, but

heard nothing. She knocked. There was a long pause before Andy finally answered.

"Who is it?"

"Of all the dumb questions!" Relief at hearing his voice made Meg snappish. "Who would it be?"

"Oh. Go away, Meg. I'll see you in the morning."

"You'll see me now. What's the matter? You can't run out like that; you scared hell out of me."

Another long pause followed. Finally Meg heard the bedsprings creak and the crackle of paper as Andy stamped through the scrapes on the floor. He had finished stripping the paper but had not yet removed the debris.

When he opened the door he stared pallidly at Meg.

"Sorry. Sorry, sorry, I'm getting sick and tired of apologizing all the time. It was a shock, that's all."

"What was a shock?" Meg almost screamed the words; if Andy had been deliberately trying to frighten her he could not have chosen a better method than the vague hints.

"Finding out what happened to the Hubers. There we were, speculating and planning complicated research problems; and the answer was right there all along, on the library shelves."

Meg began to understand. Cold spread from the back of her neck through her body.

"The book you were reading. The historic American murders?"

Somberly Andy nodded. "All three of them. The old man, the girl, and the servant. Beaten to death, on a night in October 1740. Two hundred–odd years ago tonight."

# Chapter 8

"Let me see!"

Meg made a grab for the book, which Andy was holding with his finger marking his place. He pulled it away.

"You don't believe me?"

"I hope you're wrong." Meg slumped against the doorframe and looked disconsolately at Andy. "But I guess you couldn't be, could you? I—I don't know what to say. What a horrible thing! I never thought of anything like that. No wonder . . ."

"The house is haunted," Andy finished. "It's a classic motive, all right. You might as well see for yourself. Come on in."

"Not here, the place is a mess. Come on back to the library."

"Honey bun, I don't want to sit in that room tonight. Don't you understand what I'm saying? This is the anniversary of the murder!"

They stared at one another, appalled and wide-eyed. Then Meg got a grip on herself.

"What do you expect to happen?" she demanded. "You think we'll see the murder or something? So far we haven't seen *anything* happen; only still pictures. Oh, I agree, I wouldn't want to see them lying there in their blood, but what if we did? It wouldn't kill us."

"Are you trying to shame me into showing some guts? Okay. But if you flip and run screaming out of the house, don't blame me."

Giving Andy a contemptuous stare, Meg turned her back on him and started downstairs. She heard him follow, but did not speak. When they reached the library she switched on every available light and then held out her hand.

"There. It's nice and bright, and I won't let anything get you. Give me the book, please."

Andy threw it at her. In a way, Meg didn't blame him. In silence she bent and picked up the book; still in silence, she sat down in her favorite chair by the fire and began to turn the pages.

She found the reference at once. The name—Huber— seemed to jump up out of the page at her. But the actual text was so brief as to be frustrating. The case was not discussed in detail, only referred to among a group of other crimes the writer considered related—unsolved, apparently senseless murders in remote rural districts.

Andy had been right about the date. October 11, 1740. The coincidence disturbed Meg as much as it did Andy, but she was determined not to show it. The other details, cursory as they were, were equally disturbing; it was like reading of the horrible death of people she knew person- ally. The victims—the elderly man, Christian Huber, and an aged family servant—had been found late on the night of the eleventh by a visitor. Although the house was a shambles, nothing seemed to be missing—except the third member of the family, the man's granddaughter. She had never been found, although neighbors searched the woods for days. This fact, as the author unemotionally remarked, "suggested a possible motive for the crime." The impromptu gathering which was the frontier equivalent of a coroner's jury had rendered a verdict of "murder by persons unknown."

"So she was his granddaughter," Meg said. "We should have known he was too old to be her father. That explains the mourning brooch—locket, rather. It has the hair of her parents. Why did you say they were all three killed?"

"The neighbors would have found her if she had been alive. They wouldn't have found a grave, though, not in that overgrown wilderness. The criminals had to kill her, after they got through with her, to keep her from identifying them."

"Indians?" Meg asked. "They kidnapped women and children sometimes."

Andy shook his head decisively.

"The MO is all wrong. So is the timing. The French and Indian War didn't start till about 1750. I guess there could have been isolated incidents before that; but Indians used knives and tomahawks, not clubs. They would have scalped the victims and probably set fire to the house."

"I guess so. The jury certainly would have mentioned that as a possibility if they had thought so. God, it's awful! That poor girl, dragged out into the woods. . . ."

"I wonder why they took her out of the house? With the

old man and the servant dead, there was nothing to keep them from doing whatever they wanted to her."

"The visitor," Meg said promptly. "The bodies were discovered by a visitor, later that night. Maybe the victims warned the criminals that they were expecting company, hoping to scare them away."

"Mmm." Andy nodded grudgingly. "The case doesn't smell right, somehow. I know there are psychotics in any community, but you think of rural Pennsylvania as a particularly sedate, God-fearing region—all those Quakers and Dunkards and Mennonites. It was a small-town atmosphere, too; everybody knew everybody else. Wouldn't you think criminals of such vicious tendencies would be suspected by their neighbors? Criminal lunatics don't usually stop with a single crime, either. Sooner or later they'd give themselves away and get caught."

"Maybe they were caught, later."

"Why do you keep saying 'they?' Another characteristic of criminal lunatics is that they don't usually run in packs."

"Why . . . the jury said 'persons unknown.' The usual form is 'person or persons,' isn't it?"

"Yes, I guess so. But that could be the author abridging the report. I should think one husky man could handle that pathetic crowd—two old people and a girl."

Meg shivered. The room was getting cool as the fire died.

"I'm just guessing, of course. But criminals do run in packs sometimes. Escapees from prisons or reformatories, looking for a place to hide—"

"You've got an answer for everything," Andy said disagreeably. "But you're thinking in modern terms. There were no penitentiaries or mental hospitals in colonial times. The jury would have known of any criminal gangs in the neighborhood. They didn't try to rehabilitate murderers in the good old days, they strung them up."

"You're guessing too," Meg said. "We don't know enough. We'll have to find out."

Andy gave a snort of laughter. "You're planning to solve a murder almost two hundred and fifty years old, when the people on the spot couldn't do it? I'm a crime nut myself, but I know my limitations."

"We have to try."

"Why?" Andy's eyes narrowed. "I can think of a damned good reason why we shouldn't try. You're getting obsessed, Meg. At first you were the skeptic. Now . . . maybe the word I want is 'possessed' instead of 'obsessed.' You keep this up, and you'll go crazy."

"You're the one who's crazy. What are you afraid of? Anyone with a spark of imagination would be fascinated by this business and determined to go ahead with it. But you. . . . What do you know that you haven't told me? What's your problem?"

Andy jumped up.

"I am crazy—crazy insane, to get mixed up with a weirdo like you. I must have been out of my mind to suggest this. Well, I've come to my senses. Play ghosts all you want, but leave me out of it."

He started toward the door. Meg ran after him.

"Where are you going?"

"Back to the cottage. I'm not going to sleep in this damned house tonight, and if you have any sense—which you don't—you'll come with me."

"Andy, wait . . ."

She caught his arm. He tried to pull away, but she hung on with both hands. She meant only to detain him; but she must have known, as he did, what might happen. Once it began, neither of them could move; they were held as still as the image they saw.

It was daylight in that other place. Sunlight streamed in the narrow windows and let them see more clearly than they had yet seen. A table stood in the center of the room. The old man was seated at it, and the girl sat across from him. They were eating. At least the girl was; she had a spoon halfway to her lips. The old man's head was bent over a book that lay beside his neglected plate. For the first time, Meg could see their features.

The girl was charming. Her eyes were lowered so that their color was not discernible; long lashes, of a striking dark gold, cast shadows on her delicately molded cheeks. Her face was narrow and pointed, and her parted lips showed her small white teeth.

The old man's face was as distinctive as the girl's fragile prettiness. He must have been a strikingly handsome youth, and he was still handsome, with the austerity old age gives to bones and muscles stripped of superfluous flesh. His mouth was still firm, his nose straight; his shock of white hair shone in the sunlight. The hand lying on the table had the long, thin fingers of an artist or philosopher.

Meg strained to see, as the image faded. Artist or not, old Mr. Huber would not have been easy prey for a murderer. Those lean fingers would curve knowledgeably around the hilt of a sword, and the broad shoulders had strength enough to wield it well.

Her reflections were rudely interrupted by a growl from
Andy. The image was gone, and Andy was going. Jerking
his arm away, he headed straight for the front door. Meg
was close behind him, with no clear notion of what she
meant to do. She knew better than to touch him; he would
probably knock her down if she did, he was in such a state.

Andy opened the door—and stopped, so suddenly he
rocked back on his heels. Meg felt it too, even before she
saw what was outside. It poured into the house like a flood
of evil-smelling gas.

The half-grown moon, high in the sky, cast a thin light
over the lawn. The shadows it made were faint; but those
other shadows were not the products of moonlight. Tall,
columnar shapes of blackness, they hovered in the wider,
paler shadow of the big oak. The horror emanated from
them, whatever they were—and Meg thought she knew
what they were.

She had only one aim—to close a barrier between
herself and the terror out in the night. The futility of the
gesture never occurred to her. No material obstacle can
stop the pressure of spiritual evil; but the horror had
entered when the door opened, and Meg knew she had to
get it closed.

Sure enough, the slam of the door snapped the spell.
Meg leaned against it, sick and shaking. Andy staggered
back.

"That was what you felt, the other night?" Meg whispered.

Andy nodded dumbly.

"I owe you an apology," Meg said. "That was the
worst. . . . Let's go write it down."

"You're not crazy," Andy said, staring. "You're inhuman. Write it down, she says! Give me fifteen minutes with that bottle of bourbon and I won't be able to write."

"You're going to drink—now?"

"I'm going to get drunk," Andy corrected. "Now."

"Oh, no, you're not."

"No, I guess I'm not," Andy said, after a moment. "That would be pretty stupid, wouldn't it? I guess I'm not leaving, either."

"Not unless you're braver than I think you are. I wonder what would happen if—"

Andy caught her wrist as she reached for the knob, and then dropped it, as if it were hot.

"You try to open that door and I'll break your arm."

"I haven't got the courage either," Meg admitted weakly. "I keep thinking that if we faced them. . . . What can they do to us? They're only shadows."

"Shadows of killers," Andy said. "That's what you think, isn't it?"

"They were man-shaped, man-sized. Yes, that's what I think. And you?"

As she had discovered, the way to cure Andy of his fear was to make him start thinking. His face lost some of its sickly pallor as he spoke.

"The problem in these cases is always the same. How do you separate genuine perception from hallucination based on expectation? You can start out with a legitimate experience, but almost at once it becomes contaminated. We learned about the murders tonight. Presto, chango, the murderers appear. I didn't see distinct shapes, only shadows."

"But the feeling—the horror, the dread—"

"Just what we imagine the inhabitants of the house would feel if they looked out and saw death walking toward them."

"You felt it before. Before we found out about the murders."

Andy didn't like this reminder. "Meg, I can't think anymore tonight. But I'm not going to sleep much—not till the good old sun comes up and the fatal anniversary is over."

"Silly," Meg said angrily. "You're scaring yourself, Andy, like a kid watching the late monster movie. You think the murder is reenacted on the anniversary of the day it happened? Okay, suppose it is. Shadows, striking down other shadows. They can't touch us, they don't even know we're here, if this is just a mechanical repetition of what happened in the past. But I think your hypothesis is wrong. The scene we just saw now was unrelated to the murder; it was daylight in that other room, not night. Anyhow, it's almost midnight now. The murders were committed much earlier. The visitor who found the bodies wouldn't come calling in the small hours of the morning."

"Damn," Andy said. He looked almost normal now; he even smiled feebly. "How I hate being outthought by a woman. Want to arm wrestle?"

"Anything to take your mind off your morbid thoughts. Let's go to bed. Tomorrow, come hell or high water, we are going to Reading. We're going to find out more about this. Andy, there might even be a report in the Philadelphia papers."

"I'll go to bed and pull the covers over my head, but I won't sleep."

"Oh, come on." She started for the stairs.

Andy lingered, glancing uneasily at the door. "Amazing, how it cut off when the door closed. I wonder if they're still out there."

"Go ahead and look if you want to. I don't care what's out there, as long as it stays out."

"True." Andy followed. On the landing, under the large stained-glass window, Meg stumbled. Andy's grab at her elbow was an instinctive gesture. . . .

The girl stood by a window, but it was not the rose window of the Victorian house. The walls were thick and the window was small. Its panes were streaked with rain. The girl's face was pressed against the glass. Her body strained forward, as if she were watching for something ardently desired. She was so close to Meg that the latter could have reached out an arm and touched her, but that Meg was not inclined to do. The figures appeared impalpable; but what if they were not? To touch the cold flesh of the dead, or the chilly clinging fog that was the stuff of the spirit. . . . Meg shivered, and saw the bare boards of the upper hall take shape as the girl's full skirts faded. This time the image had blotted out the real room. The visions were getting stronger.

"God damn it!" Andy said. "This is getting monotonous. Every single damned time I touch you—"

"Practice," Meg said, with a casualness she did not feel. What—or who—was it Anna Maria was watching for?

## II

Meg was awakened next morning by Andy's call.

"If we're going to Reading, we'd better get started. Hurry up. I'll get breakfast."

She heard him whistling as he went downstairs. At least he's in a good mood this morning, Meg thought sleepily. Well, the sun is shining and we survived the night; that's enough to put anyone in a good mood.

She stretched lazily under the warm blankets and tried to remember the dream Andy had interrupted.

It had begun with the image of Anna Maria standing by the rain-streaked window. Meg had given up any pretense of thinking of the girl anonymously; she was Anna Maria, Meg had no more doubt of that than she had of her own name. It was not surprising that the vision should have prompted the dream, but its sequence had been somewhat unusual. Instead of breaking up into the incoherent action of most dreams, which seem logical at the time but absurd in the cold light of day, this dream had proceeded with the slow dullness of real life. The girl had turned from the window with a sigh. The room was small, with sharply sloping eaves, and was obviously her bedroom. The narrow bed was covered with a white counterpane, delicately embroidered in shades of blue. The same pattern appeared on the bed-curtains, and even in sleep Meg felt a sharp pang of regret to think that such beautiful work had vanished.

A straight chair with a rush seat and two large chests were the only other furnishings of the room, except for a curtain across one corner, which hid the washstand with its load of china utensils and a cord on which the girl's clothes were hung. Meg knew what was behind the curtain, although she couldn't have explained how she knew it. In the dream, no explanations were necessary.

Anna Maria knelt down in front of one of the chests and opened it. It was filled with neatly folded pieces of cloth—petticoats and other undergarments. She was lifting out one of these articles when Andy's voice shattered the dream.

As Meg dressed, she debated whether or not to tell Andy about the dream. She decided not to. He would deny that a dream was a valid source of information and, after all, she had learned nothing from it—except what Anna Maria's bedroom looked like. It was precisely what she would have expected in a house of that era.

They breakfasted hastily, and got in the car. Meg couldn't see that Andy's work had noticeably improved the vehicle's performance; it groaned and jerked every foot of the way. It got them to Reading, though, and by asking at a gas station they found the building in which the Historical Association was located.

They had agreed that Andy would investigate tax and property records while Meg looked up old newspapers. American history was not her forte, but every schoolchild knows about Ben Franklin and the printing shop in Philadelphia; so Meg was not surprised to find Franklin's *Pennsylvania Gazette* flourishing in 1740. The association had microfilm copies, and Meg found the reference she wanted without difficulty. She copied it and then, her duty done, abandoned herself to amusement. The old gazette was fascinating, even the advertisements.

"Run away, on the 15th Instant, a Dutch Servant Man named Paul Clem, about five feet high. . . ."

There was a reward offered for the return of Paul to his irate master. Meg hoped he had gotten away. He wasn't even as tall as she was, poor boy.

At noon she met Andy in the lobby and they went out for lunch. Andy had had a frustrating morning; he had spent most of the time trying to figure out the system used in recording. He bemoaned his ignorance over a hamburger and coffee. Then Meg produced her copy of the newspaper article.

"It's so uninformative," she complained, while Andy read it. "Almost as if they were trying to cover up something."

"You're getting paranoid," Andy said, still reading. "To Philadelphians this was rural, backwoods news. And the paper was a weekly; by the time it was published the search for the girl had been abandoned and the self-styled jury had already met. Did you notice the date?"

"Yes," Meg said reluctantly. "You were right. October eleventh."

"Another coincidence that can't be coincidental."

"I'm not so sure about that. We saw the murderers on the eleventh; but that doesn't mean they weren't there before. Or that they won't be there—"

"Don't say it. . . . They searched for three days, then gave it up. Doesn't seem very long."

"Long enough. If she was alive and unharmed, she wouldn't have gone far from the house. If she was injured, exposure would finish her. Anyhow, there was another tragedy. One of the searchers tripped over a tree root and shot himself. That probably discouraged the others."

"Yes, I see. The report seems fairly complete; why do you say it's uninformative?"

"There's no description of the weapon. You would think they could guess that. No description of *anything*. Just that the house was in disorder. How? What kind of disorder? Was the furniture knocked over, or actually broken up? They don't say what happened to the cat, either."

Andy looked sharply at her. The restaurant was almost empty. It was a big place, with booths instead of tables, and the waitress had abandoned them to their own devices.

"What cat?"

"A black cat. It was lying on the hearth. I think it belonged to the old servant."

"I remember seeing a black heap that might have been an animal. Why not a dog? Or a pile of rags?"

"It was a cat."

Andy started to speak and then changed his mind. He glanced at her copy again.

"Look at the names of the jurymen. Solid Pennsylvania Dutch all the way. Emig—my ancestors were all over the place—Hamm, Stauffer, Neesz. I wonder how you pronounce that—an N and a sneeze? Here's a Huber, too. Wonder if he was any relation."

"It was a common name."

Andy reached for his wallet. "Let's go. Unless you want another cup of coffee."

"No, thanks. What are you going to do this afternoon?"

"Find the original land grant and the name of the owner, if it kills me. How about you?"

"I've got some shopping to do," Meg said carelessly. "Then I'll come back to the Historical Association. Meet you there—what time?"

"I want to be home before dark," Andy said.

"Five o'clock?"

"Make it four thirty."

The separated at the door of the restaurant. Meg had not told Andy what she was planning to do. She felt guilty, wasting time with trivia while Andy racked his brain over dusty records, but not guilty enough to give up her hobby. She had found the address of a needlework shop in the telephone book at the museum. A pedestrian gave her directions.

Since this was Meg's first attempt at embroidery, she decided to admit her ignorance and ask for help. She explained the project to the girl behind the counter; by the time she had finished, the other customers were unashamedly eavesdropping. Meg was accustomed to the casual camaraderie that unites women who are shopping in the same store; even in Manhattan she had often struck up a conversation with another shopper as they mutually moaned about high prices and shortages. But the enthusiastic response of the women surprised her. She was overwhelmed with advice and suggestions.

It had never occurred to Meg to calculate how much thread of each color she would need; but as one of the women explained, she ought to buy all of it at one time, since new dye lots sometimes varied slightly in shade. Another customer advised her about embroidery hoops and proper needles; a third helped her match the colors on her sample page with the silks. When Meg left, carrying a paper bag, she was followed by a chorus of farewells and wishes of good luck. She smiled as she walked along the street. A few more months of this sort of thing and she would lose her big-city cynicism and start to believe in the goodwill of her fellow man.

The shopping had taken much longer than she had expected. It was after three when she got back to the Historical Association. Looking into the library, she saw Andy hard at work. His face was smeared with dust, his hair stood on end, and he was scowling ferociously as he turned the pages of a huge ledger that lay on the table in front of him. Meg tiptoed quietly past the door.

Since she had already wasted most of the afternoon, she decided to finish off the day in style and visit the museum of the association, which was on the lower floor. There were several samplers, which she studied with patronizing interest. None of them were as nice as hers. The Pennsylvania Dutch furniture attracted her too. There was nothing like it in the attic. Probably it had been thrown away by the nouveau riche nineteenth-century Emigs.

She ended up in the little museum office, where publications of the society were for sale, and where she was received with remote courtesy by the elderly, well-dressed woman in charge of the place. Once again Meg's new hobby broke the ice. When the old lady saw the name of the shop on the bag Meg was carrying, she thawed perceptibly. She herself did needlepoint, and she told Meg all about the twelve dining-room chairs she had just re-covered, describing the patterns in detail. Meg explained her project, and the woman's capitulation was complete.

"How nice to see a young person who appreciates old

things. I myself am a member of the Historical Association—a volunteer, of course; we all help out at the museum."

She needed little urging to lecture on the early history of the colony. Elbows on the counter, chin propped on her hands, Meg listened intently. The old lady was no dilettante, she knew her history; but Meg suspected she had a tendency to glamorize the hard frontier life and her family's participation in that life.

Mrs. Adams' ancestors had been among the First Purchasers, and Meg gathered that in Pennsylvania that was the equivalent of a *Mayflower* ancestor. These sterling characters were English Quakers, the first settlers of Penn's grant in the New World in 1682. Mrs. Adams implied that the later German settlers, the so-called Pennsylvania Dutch, were admirable people too, though not as top-drawer as her ancestors. She painted a glowing word picture of the earthly paradise into which the early settlers had come. The rolling, fertile fields and the hardwood forests; the brilliantly plumaged song birds, the babbling brooks of clear crystal water; the peaceful days and quiet nights, far from the vice and corruption of the city. . . .

"Did you ever hear of a murder case?" Meg asked abruptly. "A family named Huber, back in 1740?"

Mrs. Adams' thin lips clamped together. "That was a rare exception," she said, a hint of frost entering her voice. "No, my dear, I am not interested in crime."

Meg had to apologize for several minutes. She felt it necessary to give the offended old lady a censored version of her interest in the Huber family—someone had told her, she explained vaguely, that the old house had once stood on the site of the house she was presently inhabiting.

Mrs. Adams relaxed. "I suppose it is natural that you should be interested," she said, more graciously. "But you must understand that the present owners of the land would not advertise its unsavory history. Facts of that sort do not add to the value of a piece of property. Possibly the house was abandoned after the tragedy. Being built of logs, it would quickly deteriorate. Fifty years later, even the fallen stones of the chimney would be overgrown, and the location of the house would be forgotten."

She smiled pleasantly, and Meg smiled back. She was willing to bet that Mrs. Adams knew more about the murder than she would admit. But it was unladylike to dwell on murder and offensive to local pride to recall unpleasant incidents of the past.

In an effort to propitiate Mrs. Adams, Meg bought several of the society's pamphlets. One of them, on early land grants, looked as if it might be useful. Another pamphlet, on Pennsylvania Dutch hex signs, started them on a fresh subject. Mrs. Adams explained earnestly that these painted geometric decorations were purely ornamental.

"Hundreds of years ago the more ignorant farmers did believe in such superstitions," she said, her aristocratic nose in the air. "The signs were to ward off witches. No one believes in witchcraft nowadays, of course; and I am sure the educated classes never did."

Little do you know, Meg thought, with an inner smile.

She asked about historical needlework, and Mrs. Adams produced a book on early samplers and show towels that Meg immediately coveted. The show towels tickled her; exquisitely embroidered, they were hung over the grubby family towels when company came—and woe to the dirty little son or husband who used them to dry his hands.

They were discussing the book when Andy looked in. He was scowling hideously. When Meg glanced at her watch she understood his annoyance. It was twenty minutes after the time they had agreed to meet, and Andy had probably been all over the museum looking for her.

She introduced Andy to Mrs. Adams, who looked doubtfully at his patched jeans and shabby jacket; and then Andy swept her away, mumbling apologies.

"Shame on you," Meg said, when they were outside.

"I was civil, wasn't I? I felt like slugging you. Do you know what time it is? We're going to be caught in rush-hour traffic."

"We'll be back before dark."

"We'd better be. If the monsters get me, I'll come back and haunt you."

He was only half joking; they drove home at a speed that made the car shake like a cement mixer, and Meg kept expecting to hear the scream of a siren. But Andy's luck held; they met no traffic policemen, and they pulled up in front of the house before he had to use the headlights.

Dinner was a joint project. They discussed their discoveries while they worked and ate.

Andy had found some of the information he was after. The plot of land had been part of a farm of 230 acres, sold in 1728 to a Christian Huber. After that the records seemed to be incomplete. There was no further transfer of land until the end of the nineteenth century, when the Benjamin Emig who had built Trail's End had disposed of two hundred acres and given up farming for industry. The remaining thirty acres constituted the estate on which the house was located, but how it had come into the possession of the Emig family Andy could not ascertain. A man named John Emig had owned the adjoining farm, but there was no record of any sale.

"So the Emigs were neighbors of the Hubers," Meg said.

"You couldn't call them neighbors. The houses were probably miles apart. The point is, how did the Emigs get this place?"

"What about tax records?" Meg suggested.

"Look, it took me all afternoon to get that little bit of information. You know, it takes more time to get nowhere than it does to get—"

"I don't think that metaphor is going to get anywhere either. Naturally it takes time to eliminate possibilities. But the tax records—"

"Are probably in Harrisburg—if they paid taxes in those days. I guess we could see what they've got in the state archives."

"Fine," Meg said enthusiastically. She had several more colors of embroidery thread to match. Harrisburg, the state capital, probably had a good needlework shop.

"Did you have a nice time chatting up the old lady? You're getting to be a regular small-town gossip."

"I did enjoy it. But I had an ulterior motive."

She told Andy what Mrs. Adams had said about the Huber house. He was not impressed.

"A log house, abandoned after the crime. . . . Logical guesses. Doesn't mean she knows anything."

"It wasn't what she said, it was the way she said it. If Huber had no heirs, the property would revert to the state, wouldn't it? Probably your ancestor bought the farm from the government."

"They why wasn't the sale recorded?"

"Lost," Meg said sweepingly.

It was dark outside by the time they had finished cleaning up the kitchen. Andy was in a silly mood, juggling dishes and making up impromptu limericks.

As they headed for the library, Meg said maliciously, "Want to go for a walk? It's a beautiful night."

"Ha ha," said Andy flatly.

"Well, at least we could look out the front door."

"As you said so eloquently last night, I don't care what's out there so long as it stays out. I have come to the conclusion," said Andy, "that the experience of last night was either a product of our diseased brains or else a phenomenon caused by the recurrence of the vital date. It won't happen again."

"I'm glad to hear it."

Andy sat down at the library table with the pamphlets Meg had bought at the museum. Evidently he had had enough of murders, fictional or real. Meg hovered.

"Wouldn't you be more comfortable in the leather chair?" she suggested.

Andy, leafing through the pamphlet on hex signs, looked up in surprise. "Why the sudden concern for my comfort?"

"Well, uh—I was going to work on the table myself."

"Plenty of room. Want one of these pamphlets?"

"Well . . ."

"For God's sake, what's the matter with you?"

"I don't know," Meg said irritably. "Why should I care if you see what I'm doing?"

There were cupboards under the bookshelves. Meg had

appropriated one of these for her embroidery materials; she had added her purchases in Reading to the collection when they came home. Now she began to carry them to the table. The pattern, on graph paper; the rainbow pile of embroidery silks; the square of fine linen fabric; and finally, the sampler, in its rough glass frame. Andy watched, his jaw sagging.

"May I ask what in Hades you are doing?"

"You should have figured it out by now," Meg mumbled, sorting her silks.

"Damned if I can. Unless. . . . Oh."

The change in his voice made Meg look up. He was staring at her with an expression she had seen on his face several times before. It was an expression she particularly disliked, and now she realized why. It was a look of intense suspicion.

"I'm going to embroider," she said defiantly. "I want to make a copy of the sampler. Is there anything wrong with that? What are you looking at me that way for? Haven't you ever seen anyone do embroidery?"

"Yes. I have."

"I'd be surprised if you hadn't. It's very popular."

"Is it?" After a moment Andy's face relaxed. "Yes, I guess it is. I didn't think you were the type, though."

"What's the type? Everybody does it. Needlepoint, crewel, bargello—most of my friends have workbags permanently attached to their right arms."

Andy grunted and returned to his book. Meg went on sorting thread, comparing the colors to the originals on the sampler. She had done quite well; only two of the shades failed to match. A little more brown in that rose-pink, a softer yellow. . . . She would try again in Harrisburg. Threading her needle, she started to hem the linen square. That was something she wouldn't have thought of doing if one of the friendly ladies in the shop hadn't suggested it.

It gave her some satisfaction to have begun working, but this part of the process was pretty dull. Meg yawned. After a while she glanced up and caught Andy's eye.

"What's the matter now?"

"I thought you used that colored thread," Andy said.

"I will, for the pattern. I'm just hemming the edges so they won't ravel."

"Oh."

Meg hemmed another side. When she looked up Andy was still watching her.

"What is it now?" she demanded.

"I'm waiting till you're through playing. We have a little research project, remember?"

"I can talk and do this at the same time."

Silence fell. Placidly stitching, Meg waited. The outburst finally came.

"I like people to look at me when I'm talking!"

"Sure you do. Most egomaniacs feel that way."

"God, you have a nasty tongue. No wonder you're still a spinster."

"I'm only twenty-three," Meg said humbly. "Maybe there's still a chance for me."

"Sure. Plenty of men are masochists."

"Cool it," Meg said. "If we have a fight, you'll have to walk out into the cold, dark night. Remember what happened last time?"

That ended the discussion. Andy returned to his book

and Meg sewed. She was ready for bed by the time she had finished hemming the linen, but she couldn't resist making a few stitches of the pattern. Following another suggestion from her friends in the embroidery shop, she marked off the center of the square of linen and began working out from the center of the pattern.

It was addictive as heroin. Meg couldn't stop. Her needle flashed in and out with a precision that surprised and delighted her. Blue and pale pink, buff and black and green, the motto began to take shape:

"My Life's a Flower, the Time is Morn. . . ."

She sensed that Andy was watching her. At first she was amused; after a while his steady regard began to fret at her nerves. She reached a section that had to be done in the rose-pink that had yet to be matched accurately, and jabbed her needle into the fabric.

"I'm going to bed," she announced.

Andy did not reply. He continued to watch her as she put away her materials and left the room.

### III

For the first time since she had arrived, Meg was awakened in the middle of the night by uncanny noises. In helpless half-sleep she couldn't decide whether they were the product of nightmare or ghostly intruders. Then she came fully awake. She did not know whether to be relieved or not when she realized the sounds were coming from Andy's room.

Without waiting to put on robe or slippers she got out of bed and ran down the hall. Both doors were open. There was a light in the corridor, but Andy's light was off. Meg

didn't stop to locate the switch. The closer she came to
them, the more the sounds distressed her. She crossed the
room amid a crackle of paper scraps and sat down on the
edge of Andy's bed.

There was enough light from the open door to let her see
him. His eyes were screwed shut and his face was distorted
in a tight frown of pain; he was moving and moaning,
tossing from side to side. He had thrown off the covers. He
wore pajama bottoms—a concession, Meg suspected, to
her presence in the house—but no top. His bare chest was
sticky with perspiration, as was his face.

Meg put her hands on his shoulders. He stopped
moving, but his eyes remained stubbornly shut. She shook
him. When this produced no effect, she reached out and
turned on the lamp on the bedside table.

Andy groaned. His eyes opened, but Meg knew he
didn't see her.

"Not for months," he mumbled. "I wouldn't have
moved in here if I'd thought. . . . The damned sewing,
that's what did it. Needle flashing, long trails of thread
going in and out, red and gold and—red, like blood. . . ."

"Andy," Meg said sharply. She couldn't listen to this; it
was worse than eavesdropping. "Andy, wake up."

Andy's body gave a violent start. His foggy eyes
focused.

"What the hell—"

"You had a nightmare," Meg said.

"Did I wake you up?"

"That's all right. What were you dreaming about?"

Andy's lashes flickered. Meg knew he had no recollec-
tion of what he had said earlier.

"I don't remember. Monsters, I guess."

"Well. . . ." Meg was acutely conscious of the hard pull of his muscles under her flattened palms. She stood up. "If you're okay now, I guess I'll go back to bed."

"Sorry I disturbed you."

"That's okay. Good night."

Meg went back to bed, but she didn't sleep, not at first. She had suspected for some time that Andy's illness had not been physical. "Nervous breakdown" was a good loose term that could cover any number of mental ailments. And it had something to do with a girl—a girl who had embroidered, as she had done that evening. She ought to have known from Andy's reaction when she began. The poor devil had actually thought she was doing it to taunt him or to remind him of an incident that he wanted desperately to forget.

Meg rolled over and wrapped both arms around the pillow, hugging it to her like a comfort blanket. No wonder Andy had been so anxious to find an alternative explanation for her hallucinations. He had seen them too. He must have wondered whether he was cracking up.

To her surprise Meg began to get drowsy. With all the things I have on my mind, she thought sleepily, you'd think I couldn't sleep a wink. Here I am in a haunted house with a man fresh out of a mental hospital. . . .

As she drifted off to sleep, Meg was not thinking about the house or its shadowy occupants. She was wondering what sort of woman could have such a devastating effect on a man that he still suffered from nightmares months after losing her.

# Chapter 9

When Meg came down the next morning, Andy was making coffee. She had no intention of referring to his nightmare, but as she watched him fidget, she realized he wouldn't be able to leave it alone. His first remark betrayed his real concern.

"Sorry I woke you up last night. Was I screaming obscenities, or what?"

"Just groaning and thrashing around."

"I didn't . . . say anything?"

"Nothing that made any sense."

"Oh." Andy wiped a single drop of spilled coffee from the table. "I used to talk in my sleep when I was a kid."

"Did you? What did you talk about?"

Andy laughed hollowly. His drawn face and sunken eyes contrasted painfully with his attempt to appear casually amused.

"Oh, I made up all kinds of stories. Even at that age I had literary talents."

174

Meg decided to put an end to the conversation. Not for worlds would she have indicated to Andy that she had inadvertently intruded on his private agonies. It did not occur to her then to wonder why she was so tender of his feelings; under the circumstances she might have been excused for trying to discover what his problem was and how it might affect her.

"I meant to ask how the novel was getting along," she said brightly. "You haven't had much time to work on it, have you?"

"I thought I might put in a few hours today. I could work in the library, if that wouldn't bother you."

"Oh, don't be so bloody polite. It doesn't suit your character."

Andy grinned. "I'll go get my stuff."

Meg sat at the kitchen table for a while, trying to decide what she ought to do next. What she really wanted to do was embroider. The sampler drew her like a magnet. But she resisted; the embroidery was for relaxation, she ought to get some work done first. Until Andy helped her move the old piano, there was nothing more she could do in the room where she had found the sampler, but there were acres of objects in the attic to be rearranged. Sylvia must be persuaded to sell some of them, just to clear enough space in which to work on the others. As it was, they would have to shift mountains of furniture back and forth every time they wanted to examine a particular piece.

First on the list, however, was some housecleaning. She had neglected the everyday chores of vacuuming and dusting in recent days.

Accustomed to working in a one-room apartment, Meg

was appalled at how long it took to get even a few rooms into reasonably good order. Betty Friedan is right, she thought, as she began to dry-mop the bare drawing-room floor; housework does expand to fill all the available time. It wasn't hard to understand why women fell into the trap, though. Barraged by TV commercials that imply that dirty collars are more disgraceful than infanticide, infected by the ancestral Calvinist doctrine that puts cleanliness next to godliness—no wonder women slaved over dishes and T-shirts that would be dirty again next day. They were brainwashed by a deadly combination of advertising and outdated morality.

Inspired by these critical thoughts, Meg wielded her mop with more speed than accuracy; she had no intention of spending any more time on the job than was absolutely necessary. The floor did need dusting, though; they had tracked in an amazing amount of litter in the past week, and the house hadn't been properly cleaned for months— since before the Culvers had moved in.

After finishing the drawing room she went into the dining room, which connected with the drawing room by means of wide double doors. Meg had only been in the room once before, when she had explored the house that first day. She hoped it wouldn't need much cleaning; but dust was bound to accumulate even in an unused room.

Like the drawing room, the dining room was sparsely furnished and had no carpets on the floors. The room hadn't been used much. It hadn't been swept, either; a weird mixture of lost objects rolled out into daylight as Meg probed under the heavy sideboard. Hairpins, stubs of pencils, crumbs innumerable, fifty-four cents in change, a comb with most of the teeth missing—and a square black box that went sliding across the floor and struck a chair leg.

Meg knew what it was before she stopped to pick it up. With an uncomfortable sinking sensation in her stomach she pressed one of the white plastic buttons. The familiar chords of a Mozart minuet filled the room.

It was a cheap tape recorder. The quality was poor and scratchy, but at a distance a susceptible listener might not notice that.

Meg left her mop where she had dropped it and went storming into the library. Andy was typing. He was so absorbed he didn't hear her come in. When she threw the tape recorder down on the desk, he jumped half out of his chair.

"What the hell—"

"Cute," Meg said, panting with anger. "That's really cute. Setting this thing to go off so I'd think of supernatural harpsichordists. How did you manage the optical illusions?"

The strains of Mozart interrupted her. Andy had pressed the switch. He pressed the off-switch almost at once.

"Where did you find this?"

"In the dining room, under the sideboard. Where you left it—"

"Just calm down, will you? I don't know what the hell you're talking about."

He was either the world's greatest actor, or he was honestly bewildered. Meg's anger cooled a little. She was still too angry to speak coherently, however, and her silence gave Andy time to think.

"Wait a minute," he muttered. "I remember hearing that . . . but you played it on the piano. Mozart, isn't it?"

"Yes. I played it—after I heard that tape. I didn't know it was a tape, of course; but I knew the music wasn't performed on a piano. It's a harpsichord."

"I see. Ghostly music, and all that crap." Andy leaned back in his chair, turning the tape recorder over in his hands. "I suppose you would suspect me. I can clear myself, though, if you'll give me a chance."

"Go ahead."

"To begin with, I wouldn't own a piece of junk like this. It's only good for listening to the news or to very loud, very crummy pop music where the quality doesn't matter. If I had bought this to perpetrate a trick, it would be new. This is battered and banged up. Maybe that's not convincing. Try this, then. If I planted this on you, I'm responsible for the next of the funny tricks, right? The whole complicated fictitious plot involving a family that lived here back in 1740. Do you really think I'm dumb enough to include a piece of music written by a composer who wasn't born till 1756?"

Meg's mouth fell open. "How do you know when Mozart was born?"

"I don't suppose you remember I used to play French horn—"

"Don't I, though. You used to sneak up on me and let off a blast in my ear."

"Nevertheless," said Andy, with dignity, "I took lessons for ten years, and my teacher was a fanatic about music history. I had to memorize a lot of that stuff. Don't know why it should stick in my mind, but it did. Do you know when Beethoven was born? In 1770. He died in 1827. Vivaldi—"

"Okay, okay. I'm convinced."

"Mozart was an infant prodigy, admittedly," Andy said. "But he didn't compose prenatally. If I were going to produce ghostly music for you, my girl, it would have been Bach. I don't make sloppy mistakes like that."

"Then who—"

"Who else? It's the sort of imaginative, careless scheme Culver would think up. This looks like his kind of tape recorder, too—cheap, crummy, kicked around. As a matter of fact—" Andy hesitated.

"Well?"

"I don't want to scare you," Andy said slowly. "But this gadget doesn't have a remote-control mechanism or an automatic cutoff. It's still working, so the batteries didn't run down. . . ."

"Oh. You mean, he was in the house."

"Must have been. I wonder why he left this here?"

"I suppose he planned to use it again," Meg said uncomfortably. "Lord, that's a nasty thought."

"I wouldn't worry about it. That was before I moved into the house. But we might be a little more careful about locking up. Meg—you believe me, don't you?"

"I guess so. You don't think Culver could be responsible for the other phenomena, do you?"

"I'll be damned if I can see how. I suppose you could rig up machines that would produce effects like the ones we saw, but the equipment would be hard to hide; we'd be tripping on cables and wires all over the house. No, I think the music was an additional goody, nothing to do with the main problem."

He went back to his typing and Meg, feeling the need for distraction, got out her embroidery. She looked at her work with pleasure. It did look nice. Her smugness received a slight check when she noticed a mistake, in the third row from the center. Sighing, she began to pick it out. No sloppy work allowed; this was going to be a master-piece even if she had to redo every stitch.

She worked for almost an hour, undisturbed by the rattle of the typewriter. The embroidery had its usual calming effect. She decided she had been unfair to Andy. His explanation made sense. As for Culver, Andy was right about him too. He wouldn't break in while there was a man in the house.

.           II

Once wooed, the muse continued to inspire Andy. For the next few days he typed from morning till night, pausing only for the meals Meg thrust at him periodically. Except for feeding him she left him alone. Writing seemed to be as therapeutic for him as embroidery was for her, and in her year at the publishing house she had learned that writers were strange animals who had to be handled with care. They might scratch and snarl if they were interrupted while genius was burning; it didn't burn very often, and the rare interludes had to be used while they lasted. Eventually Andy's inspiration would run out.

In the meantime Meg had plenty to do. On Sunday, she cleaned house again. Georgia was due on Monday, and she wanted to impress Georgia with her industry, in case that amiable busybody decided to report to Sylvia. Andy was beginning to run down; the periods of silence between the frenzied bursts of typing came more and more frequently.

In the afternoon Meg went up to the attic. She had discovered several boxes filled with Victorian ornaments which she wanted to unpack so Georgia could look them over. She dusted a tall corner whatnot of carved walnut and began removing the objects from the excelsior in which they had been packed. Wax flowers under a curved glass dome, a pair of hideous china pug-dogs, pop-eyed and drooling; and a collection of nineteenth-century needlework that amused Meg as much as it offended her aesthetic sensibilities. Some of the doilies in the box might have been pretty if they had been crocheted in plain white thread. The most subdued had five different shades of scarlet, from brownish red to cherry, plus lilac, green, and gold.

Some embroidered cushions in equally garish shades made Meg yearn for her sampler. She hadn't done much work on it in the last few days because she still lacked some of the colors. Without a printed pattern it was difficult to skip sections of the design. Meg missed it—and its former owner. Andy had been working so industriously she hadn't wanted to harass him, but it seemed like a long time since she had seen the slim blue-clad figure that was beginning to seem like a normal inhabitant of the house. . . .

With an exclamation Meg got to her feet. Why hadn't she thought of it before? Actually, she had thought of it, and had meant to pursue the subject; but something had happened, she couldn't remember exactly what, and she had gotten sidetracked. Yet it was an important point, one that might lead to new discoveries.

She ran downstairs. As she approached the library she was encouraged to hear that the typewriter had stopped. If Andy had reached an impasse in his work he wouldn't mind an interruption. She was too full of her new idea to wait, and she wanted him to be in a receptive mood.

He looked up as she entered, his gloomy face brightening. "Time to eat?"

"No. I've got an idea."

"Out with it then, before it injures your brain."

"I was in the attic just now," Meg began, "and it dawned on me, I've never seen any visions up there. When we're in this room, we consistently see the same room of the other house—the kitchen. In the drawing room, it's another room—the parlor, probably. You said the other day we're seeing the house as it once was, occupying the same space as this house. Andy, we could draw a plan of it, practically."

"Hmmm." Andy scratched his chin. "Maybe we could. But why should we bother?"

"We might learn more if we saw the rest of the house," Meg argued. "We don't even know how many rooms it has."

"That's true." Andy reached for a pen and a sheet of paper. "Let's see. This house is divided by the hall and the stairs. On one side is the drawing room with the dining room behind it; across the hall we have, from front to back, the small parlor, the library, and the kitchen. If the kitchen of the old house was here"—he reached for a red pen and began drawing over the black lines of the first sketch—

"and the parlor was here, where our drawing room is . . . Yes, it fits. The back part of the drawing room is just across the hall from the library, which was their kitchen. The old house occupied an area that lies smack in the middle of this house. Do you know anything about the architecture of that period? How many more rooms should we expect?"

"I imagine a farmhouse of that early date, almost anywhere in the American colonies, would have been small and simple. Two rooms on the ground floor and two bedrooms upstairs. They cooked in a separate building, a smokehouse and bakehouse combined, outside; in cold weather they would use the kitchen fire. There would be outbuildings, too—sheds, barns. . . ."

"Servants' quarters?"

"Outside, maybe. A shed next to the kitchen."

"We haven't seen the bedrooms," Andy said thoughtfully.

"We have! We saw Anna Maria's room. Remember, that time on the stairs? I saw her bedroom again in a dream, but I guess you won't count that."

"Dreams aren't kosher evidence. However, the episode on the stairs is interesting. The old house would have had lower ceilings than this one. Which would put the bedrooms about midway between the first and second floors of this house."

"Right. And if her bedroom was near the landing, where the stair turns . . ." Meg watched Andy scribble on his plan, which was beginning to look like an unholy mess. "It's hard to visualize in three dimensions. The landing isn't halfway up the stairs, it's about three fourths of the way up. The upper-floor level of the old house was—oh, say about four feet below our second-floor level. The stairs turn to the right; so her room was above the kitchen—the library. The other bedroom must be over their parlor."

"That makes it out of bounds for us," Andy said, scowling at the plan. "It's hanging somewhere near the ceiling of the drawing room."

"What's above the drawing room in this house?"

"One of the guest bedrooms."

"Well?" Meg looked challengingly at him.

"You mean—go up there and—"

"Yes. That's a room we never go into. Let's try."

The room was the central one of the three that, with the bathroom, filled this side of the second floor. It had no rug on the floor—Sylvia seemed to have a fetish about the rugs—and was furnished with a brass bedstead, a battered chest of drawers, and a table. . . . Meg did a double take. The chest of drawers had a serpentine front and broad fluted corners.

"Gostelowe!" Meg exclaimed.

"Abracadabra," Andy answered. He eyed her warily. "What happens now, do you turn into a zebra?"

"Jonathan Golstelowe of Philadelphia, flourished about 1765," Meg said. She ran her fingers over the surface of the chest. "I'll eat my hat if this isn't his work. It's solid mahogany. Wouldn't you know Sylvia would outfox herself? Imagine leaving a thing like this down here! There's a chest very similar in the Philadelphia museum."

"Are we going to hold hands or look at furniture?" Andy demanded. "Let's get this over with."

"Hold hands, is it! What a euphemism."

Meg's amusement faded as the image formed. The overlap of the two houses, which had been mildly disturbing on the lower level, was much worse here, where the floor levels were utterly uncoordinated. The legs of tables and chairs, the lower part of the bed went down below the floor level of the room in which they were standing, and faded into invisibility.

This was a room they had never seen before. It was unoccupied, but it was obviously a man's room. Yet it was a strange room to find in a primitive farmhouse. Hanging bookcases held rows of heavy volumes. Tables were covered with an odd assortment of objects—books and papers, boxes large and small, bottles of all sizes and shapes, filled with a variety of substances. Over the whitewashed chimney hood hung a sword, its hilt gilded.

The image faded before Meg had time to see more.

"How about that," she said triumphantly. "Our plan was correct."

"Are you sure we've got the right house?"

"The right house and the right room. And I was right about Herr Huber. He was no simple farmer."

"No."

"Not all the settlers were uneducated," Meg said. "Mrs. Adams was telling me about that the other day. Pastorius, who led the first group of German immigrants, was a distinguished scholar and theologian. There were thirty printing houses in Pennsylvania before the Revolution; did you know that? The first Bible printed in the colonies was Christopher Sauer's German Bible. And Mrs. Adams says—"

"You really did pump the old lady, didn't you?"

"I got a letter from her yesterday," Meg said, following him out of the room.

"You're kidding."

"No, I'm not. She invited us to tea on Wednesday."

"Us!"

"Yep. It's your clout that got us the invitation. She's discovered that you are the grandson of her dear old school chum Matilda's brother. She apologized profusely for not having recognized your name—"

Andy's comment would have made Mrs. Adams regret her invitation.

"Don't be vulgar," Meg said. "I don't know why she should apologize. You didn't give her time to say yes, no, or boo; you just dragged me out. I take it you are the grandson of her dear old school—"

"I had a great-aunt named Matilda. Damn it. Look, if you think I'm going to have tea with a little old lady, you're crazy."

"She says she knew your mother quite well. And she remembered you as an adorable curly-headed moppet. . . . She's the one who's crazy, poor thing. Anyhow, it was sweet of her to ask us. She says Wednesday is her day off—she put quotes around the phrase—and not to bother to answer, she knows we must be busy, just come if we can."

"We can't," said Andy, and led the way to the kitchen.

## III

Georgia arrived next morning at nine o'clock. Meg had not expected her till much later; she was brooding over the presumed Gostelowe chest when a hail from below in-

formed her of Georgia's arrival. Meg yelled down and
Georgia came up.

She agreed that the chest might well be by the Philadelphia cabinetmaker, and then demanded, "Don't you
lock your doors around here? Somebody even uglier than
me could walk right in."

"I unlocked it this morning when I went out to sniff the
weather," Meg said. "I thought this was the safe country-
side."

"Culver was in town this morning, looking for trouble."

"I don't have to worry about him now that I have a
resident hero," said Meg, glancing at the doorway, where
Andy lounged against the doorframe, looking as boneless
and unheroic as any man could look.

"Hi," said Andy to Georgia.

"Hi," said Georgia.

"Coffee?" said Andy.

Georgia's jowls quivered.

After she had been primed with coffee, Georgia cheered
up, and they put in a long, productive day. There was only
one thing Georgia didn't see. The box and its contents,
except for the sampler, was at the back of Meg's closet
covered with dirty clothes.

Georgia's most useful suggestion was that they move
some of the furniture from the attic down to the empty
bedrooms on the third floor. They cleared two of the
smaller rooms this way, leaving only the heaviest objects
in place, but the chief discovery of the day was found in a
tiny back bedroom that had belonged to a son or daughter
of the nineteenth-century Emigs. Painted a dull brown, it
was about the size of a cedar chest and had probably been

used as a toy box. It was Georgia who spotted the sunken arched panels on the front. She looked at Meg with triumph in her eyes.

"Dower chest," she said.

Meg stared doubtfully at the ungainly object. "One of those beautiful painted chests, with unicorns and tulips and birds? How could anyone be vandal enough to slap brown paint on something like that?"

"Not just brown. There are two or three coats of paint. It's almost two hundred years old, and for most of its history this style of work was considered crude and ugly. It's a good solid piece of furniture, though, too good to throw away."

"What a shame!"

"Not necessarily. Project for you, Andy. . . ." And she proceeded to explain the technique of removing the paint, layer by layer. "It may work or it may not," she concluded. "But it's worth a try."

"Thanks a lot," said Andy.

They had a late lunch. Meg had baked the night before, amid a barrage of sarcastic commentary from Andy, but he ate the chocolate cake with relish, and Georgia had three pieces. It was a pleasant, relaxed meal; they were all on casual terms by now. Georgia seemed genuinely reluctant to leave.

"I'd better get started," she said finally. "It'll take me an hour to walk back."

"What happened to the bike?" Andy asked.

"Wheel's bent."

"I'm not surprised, the way you throw it around. You

can't just get off the thing and walk away, like you do with a horse. Come on, I'll drive you home."

Georgia made token protests, but allowed herself to be overruled. Meg agreed to come along for the ride. Andy went off to get the car, and the two women waited on the porch. It was a bright, balmy day, but Georgia looked pessimistic when Meg rhapsodized over the weather.

"It's due to break anytime. You've had the best of it, girl. I hope you don't chicken out when the rain and snow begin. It can be pretty dreary out here in winter."

"I'm looking forward to it. Peace and quiet magnified. Reading, and working on the house, and my embroidery—"

Meg stopped short. She had not mentioned her project of copying the sampler, and felt a strange reluctance to have Georgia find out about it. But Georgia heard nothing unusual in the list of hobbies.

"You really like it here, don't you?" she asked, with a sharp glance at Meg.

"Yes," Meg said, surprised. "I never really stopped to think about it, but . . . yes, I do."

"How are things working out with Andy?"

"We get along pretty well."

Georgia nodded. "He sure has improved. I think I could learn to like the guy. He was a mean little kid."

"He used to tease the life out of me."

"He had problems," Georgia said with a sigh. "I used to blame him for being so rotten to Sylvia; but now I can see the kid's life wasn't all that easy. He was nervy and sensitive, and Sylvia—well, she isn't the maternal type."

"No."

"Boy, that sure was a loud and hearty no. I guess you didn't get much TLC from her either."

"She was always perfectly correct," Meg said slowly. "Never unfair, never cruel. But . . . she never had children of her own. You'd think she would have been overly affectionate with a stepson, and later, with me. But there was never any warmth. Never any love."

"And you resent that?"

"No." Again Meg was surprised at her own feelings. "I feel sorry for her. You can't give what you don't have. And it's worse not to give love than not to get it."

She glanced at Georgia and saw that the older woman's eyes were damp. What a sentimental old cuss she is, Meg thought affectionately. She knew Georgia would hate to be caught in a display of maudlin emotion, so she gazed interestedly out across the lawn while Georgia got herself under control, and then said briskly,

"Tell me something, Georgia. How the hell did Sylvia talk Andy's father into leaving this place to her? Wasn't that an outrageous thing to do?"

"Especially since the estate belonged to Andy's mother," Georgia agreed. "It isn't as bad as it looks; I mean, Andy wasn't disinherited. There was some property in California and some money. Andy gets it when he hits thirty."

"Thirty! Why so long?"

"His dad thought he was too immature to handle money. He was in with a pretty wild crowd when the old boy made his will; they were afraid he'd be conned out of it or spend it on riotous living."

"You gave yourself away with that 'they,' Georgia. It

was Sylvia who decided Andy was too irresponsible to handle his inheritance, wasn't it?"

Georgia's face was a study, a blend of enjoyment and guilt.

"Oh, hell, so long as we're letting our hair down—you know Sylvia as well as I do. Andy's dad was a meek, good-natured spineless darling. Any woman could wrap him around her little finger, and Sylvia is an expert. I've wondered for years how she does it. What's she got that I haven't got?"

"I've wondered myself," Meg admitted.

They exchanged conspiratorial grins.

"Meow, meow," said Georgia cheerfully. "God, I adore gossip. Next to drinking and fornication it's more fun than anything. I don't shoot my fat mouth off to everybody, Meg, don't think that. I'm going to enjoy having you around to talk to."

The car came around the corner of the house just then, ending the conversation. Meg noticed that Georgia was particularly nice to Andy during the drive—nice in her own way, which consisted mostly of friendly insults. But she did not invite them in, explaining that it was time for her to start her serious drinking, an activity that required privacy and concentration.

Andy left the car in a vacant lot next to Georgia's and they walked to Main Street to buy a few groceries.

"I wonder what she really does when she's alone," Meg mused. "She can't really drink that much; she wouldn't brag about it if she did."

"Oh, yes, she would. Most people lie about their secret vices, but there are a few rare birds who flaunt them just for the hell of it. Georgia is probably one of the few honest people you'll ever meet."

"Do you like her better now?"

"She has her charms. All this sweetness and light is beginning to get to me," Andy said aggressively. "I can't concentrate on hating people with your cooing and making excuses for them all the time. A few more months with you and I may even have a kind word for Sylvia."

Like many men, Andy objected strenuously to going grocery shopping and then had to be forcibly restrained from buying bagfuls of exotic food. Meg finally pried him away from the pickled artichokes and they started back to the car. As usual, the few groceries had stretched into two large brown bags. Andy had offered to take them both, but Meg made remarks about male chauvinists and flexed her muscles, to the unconcealed amusement of everyone in the grocery store. They left each carrying a bag.

Georgia's house had a closed-up look; the shades were all pulled. A strip of trees hid the house on the other side of the vacant lot. There were no spectators, therefore, when Culver stepped out from behind the car and confronted them. Cherry followed him. She was uneasy, although she tried to conceal it under a sullen glower. Culver was higher than a kite on a breezy March day. He wasted no time in preliminary courtesies.

"This is your last chance," he said loudly.

"Good." Andy stopped; Culver was standing in front of the car door. "You mean you'll leave town when we say no?"

"What are you gonna say no for?" Culver asked, looking confused.

"No to anything you suggest."

"Okay, I gave you your chance. It's your fault now if you get hurt."

Sunlight flashed off the blade of the knife as he pressed the switch.

Meg gasped. Andy dropped the bag of groceries.

It split and bounced; for a few seconds Meg saw nothing but oranges, gyrating like a conjurer's balls. When the bruised groceries had settled, Culver was on the ground. Andy stood over him, his foot planted on Culver's wrist. Andy wasn't even breathing hard.

Cherry let out an inarticulate howl and sprang at Andy. He backed away, his arm raised to shield his face against her clawing nails. The chipped, scarlet polish looked like blood.

Meg put her bag of groceries carefully on the ground. She had to force herself to touch Cherry; it was not that she feared being hurt, she simply loathed coming in contact with the unwashed body. Cherry had no such compunctions. She lashed out with a booted foot that caught Meg on the shin and sent her sprawling. Andy lost his patience. He slapped the girl twice. She sat down with a reverberant thud. Culver had gotten to his knees but he made no attempt to rush to his lady's assistance; in fact, as Andy turned toward him, he started crawling backward.

Andy picked up the knife, retracted the blade, and put it in his pocket.

"You all right, Meg?" he asked. Cherry had marked him; his shirt sleeve was torn and three parallel scratches on his left cheek oozed blood.

"I'll be limping for a few days," Meg said, nursing her calf. "But I don't think anything is broken."

She looked around to see Georgia trotting toward them. The shaded windows had been misleading; Georgia didn't keep up with local gossip by avoiding the windows.

"I'll call the cops, Andy," she wheezed, glaring at Culver, who was now peering at them from behind the protection of the back fender.

Cherry snarled.

"Sure, you call the fuzz. Wait'll I tell how he hit me. Right in the face. I bet I'm all bruised."

"Wait, let's not lose our tempers," Culver said.

Andy began to laugh. "No, we wouldn't want to do that. Forget it, Georgia. Just get out of town, Culver," he added, out of the corner of his mouth. "If you don't, I swear I'll get you!"

"It isn't funny," Georgia snapped, advancing on Cherry.

"Wait a minute, wait a minute," Cherry whined. "We'll go. People like us never get a square deal."

"Sure, we'll go," Culver said. He held out his hand. "Gimme back my knife, okay?"

The request set Andy off again; he bent over, gasping with laughter. Meg still didn't feel like laughing, and Georgia was crimson with fury. She picked up a can of tomatoes and threw it at Culver. The can whizzed close by his head and crashed against a rock. Georgia reached for another can, and the Culvers fled.

"Did you ever pitch for the Phillies, Georgia?" Andy was still grinning. "Forget about the police. Those two won't bother us again."

"Andy, you have to file a complaint," Georgia said. "The whole town has been waiting for an excuse to get rid of that precious pair."

"She's right," Meg said. "Culver may try to get back at you, Andy. Good Lord, you can buy a gun in this country as easily as you can buy a pack of cigarettes. Suppose he takes a shot at you from behind a tree!"

"Okay, okay. Anything to shut you girls up."

Georgia helped them retrieve their scattered and bruised supplies, and then they started for home. Neither spoke at first. Andy was whistling softly under his breath as he drove. His torn shirt and the ragged scratches on his face made him look like a brawling schoolboy. The whole encounter seemed to have cheered him, in some incomprehensible male way. Meg was a little impressed. Whatever Andy's other failings, he was not a physical coward.

"How did you do that?" she asked finally.

"Do what?" Andy's eyes were intent on the road.

"Knock him down. Was that judo, or what?"

Andy smiled. "I'm tempted to brag about my black belt. No, honey, a ten-year-old in reasonably good condition could take Culver; he's an undernourished slob and his reflexes are shot to hell. Cherry is a different story. I'd hate to tangle with that girl if she had a knife. You noticed how I tried to run when she jumped me?"

"I noticed your gentlemanly instincts held you back far too long. Why didn't you clobber her before she scratched you?"

"I don't mind the scratches so much," Andy said. "But I'll never forgive her for ruining my one good shirt."

"Oh, damn the shirt. I hope your tetanus shots are up to date. You could get lockjaw just from breathing the same air she does."

# Chapter 10

By the time Meg had finished smearing iodine on the scratches, Andy said he looked like an Indian on the warpath. He insisted on getting dinner, pointing out that she had been feeding him for the past few days. Meg assented with a smile and an inward groan; Andy really was a terrible cook, but she was feeling kindly toward him just then. She was secretly amused at her feelings; all a man has to do is flex his muscles, she thought, and we poor females flip.

The muscle flexing, or something, had done wonders for Andy's disposition. When they went to the library after dinner he came over and looked at her embroidery.

"How do you do that?" he asked. "Don't you need a pattern or something?"

"Sometimes you work with a pattern printed on the cloth. But I'm doing it the same way Anna Maria did—counting threads. Two each way, up and down and crosswise, form a square. It's cross-stitch."

"It looks nice," said Andy graciously.

"Thank you. Aren't we polite this evening?"

"It's high time." Andy sat down across from her and reached for a book.

"Go ahead and work on the masterpiece," Meg said, determined to match him in courtesy. "The typewriter doesn't bother me."

"I'm not in the mood. Don't faint—but I think I'll get back to ghost hunting."

"I thought you'd given that up."

"I have ambivalent feelings about it," Andy admitted.

"So I noticed."

They smiled at one another.

"Maybe we ought to discuss it for once when we're both in a reasonably good mood," Andy said. "It's funny, the way the thing has developed. It was my idea to begin with. Then I got cold feet and you got interested."

"How do you feel about it now?"

"I'm still mixed up. But I have to admit the evidence for genuine occult phenomena is just about incontrovertible. You haven't had one of your old-type hallucinations since you got here, have you? I mean, like elephants in the drawing room."

"No. In fact, I haven't seen anything at all, except when you were with me. That's significant, I think. We've both experienced emotional states—that feeling of anticipation I told you about, for me. And you—"

"You know about my emotional states. Lucky you. But so long as we're leveling with each other. . . ." Andy looked sheepish. "That first hallucination you had, the day you got here. I saw it too. Then I—well, I chickened out. I was afraid to admit it."

Meg waited, hoping he felt secure enough now to explain why he had been afraid to admit it. But he said no more and she didn't want to shatter their confidential mood by asking the wrong questions. Still, she was disappointed. He wasn't ready to trust her yet.

"One funny thing about the visions," she said. "They are without sound or motion."

"Yes. What that means, if anything, I can't imagine. I can't see any time sequence either. But we seem to be seeing these people over a relatively short period of time; I mean, they don't age visibly, or change in appearance."

"The visions seem so inconsequential," Meg complained. "We just see people engaged in ordinary daily activities. According to all the ghost stories I've ever read, restless spirits don't linger unless they have a problem. Oh, I know; murder victims make fine ghosts. But wouldn't you think we would see them do something significant— being murdered, or about to be murdered, or—"

"I've wondered about that too. Another thing that puzzles me is that the anniversary of the murder went by with no particular fuss."

"We made quite a fuss."

"That was the first time we saw—them. But was it the first time they were there? They are still there, Meg. Every night."

"I know," Meg said, in a low voice. "I've seen them too."

"Why didn't you say something?"

"Why didn't you?"

There was no need for either of them to answer.

"Have they always been here?" Meg asked, after a while.

"They sure as hell weren't when we used to live here," Andy answered. "Or if they were, they were better behaved. Dad and Sylvia did some entertaining, and I don't recall any of the guests having a fit when they left after a party. Far as that goes, I've been back and forth at night all summer. I never felt a thing, till the experience I told you of."

"Maybe they'll go away."

"Or maybe they won't. Maybe we've raised something we don't know how to dismiss."

"Now we come to it," Meg said. She didn't look at Andy; she concentrated on sliding her needle in and out. "This isn't just a question of finding out what happened. We have to do something about it."

"Or else move out. We can't spend the whole winter hiding in the house between twilight and dawn. The nights are getting longer."

"What do you propose?"

"I propose to fight it out on this front if it takes all winter."

Meg dropped her embroidery and looked up. "Oh, Andy, I'm so glad. I don't want to give up; but I didn't think I could stick it out alone."

Andy was smiling; now his face grew serious. "I've only one reservation about this, Meg, and I'm going to be honest about it even if you get mad. I'm worried about you."

"Why, for heaven's sake?"

"You've changed. You can't see it, but I sure can. When you got here, you were a city girl—cynical, uptight, sarcastic. Now look at you." He gestured at her embroidery. "You're turning into a crazy-clean Dutch housewife. Baking, sweeping floors, getting chummy with Georgia and gossiping with little old ladies about the best way to hem dishcloths. . . . Jim Stoltzfuss thinks you're a nice little girl. Nice little girl, for God's sake!"

Meg couldn't help laughing. "Andy, that's ridiculous. Why shouldn't I embroider if I want to?"

"Oh, it isn't the damned embroidery. . . ." Andy flapped his arms distractedly. "I can't explain it. It's your whole attitude. Hell, you haven't even made a nasty remark about Sylvia lately."

"I feel happy here," Meg said. "I'm not mad at anybody these days. I feel as if I've come home. . . ."

The words startled her a little; but they had a devastating effect on Andy. His face went white. The iodine-stained scratches stood out like a brand.

"Why don't you be honest?" Meg asked. "That's what you're afraid of—you think Anna Maria is taking me over. Andy, that is so foolish! Don't you think I would know if somebody were trying to move in on my mind? Of course I identify with the girl; any woman would. She was young and pretty and in love—"

"Aha!" Andy pointed an accusing finger. "That's what I mean. That's what worries me. Sure, it's natural for any woman—or man, my God, we aren't all monsters—to sympathize with a girl who was brutally done to death. But how do you know all these things about her? You keep coming up with statements, flat statements based on nothing. Why do you say she was in love?"

"Oh, for God's sake, haven't you ever heard about hunches? She was young and pretty; what girl of seventeen isn't in love? We saw her once looking out the window, as if she hoped to see someone coming. . . . That's enough for a good imagination to work on. Now are you going to stop cross-examining me?"

"All right, I'll lay off. Shall we assume that the house is haunted because the spirits of the victims can't rest? We could have a nice friendly exorcism, or call up a medium—"

"No."

"I'm inclined to agree. Then we can go on as we've been doing. Try to find out what really happened. Though if a jury—"

"We've got sources of information the jury didn't have. If we keep on . . . looking . . . sooner or later we're bound to *see* what happened. But maybe we don't have to wait that long. Suppose this was a real case, I mean a contemporary murder case. Or suppose you were writing a mystery story. How would you go about solving it?"

"That isn't how you write a mystery story. You imagine the crime first and then plant clues so the detective can solve it." Andy's expression was thoughtful; as always, he was distracted by an appeal to reason. "But in a real murder case. . . . What have we got? Three people killed—"

"Two. A third missing, presumed dead."

"You're a stickler for details. But it's barely possible that the girl did survive, isn't it? Suppose she escaped, fled from the house while the killers were butchering the others. The shock alone would be enough to make her lose her wits, even her memory. She might wander in the forest for days."

"You're getting off the track," Meg said. "Two people dead, one missing. The method, the usual blunt instrument. Motive?"

"That has bugged me all along," said Andy, now completely absorbed. "A frustrated lover might attack the family in order to get at the girl; but a whole group of unsuspected sex maniacs? It's unlikely. The most obvious motive is robbery."

"Surely the newspaper would have mentioned it if anything had been stolen."

"Right. The more you think about it, the more puzzling it is. They were the most harmless people—an old man, an old woman, a young girl. Why should anyone want to wipe them out?"

"Lust, greed, revenge, fear," Meg recited. "Aren't those the usual motives? You've eliminated lust and greed—"

"Not eliminated. Merely reduced them to improbabilities. That leaves us with revenge—"

"But as you say, they were so harmless."

"Well, we don't know that they were as harmless as they looked. It would be easier to find a motive if there had been only a single murder. The fact that the whole family was attacked almost suggests a kind of feud."

"Did they have feuds?"

"Everybody always had feuds," Andy said sweepingly. "The feud came from Europe. In Sicily it was called a vendetta—"

"None of the people around here were Italians."

"What does that have to do with it? The Scots were great on family feuds. Some of the settlers were Scotch-Irish—"

"That would imply that the roots of the trouble lay in Europe. Like, if old Mr. Huber was the last member of a family which was feuding with another family that had also moved to America."

Andy laughed. "Sorry. The Huber-Schutzfuss feud? Not only is it ridiculous, it's too coincidental. So far as I know, the bourgeoisie of central Europe didn't indulge in such wasteful activities as feuds. And it would be too much if Huber happened to move into an area where his deadly family rivals had also settled."

"But there wouldn't be any other reason for revenge," Meg argued. "What harm could he do anyone personally, a noble-looking old man like that?"

"Then there's only one motive left," Andy said. "Fear."

The word echoed in the shadowy room. Meg shivered.

"That's just as ridiculous as the idea of revenge," she said, raising her voice to overpower the faint echoes of a word. "Why should anyone fear a kindly old man like that?"

"It isn't ridiculous, it's hopeless. I can think of a dozen reasons, and we'll never be able to substantiate any of them. Mr. Huber recognized one of the neighboring families as well-known European criminals; they were afraid he'd turn them in. He was a usurer—a man's features don't reflect his character, Miss Innocence—and held a mortgage he was threatening to foreclose. He had seduced a neighbor's daughter—"

"Oh, stop it. That old man?"

"They're the worst," Andy said.

"All right, I see what you mean. Maybe we'll never find out, but we can try, can't we? When you said the trouble might go back to Europe, where these people came from, I had a flash of intuition. We don't even know when Huber arrived in this country."

"He bought the property in 1728."

"He could have been living in Virginia or New England before that."

"I doubt it. The earliest settlers were English or Dutch. The Pennsylvania Dutch didn't come from the Netherlands; they were German—*deutsch* in their own language. When did they arrive? My history teacher always told me I'd be sorry if I didn't study. . . ." Andy reached for a reference book. "Here it is. Penn went to the Rhineland in 1671, trying to drum up immigrants. The area had been wasted by religious wars, and many of the people were followers of a sect that had a lot in common with the Quakers; it's no wonder they responded to Penn's descriptions of a fertile new land where every man had the right to worship as he pleased. The waves of immigration started in 1683 and went on up to the French and Indian War. It was a rough trip. The ships were packed so full that passengers died like flies. Rats used to lick the sweat off the faces of sleeping men and women. The ones who didn't die of typhoid and malnutrition and fever often had to sell themselves as indentured servants. Seven years of your life in exchange for passage across the Atlantic. . . ." Andy's voice had changed. "I wonder if that's how my ancestors got their start."

"So what if they did?"

"What kind of snob do you take me for? I was just thinking how the old stock has deteriorated. Anyhow, the point is that Christian Huber must have been among those later immigrants. 'Devout, simple, honest people, most of them very poor. . . .'"

"He was an exception, then," Meg said. "That old man was not a simple, devout farmer."

"You're thinking about the crest, aren't you?"

"Oh, Andy, there are all sorts of indications that Huber's background was more distinguished than that of his neighbors. The sword over the mantel in his room; all those books. And remember the clothes he and Anna Maria wear—wore? A farmer's daughter would wear homespun. That pale-blue dress is completely impractical for a pioneer girl. Old Mr. Huber goes around in silver buttons and white shirts; we have yet to see any indication that he was farming his land. And the servant—how many settlers had servants?"

Andy looked impressed.

Meg went on, with growing vehemence, "The motto on the sampler is in English, not German. Would a German peasant's granddaughter know English? He must have sent her away to school. There were ads in the *Gazette* for boarding schools, where they taught embroidery and languages in addition to the usual school subjects. Not everybody came to America for religious freedom. There must have been political refugees even then. If a Count or Baron von Friedland fled to America after the failure of a plot in which he was involved, he'd change his name, wouldn't he?"

"Boy, that is really farfetched!"

"I don't see why."

"But, Meg, we'd never be able to check that out. All those petty little duchies and kingdoms and their petty local politics. . . . You're a frustrated romantic, that's your trouble. You want your pretty little ghost to be of noble blood."

"We're looking for a motive for a murder," Meg insisted. "Aren't we more likely to find one for a complex, educated man than for a simple German farmer?"

"You're not only a romantic, you're a snob. Common people murder each other just as often as aristocrats."

"I just might murder you!" Meg jabbed her needle viciously into the cloth, and stabbed her thumb. "You're so stubborn!"

Andy was silent for a moment. Meg stealthily staunched the flow of blood and went on stitching.

"All right," Andy said, in a mild voice. "We'll think about it. Suppose we go to Harrisburg tomorrow."

"Okay." Meg didn't look up. After a while Andy picked up a book and started to read.

They sat in silence for almost an hour. Meg finished the motto. Getting bored with letters, she moved down to the lower section and began embroidering a tree.

Finally Andy closed his book. "You're really going great guns, aren't you?" he said, looking at the sampler.

"It's a lot easier than I expected." Meg smoothed the fabric and admired her symmetrical green tree. "I guess I'm improving with practice."

And then, since he had shown an interest in her work, she inquired amiably, "What are you reading?"

"That pamphlet on hex signs. You know, some writers sill insist they had a purely decorative function. It's funny, how people hate to admit their ancestors were superstitious."

"People are still superstitious."

"You know it and I know it; but people like to think of themselves as rational—especially when their irrational ideas lead to violence. Remember that hex murder we were talking about the other night? The writer who resurrected the case some years later had harsh criticism for the judge and the prosecutor of York County. They refused to allow any reference to witchcraft or hexerei as a motive. If the defense could have proved the murderers acted out of superstitious fear, they would have been sent to mental institutions. Instead they were convicted of murder in the first degree. Motive, robbery. The sum involved was only a couple of dollars."

"Murders have been committed for petty sums."

"Not this one. The chief killer, Blymire, was a pathetic man who had been raised in a community where everybody believed in powwowing and hexerei. He was a fourth-generation witch himself—"

"I thought witches were all female."

"Warlock is the correct term for a male witch, but apparently it wasn't used around here. Blymire called himself a witch. He was lousy at it, though. He was lousy at everything, poor devil. After half a lifetime of illness and failure he decided some other witch had put a hex on him. He talked two other innocents into going with him and helping him break the spell. You can do that by getting a lock of the witch's hair. The guy refused to cooperate, and in the ensuing struggle he was killed."

"What a fantastic story."

"No more fantastic than some of the things that have been done in the name of religion," Andy said. "The interesting point about the case is why the legal authorities tried to suppress the hex angle. The big-town newspapers had a field day, jeering at the dumb peasants of Pennsylvania, and the judge refused to admit that such things could go on in his home town."

Meg laughed shortly. "Maybe we should nail up some hex signs. Do you think it would get rid of our ghosts? I don't mind the ones that are already inside."

"We could try garlic or holy water," Andy said. "Or maybe we should look for a hostile witch. Do you think Culver would let us cut off a lock of his hair?"

"I wouldn't touch his hair with rubber gloves. How about Georgia? She'd make a cute witch."

"Speaking of witches," Andy began—and broke off in mid-breath. His eyes took on a glazed stare.

"What is it?" Meg asked curiously.

"Nothing. . . . Something just ran through my mind, but it ran right on out the other side. Are you about ready to quit? We should leave early."

"I'm not tired."

"I want to try something."

Meg looked up. Andy had extended both hands across the table.

"Oh," Meg said. "Now?"

"I want to try something," Andy said again.

Slowly Meg extended her hands till they touched Andy's.

The last thing she saw before the image formed was Andy's face, intent, frowning, his eyes narrowed.

Earlier she had complained that the incidents they had witnessed were inconsequential. It was not true of this scene; something had happened, but she was at a loss to understand the violent emotions that marked the faces of the players.

The old woman, in her black dress and white cap and apron, sat huddled on one of the benches by the kitchen fire. Meg could see the purple veins in the backs of her old hands, but she could not see the object they held. It was partially hidden under her apron.

The wrinkled, toothless old face looked malignant, but the pose was one of guilty shock. She was looking up over her shoulder at a man who stood in the doorway behind her. Drawn up to his full height, Huber was a rigid statue expressing indignation and anger. He was, as always, dressed with an elegance that did not suggest a working farmer. The silver buttons on his blue coat sparkled; the crisp white linen at his throat looked freshly starched.

As the image faded, Meg thought it had resembled one of those story paintings of which the Victorians were so fond. It might have been entitled—

"Caught in the Act," she said aloud, and saw Andy's face before her in the lamplight.

Andy nodded.

"But what was she doing?" Meg asked. "He was angry and she was trying to hide whatever it was she held. . . ."

"It was a doll. With pins sticking in it."

"A doll . . . Oh! Damn it, Andy, you did that on purpose. We were talking about witchcraft, and you—"

"I wanted to see if I could control it," Andy admitted, looking worried.

"Control—or wishful thinking?"

"Aye, there's the rub." Andy made a vaguely Hamletian gesture. "The problem all psychic investigators run into. But I didn't really want to see that. I was hoping I wouldn't."

"Let's try again." Meg held out her hands.

"I'm tempted to agree, if only to find out what's in your mind. What is it you want to see, Meg?"

"Never mind." Meg began to fold her work. "We'll have to get an early start. I'm going to bed."

But as she climbed the stairs Andy's question came back to her. What was it she wanted to see? She knew the answer, but did not like to admit it, even to herself.

## II

They arrived in Harrisburg just as the stores were opening. Andy looked as if he were on his way to the dentist.

"I hate this dusty, squinting research," he grumbled. "The least you could do is come along and help."

"We'd just get in each other's way."

"What are you going to do this morning?"

"Oh, I don't know," Meg said, trying to conceal the big bag that contained her embroidery. "Maybe I'll go to the library and look up eighteenth-century German plots, conspiracies, and failed revolutions."

She was surprised when this feeble attempt at distraction succeeded. Andy looked thoughtful.

"See what they have, anyway. Intellectual history, biography, whatever. And while you're at it . . ."

With dismay Meg saw her empty morning being filled with work.

"You had better meet me there," she interrupted. "If you have things you want to look up too."

They arranged to meet at noon. Squaring his shoulders, Andy marched into the archives building, and Meg started walking. And thinking.

The "candid" discussion she had had with Andy had not really been wholly candid. Andy was reticent about his past, and Meg had not told him of the sensations she had experienced in the past few days. The feeling of waiting, of expectation, was intensifying. It was not a feeling of fear. It was more like—Meg fumbled for a comparison—like the week before Christmas, when she was a child. Like the long, dragging morning, back in junior high, before the math class in which she would see *him*. What was that boy's name? She had been desperately in love with him when she was thirteen. . . .

A boy on a bicycle zipped by, brushing her arm; a lady with a shopping bag muttered something as she circled Meg's motionless form. She had stopped in the middle of the sidewalk, blocking traffic.

Desperately in love. . . . Was that why she had insisted on Anna Maria's being in love—because the feeling in the house was that of a girl watching for her lover? Far-fetched, Andy would say. But Meg's reasoning wasn't that bad; every girl of seventeen is in love, or thinks she is—which is the same thing. Who was Anna Maria's lover? An awkward young farmer—an Emig or Stauffer from a neighboring family? And why, if he was a frequent visitor, hadn't they seen him?

Meg wanted to see him. That was the image she would have tried to produce, if Andy had cooperated. Anna Maria's lover.

I'll try tonight, she thought. I'll make Andy try. She started walking again, heading for the center of town—where the shops were.

The shop sold fabric and patterns as well as needlework, but there was a whole back room devoted to the latter pursuit, and a class was in session. The group broke up when Meg produced her work, and she swelled with pride at the admiring cries of the women. They were all novices, learning basic stitches, but the instructor was an expert, and she examined Meg's pattern interestedly.

"It is genuine, isn't it?" Meg asked anxiously.

The instructor, a pleasant-faced woman in her mid fifties, laughed.

"I'd have to see the needlework on the original to be certain, but don't worry; so far the forgers haven't contaminated this field. Some of the motifs are very unusual, though. Tulips, the Tree of Life, animals—common enough. Crosses are not, although many of the mottoes are religious. This is a cross, isn't it—with something in the center?"

"It's supposed to be a flower," Meg said humbly. "I guess my copy isn't—"

"And what is this? Gracious, it looks like a snake."

"No snakes?"

"One might find the serpent in the Garden of Eden. Some samplers depict Adam and Eve. But if I were you, I would look at the original again."

When Meg finally glanced at her watch she was horrified at the time. She asked for directions to the library and made it to the rendezvous only moments before Andy arrived. He looked at her suspiciously.

"You're very pink-cheeked and healthy looking for a girl who has been pouring over books all morning. Did you find anything?"

"I—uh—"

Andy looked pointedly at the paper bag, and Meg began to laugh.

"Caught in the act. Okay, so I wasted the morning. Want to make something of it?"

"I'd beat you, only I'm too tired. Let's go eat."

"I know a place."

One of the women in the embroidery class had recommended it. A shabby exterior made Andy look dubious, but the food was superb, the genuine Pennsylvania Dutch variety which is scarcely ever found except in country farmhouses. They finished with an apple pie whose only resemblance to the "Dutch apple" types found in stores and restaurants was in its name. The apples, thickly sprinkled with sugar and cinnamon, were embedded in a rich creamy custard. Andy pushed back his empty plate and sighed.

"I am replete," he announced. "And conciliated. If you pick up tips like this from your lady friends, it's worth it. Take advantage of my good mood. Tell me about your useless activities."

"I found the colors I needed," Meg said seriously. "The rose is a little too pink, but it has the subtle undershade of rust brown that I—"

"That's enough."

"I had a nice time," Meg said. "The ladies admired my

sampler. The teacher—I told you there was a class, didn't
I?"

"You did."

"The teacher said it was very unusual. Some of the
motifs are unique. A cross with a flower in the middle—"

"Oh, come on, Meg, I don't really want to know—What
did you say?"

"I said a lot of things," Meg answered.

"A cross with a what in the middle?"

"A flower. At least I think it is. The teacher was
skeptical about some of the other motifs too. A snake—"

"Shut up a minute," Andy said.

His tone was inoffensive, so Meg shut up. Andy thought.
His face could not be called enigmatic; it showed every
passing emotion, and Meg was learning to read them. Doubt,
excitement, and severe cogitation followed one another in
rapid succession.

"Check," Andy said suddenly.

"Check what?"

"The check. The bill. Toss you for it."

"You paid last time," Meg said. "I'll get it."

Andy's pensive look was replaced by one of amusement.

"Liberated, eh?"

"Hadn't you noticed?"

"At least you're consistent. I can't stand the women who
want to be freed of the oppression of male domination but
howl if you suggest splitting the check."

"None of us really liberated types do that," Meg said
severely. "It's the crypto-pussycats who cheat. What are
you in such a hurry about?"

"I just had an idea. Let's go back to the library."

The restaurant was on a back street. There were few pedestrians, so they walked side by side, taking their time.

"You've been so busy lecturing me you didn't tell me how you got along this morning," Meg said. "Any luck?"

"Yes and no."

"Typical masculine vagueness. If men would learn to think logically, the way women do—"

"I mean it literally. I found out some facts, but I don't know how to interpret them. The taxes on that farm were paid by one John Emig from 1740 to 1765. After which the payee was Jacob Emig—son and heir, I presume. And what do you make of that?"

"Emig must have bought the farm after the murders."

"Who from? Everybody was dead."

"The state."

"There wasn't any—"

"Oh, all right, the colony, or the Crown, or whatever it was. Huber was dead and so was his only heir; the land would revert to the government. We talked about that before."

"Then why wasn't the sale recorded? I've got a theory. After Huber died, the farm belonged to the girl, and she was missing. I don't know what the law was in those days, but today you have to prove death before you can take over somebody's property. The usual period is seven years, but it takes a formal court decision to transfer title. Suppose Emig was a friend. He paid the taxes to keep the place from reverting back to the government, hoping maybe the girl would turn up."

"I suppose he was one of your ancestors?"

"What does that have to do with it? I can't remember, to tell you the truth; I didn't pay much attention to that genealogy book."

"Well, you make him sound awfully noble. They were poor people. Why should he shell out hard-earned money for a neighbor?"

"I don't say his motives were purely disinterested. He probably moved in—farmed the land and kept the profits."

"I still don't see how he could—"

"Look at it this way. Emig was Huber's neighbor and pal. He had a son. Maybe the son and Anna Maria were engaged. Hell, they might have been married, for all we know. That would explain how the property came to the Emigs. A woman's property belonged to her husband."

"Prove it. Find a marriage certificate."

"I'll bet we could at that. To find the record of a marriage you have to know the date and the name of the groom. I could look under Emig. That's a damned good idea."

Andy continued to crow until they reached the library. They separated, Meg to search for books on European history, especially "plots and conspiracies and unsuccessful revolutions," while Andy went off on some unspecified research of his own. He was disgustingly coy about the nature of that research; when they met, some time later, he had an armful of books, but refused to let Meg look at the titles.

"Are you going to read them all now?" Meg asked.

"I hope not. Watch this."

Andy advanced on the librarian's desk. Meg stood at a

respectful distance and watched. She had never seen him exert his full quota of charm before. It was an impressive performance. He did everything but kiss the dazzled old lady's hand. He also produced mysterious cards and documents from his wallet. He walked out with the books, including a few Meg had selected.

By the time they started home it was midafternoon. Andy was in an excellent mood; his expression was positively smug.

"You've got a theory, haven't you?" Meg asked.

"Uh-huh."

"What about?"

"The motive for the murders."

"Really? Something we hadn't thought of?"

"I'll tell you when I figure it out."

"You've got a nerve. I tell you my wild hunches."

Andy's smile disappeared. "Do you?"

When they got back, Andy headed for the library with his pile of books, pausing just long enough to ask, "What time is dinner?"

"I'm not planning to have dinner," Meg said coldly. "That was an enormous lunch. I'll make a sandwich when I get hungry."

"Don't let malice destroy you, child," said Andy.

Seething, Meg put on old clothes and went outside. For several hours she worked on the lawn, muttering rude comments to herself about Andy's inadequacy as a caretaker. Of course the place was too big for one man, even full time; but he might have tried to pick up the worst litter. Meg staked and cut back drooping dahlias and chrysanthemums, and picked up armloads of dead branches blown down by the rain. In all honesty she had to admit that her efforts had little effect, but she worked off a lot of steam in a useful fashion.

She didn't go in until the gathering twilight reminded her of what else might be gathering, under the boughs of the oak tree. She was ready to forgive Andy by then—for what, she wasn't quite sure. She went to the library door and looked in.

Andy was standing, bent over the table. His hands rested on its surface and he was looking down at an object that lay between them. He glanced up.

"Hi," he said abstractedly. "When did you say dinner was going to be ready?"

"My sampler!" Meg exclaimed. "What are you doing with my sampler?"

"What was it your girl friend said, about these motifs being unusual?"

Meg took full advantage of the question, giving him a lecture on the patterns and their symbolism. Andy listened meekly.

"The tree is the Tree of Life," he repeated. "And the peacock symbolizes immortality. Not all the designs were symbolic, though, were they? I mean, flowers are just for pretty."

"You're talking like a Dutchman," Meg said, with a smile. "Even the flowers had meaning. So did colors. White for purity, red for the passion of Our Lord Jesus, and so on. Hey, there's one of the motifs the lady in the sewing shop questioned. I was right, too; if that isn't a snake I'll eat it. It can't be a vine; it's got eyes."

"It's a snake." Andy's voice sounded odd, but when

Meg looked at him his expression was equivocal. "Coiled around a tree. The tree is not the Tree of Life, in that case, but the Tree of Knowledge. And here's your cross with a flower. Funny color for a cross—gray-black."

"Death and sorrow," Meg said glibly. "And the red flower in the center signifies the Passion. What are these funny shapes here? They look like Greek letters."

"I'm hungry," Andy said suddenly. "I'm going to make a sandwich. Shall I make you one?"

"I'll come in a minute."

As soon as Andy had left the room Meg examined the books he had been reading. They were scattered all over the table. The titles did not enlighten her; they were a weird mixture, from a history of magic to a ponderous tome on eighteenth-century rationalism. What was Andy up to? He had not taken notes; several sheets of paper lay among the books, but they were blank.

She followed Andy into the kitchen and saw that he had covered the kitchen table with a wild variety of ingredients—cheese, cold cuts, a can of tuna, pickles, onions, anchovies. . . .

"You're not going to put all that in one sandwich!" she exclaimed.

"That and more." Andy took lettuce and tomatoes from the refrigerator. "Haven't we got any smoked oysters?"

They ate sandwiches and drank beer, from what Andy described as his private stock. Meg was carrying the dishes to the sink when the telephone rang.

It rang so seldom that it startled her. She dropped a plate, and swore as she bent to pick up fragments of lettuce and bread crust.

Andy went to get the phone. He was back almost immediately. "It's Sylvia," he said, his face expressionless. "She wants to talk to you."

"Somebody must be dying," Meg said. "Sylvia never calls. What do you suppose—"

"If you answer it, maybe you'll find out."

The telephone was lying on the desk in the library. Meg picked it up with the tips of her fingers. She had a premonition of bad news, which was perfectly understandable. Sylvia was probably mad because she hadn't written.

"Goodness, it took you long enough to get here," she snapped, as soon as Meg had said "hello." "This is long distance, Meg. It costs money."

"I'm sorry. I was in the kitchen."

"How are you?"

"Fine."

"No more hallucinations?"

Meg had a wild desire to laugh. If Sylvia only knew!

"No," she said firmly.

"Good. I knew they would stop when you got away from New York. The reason I'm calling is that I've decided to come down and look at some of the things in the attic. Georgia says there's a Duncan Phyfe dining-room set."

"I'd like to keep that," Meg said firmly. "The dining room set downstairs is junk—that heavy carved mahogany with bunches of grapes all over it like goiters. With the Duncan Phyfe we could fix up the dining room to be quite attractive."

"Oh. Well, that's the sort of thing we have to discuss. You had better make a list. I won't have much time. I have a doctor's appointment in New York on Saturday."

"When are you coming?" Meg asked, trying not to sound as depressed as she felt.

"Friday. Just for the day. I'll spend Thursday night in Philadelphia and drive out early Friday morning. This is costing money, Meg. I'll see you Friday."

Meg turned from the phone to see Andy hovering in the doorway. She was annoyed; if he wanted to eavesdrop, why didn't he do it openly? She was also a little ashamed of herself for not asking about Sylvia's health. When someone mentioned a doctor's appointment it was only courteous to express concern, although the appointment was probably only for a checkup. Sylvia took excellent care of her health. She went to the doctor so often and took so many pills that Meg suspected her of mild hypochondria.

"What's up?" Andy asked.

"She's coming."

"Hell. When?"

"Friday." Meg relented; he had every right to be curious, the whirlwind visit would be as vexing for him as it was for her.

"She'll arrive in the morning—if I know Sylvia, about six A.M. She says it's just for the day, so I suppose she'll leave about five. You'd better brace yourself, my lad; Sylvia intends to do a week's work in one day."

"God, yes," Andy groaned. "Damn it, that means we've got to slave for the next couple of days. I wouldn't want her to decide to stay over because we didn't have everything ready when she came."

"I don't feel like starting now, though."

"Bright and early tomorrow morning, then. That means I've got a lot of reading to do tonight."

He dropped in his chair and reached for a book. Defiantly Meg took up the sampler. If she wasn't going to have time to embroider in the next few days, she would indulge herself this evening.

It was like so many other evenings they had spent together: darkness deepening outside the windows, the smooth hypnotic movements of Meg's needle, and the growing patches of color on the linen fabric. Very domestic and peaceful, Meg thought—and to close the evening's entertainment, a glimpse into the unknown, a conjuring of scenes and people long dead. With one of the flashes of incredulity that hit her sometimes, she thought, it's crazy. Really crazy, what we're doing.

As Andy turned from book to book, he began to read excerpts to her. Meg was perfectly willing to talk; but Andy's comments seemed to have no bearing on the subject uppermost in her mind.

"I bet you didn't know that, before the Fall, Adam never had to go to the toilet."

"I can't say the question ever entered my mind."

"Some of the religious types who settled at Ephrata, north of here, tried to get back to Adam's state of grace by restricting their diets."

"I've heard of Ephrata. It was a celibate community that had one of the first printing presses in the colony."

"Good schools, too. And a certain small percentage of fanatics."

"How did fanatics do with their back-to-Adam project?"

"They got constipated," said Andy. He turned the page.

"The Society of the Woman in the Wilderness was a monastic community too. They perched on a hill above Germantown watching the skies for signs of the Second Coming. Many of them were learned men who were kicked out of the German universities for their heretical views. They practiced astrology and alchemy."

"Simple, pious farmers," Meg jeered.

"Most of 'em were. Not all of them were pacifists, either, although the Mennonites and some of the other German sects shared the Quakers' views about killing. Did you know that the famous Kentucky rifle was really developed by Pennsylvania Dutchmen?"

"Do tell."

"The companies of riflemen in the Revolution were almost all Pennsylvanians. They were the best shots in the country."

"You sound like Mrs. Adams bragging about her ancestors."

"They weren't so bad," Andy muttered. "The Germans formed one twelfth of the population, but they made up one eighth of the Patriot army during the revolution. And don't get smart. They're your ancestors too."

He slammed the book shut and tossed it aside. After reading for a few minutes in the next volume, he remarked in a conversational tone.

"Woman is the vegetative passive element. The generative, active male element must be united with the female in order to become the perfect Unity."

"I don't know what you're talking about."

"The specter of the rose."

"That's a ballet."

"Is it?"

Meg put down her embroidery.

"Andy, I think you're cracking up."

Andy went on reading. "Do any of these names strike a familiar chord?" he asked. "Swedenborg, the Count of St. Germain, Cagliostro, Christian Rosenkreutz?"

"Cagliostro was a magician, wasn't he? If you don't stop it, I'm going to bed."

"Wait, don't go away. We haven't had our evening séance yet."

"We aren't going to have one unless you play fair."

"What do you mean?"

"I mean, no fair trying to control the vision. I want to try something. It's my turn."

"Okay, your turn first. Although I must say that's a childish way of looking at it."

Once again the shadowy kitchen took shape. It was so familiar to Meg that she could have sketched it from memory. The brick fireplace, the mantel with its row of ornaments, the massive cupboard. Meg felt a violent stab of disappointment. The only inhabitant of the room was the old woman. She concentrated as hard as she could, but to no avail. Not only were the people she had hoped to see missing, but the scene was even duller than usual. The old woman was picking over a pan of beans. She sat motionless, the firelight shining on her white apron and snowy cap.

The vision faded. Meg pulled her hands away from Andy's.

"You cheated," she said angrily. "It didn't work!"

"Well, don't get all uptight about it. What was it you wanted to see?"

"I know," Meg said suddenly. "I know one thing that's wrong. We always do this in the library, so all we see is their kitchen. They wouldn't entertain company in the kitchen. . . . Come on."

"Where are you going?"

"We'll try the drawing room. That's where their parlor was."

Andy remained seated.

Meg, on her feet, gestured impatiently. "Come on, Andy!"

"Don't you think once is enough for tonight?"

"No."

"I do. One of the reasons why I've avoided the parlor is that I think that's where the murder took place. Do you want to see that?"

"Oh, you're impossible! All right, if you won't come, I'll try it by myself."

"You can't . . ." Andy began.

But Meg was already on her way.

The drawing room looked eerie with moonlight sliding in through the high windows. Meg hesitated; her anger and excitement were chilled by a sudden sensation of cold. Walking more slowly, she went to the window.

It looked out over the front lawn. The shadows were there, under the tree.

Meg shivered, but she felt none of the horror that had surged into the house that first night of seeing the figures. With a quick movement she pulled the heavy draperies across the window.

In the near darkness she waited. Darkness or light, it

made no difference; the other house had its own illumination. She was convinced of her ability to conjure up the visions by herself; in fact, she wondered whether Andy was a hindrance instead of a help. Perhaps he had been deliberately controlling the visions all along, preventing her from seeing what she wanted to see. She strained forward, her hands clasped tightly together.

It was not as easy as she had hoped. Instead of the smooth, complete manifestations they had been getting, she caught flickers of light and color that faded out and then strengthened, like a badly adjusted television set. Meg's nails dug into her palms.

"Please," she whispered. "Oh, please . . ."

A shimmer of blue.

Meg focused on it, concentrated all her will. She could feel beads of perspiration streaking her face, trickling down her body. The blue strengthened and took shape. A dress—a woman, wearing a blue dress . . . Slowly the rest of the scene formed, but it was hazy and transparent.

The sun shone in through the windows of the other room. The blue linen dress shone palely in its light, like satin. The girl had been caught in the middle of a curtsy, her skirts lifted, her fair head inclined; but her eyes were fixed on the man who stood facing her.

He was tall and young, his dark hair gathered at the nape of his neck by a black ribbon. His clothing was sober but well cut: a blue coat with facings of white, dark breeches, polished boots. A sword hung at his side. One hand rested on the hilt of his sword as he bowed in response to the girl's curtsy; the other arm held his hat, a black three-cornered hat like the ones Meg had seen in portraits of Washington. His face . . .

Meg was conscious of a faint disappointment. He was handsome, certainly—straight, regular features, broad shoulders, thick, shining hair. But he didn't look quite as she had expected him to look.

The picture began to fade. Meg fought to hold it. She wanted to see more, she had been so absorbed by the lovers that she had not noticed other details. The old man was there; naturally, a young lady did not receive male visitors unchaperoned. The sampler, bright and unfaded; a small table with curved legs, a flowered carpet . . .

A brilliant flash, like lightning, cut across the scene and destroyed it. Meg swayed. The backs of her knees struck a chair and she fell into it. Breathing harshly, she narrowed her eyes against the light. Andy stood in the archway, his hand resting on the switch that had turned on the chandelier.

"Do you know how long you've been in here?" he asked.

"No. Why couldn't you leave me alone?"

"I've been watching. Timing you. You were in a trance—or whatever you want to call it—for almost five minutes, Meg. How much longer would you have stayed there if I hadn't stopped it?"

"I don't know. What difference does it make? I did it, Andy, I did it all by myself!"

"What did you see?"

Andy was disturbed, but he was also immensely curious. The latter emotion won out; he listened intently as Meg described the scene.

"Blue coat with white facings, sword, boots. . . . He sounds like a soldier."

"He certainly wasn't a local yokel. Andy, let's try again. Right now. Together we could really get results. Please, this is the right place. We should have used this room before."

Her weakness gone, she got up and walked toward Andy, hands out. He stood watching her, his face a mask of mingled fascination and revulsion. As she reached him, he struck out violently, knocking her hands away.

"I know this is the place," he said. "That's what I'm afraid of. One of us has to fight this thing, Meg—keep it under control. Otherwise . . . I can see Georgia breaking in here a few weeks from now and finding us sitting like mummies in those two chairs, starved to death in a catatonic trance. 'Tell them I came, and no one answered. . . .'"

"Of all the morbid ideas," Meg exclaimed. "What's wrong with you?"

"I don't know," Andy mumbled. He was shaking from head to foot. "I hate this room. I always have hated it. I feel sick with despair and guilt when I come in here. Don't you feel it? Don't you know what's out there, under the oak tree?"

"Andy?" Meg reached out for him. Andy jumped back, stumbled, caught himself by catching at the wall.

"Don't touch me!"

Meg was afraid to move or speak again. She was terrified—not by any ghostly menace, but by simple practical fear of a man on the ragged edge of sanity. She was not afraid for herself; it never occurred to her that

Andy would harm her. She was afraid of what he was doing to himself.

After a minute that seemed like a month, he let out a long, shaken sigh. His face was gray under the summer tan, but when he spoke she knew the worst was over.

"All right. It's okay. I'm sorry, I didn't mean to frighten you."

"I wasn't afraid."

"Oh, yeah?" Andy smiled faintly. "You should see your face. It's green. Clashes with that blue dress."

"Do you remember what you said?"

"Yes." Andy wiped his wet forehead on his sleeve. "I got a little excited, but basically I think I'm right. This habit of summoning up the past can be damned dangerous, Meg. Schizophrenia, or possession, or morbid obsessions—what we've been doing can get out of hand. We don't really know what we're doing. That's why we have to be careful. You do understand, don't you? You aren't mad at me for losing my temper?"

"No. Do you remember saying that you hate this room? That you've always hated it?"

"That's silly. It used to be one of my favorite rooms. Not that I was allowed in here much. Sylvia kept it in apple-pie order. I was supposed to make my messes outdoors."

"That sounds like Sylvia." Meg tried to speak casually. "And speaking of Sylvia, we'd better get some sleep if we want to get the house in shape before she comes. A certain amount of yard work is in order, too."

"Yes, I've let that go to pot the last few weeks. We've also got to get those antiques out of the big room. . . ."

He talked collectedly and calmly as they went upstairs,

but Meg noticed he was careful not to touch her. She kept up her end of the conversation; but when she was finally alone in her room she dropped limply onto the bed.

He's right, she thought. It is dangerous. But not for me. He's the one who's in trouble. I should have realized it before. The way he keeps changing, from enthusiastic interest to horror. . . . A psychiatrist could explain it, maybe. I can't. . . . Oh, yes, I can. But I don't want to believe it. I've got to be careful—watch him, stop pushing when he gets angry or panicky. I'll get him back in that room yet. Together, we can. . . . But I'll wait. I won't insist. There's plenty of time.

But there wasn't time. As her conscious will relaxed in the drowsiness that precedes sleep, a small inner voice denied the assumption. Time was running out and the house was still waiting, with a mounting intensity that would soon reach its climax.

# Chapter 11

Andy was in a cheerful mood next morning, as if he had completely forgotten his gray-faced horror the night before. Naturally Meg did not refer to it, and Andy worked her so hard she had little time for introspection. The old piano that had blocked her progress for so long was moved grudgingly out against the wall; tables and sideboards were shifted. They didn't try to clear the room completely, only to move things into positions from which they could be readily approached. They made considerable progress, but there were still several heavy pieces to be shifted when Andy called a halt for lunch.

"Better get cleaned up if we're going to Reading," he said casually.

"Go to Reading?" Meg repeated in surprise.

"I thought you were going to have tea with old lady Adams."

"Good lord, I completely forgot. Maybe we shouldn't take the time."

"We can make it up by working tonight. There are a few things I want to look up anyway, while we're there."

Meg glanced obliquely at him. His face was calm; he poured milk into two glasses, clear up to the brim, without spilling a drop. He looked so normal she found it hard to believe what had happened the night before; and when he looked at her and smiled, she felt a ridiculous, illogical sense of well-being.

"I'll be ready in fifteen minutes," she said.

As they drove along, Meg was still trying to figure out why he had suggested the expedition. She had expected him to give up his research for a while; but finally she realized that his fear was a very specific fear of one room and what might happen in it. If he kept her busy with other things, there wouldn't be time for occult experiments. Well, she had decided she wouldn't push him. Not for a while, anyway. In the meantime, it was nice to have him in a good mood.

Meg had donned a dress she hadn't worn since she left New York—a sedate, brown dress that, according to Andy, made her look like a timid wren. It had a white collar and cuffs and a wide patent leather belt in a darker brown, and it was the closest thing Meg owned to an "afternoon tea" dress.

Mrs. Adams clearly approved of it. When Meg saw the elderly woman's face brighten at the sight of her, she felt slightly ashamed. Her motives for calling on Mrs. Adams were purely selfish; she had not realized how much the old lady had looked forward to her visit. She said as much, with a graciousness that had no marring tone of self-pity.

"My dear, how nice! I hardly dared hope that a busy young thing like you could spare the time to visit me."

She had prepared lavishly, however. When Meg saw the tea table, with its fine china and dainty little sandwiches, she felt another qualm of guilt.

"Your young man couldn't join us? I know men hate tea parties; but dear Matilda's grandnephew is always welcome."

"He had work to do," Meg said, smiling. "But he sent his regards, and hopes to see you again soon."

The last part of the speech was Meg's addition, but the older woman nodded as if she expected such courtesy from Matilda's grandnephew.

"I was very fond of Matilda," she said, and launched into a spate of reminiscences. Meg listened sympathetically. If she intended to interrogate Mrs. Adams about murders, the least she could do was listen to a few stories about the good old days.

"Historical research is fascinating," Mrs. Adams said, pouring Meg another cup of tea. "Try one of these cookies with the nuts, my dear; I'm sure you don't need to worry about calories, you're so slim. . . . Yes, I don't know what I'd have done without such a hobby, and my work at the museum, after my dear husband died. Friends pass on, and one's physical infirmities increase. That is why it is all the more important to use the mind, you see; that part of one's anatomy stays flexible, I am happy to say, long after the knees and back stiffen! I can't help laughing, sometimes, when I think how bored I was by history in school. But of course it is more interesting when it is personal;

when one realizes that historical personages were one's own ancestors."

"I find it fascinating even though they aren't my ancestors," Meg said with a smile.

"Ah, but how do you know they aren't? And of course you take an interest in local genealogy because of Andrew. It is very sensible of you. After all, one never knows! There are families, even in Reading, which I would hesitate to allow a daughter of mine to become connected with."

In the nick of time Meg managed to keep her jaw from dropping. So that was how the land lay! She hesitated, trying to decide whether or not to take advantage of this innocent error. Mrs. Adams mistook her silence for maidenly modesty.

"I hope I'm not speaking out of turn. To a young person these ideas may seem shockingly hardheaded; but it wouldn't do to take chances with—with children, would it?"

"Nothing is settled yet," Meg mumbled, dropping her eyes to hide the amusement in them.

The mixture of old-fashioned delicacy and hard practicality in Mrs. Adams' speech was almost too much for her composure. But why should she assume that her generation was the first to concern itself about dangerous genes? The old grandmothers hadn't known about blood types and congenital diseases, but they had a folk wisdom that served the same end. No, it wouldn't be sensible to select the father of your prospective children from a family whose members were conspicuously defective.

Happily aware of Meg's thoughts, Mrs. Adams went on

talking. "I hope you won't wait too long. I never believed in long engagements. I understand you are both doing a splendid job remodeling the Emig house. It's a pleasure to see young people going back to the old family home instead of moving into one of these horrid modern apartments."

Meg's head began to spin. This was leaping to conclusions with a vengeance.

"The house is so big," she said tentatively. "Too impractical, I'm afraid. Actually, I believe Sylvia plans to donate it to the Historical Association."

Mrs. Adams shook her head.

"Your cousin is playing a little joke on you, my dear. The association couldn't possibly manage a place like that unless the donation were accompanied by a very substantial endowment. Besides, it wouldn't be proper. The house should belong to Matilda's grandnephew. As for practicality, you might consider opening the house to the public on certain days, or even running an antique shop, as so many have been forced to do. But I understand Andrew's writing has been very successful. And such an ideal location for an author, my dear."

Meg stared. Mrs. Adams didn't look like a witch. Her wrinkled face was pink with animation, her eyes showed only kindly interest.

"Andy's writing . . ." she began.

Mrs. Adams blushed. "Of course I know his novel was published under a pseudonym. Very properly—it was not a—it was a very *modern* novel. I have not read it, of course. But these days, unfortunately, it is necessary to be coarse in order to sell, and I'm sure Andrew will write a book that is worthy of him one day. When a young man is thinking of starting a family, he must be practical."

Meg was so stupefied by the barrage of facts—true or false—that she almost forgot what she had come for. She accepted another cup of tea and lost track of the conversation for a while as she grappled with the new ideas. Mrs. Adams babbled on, unaware of her abstraction. Then Meg heard a word that woke her up with a vengeance.

". . . murder. One doesn't like to think of such things. But if you are marrying into the family, you have the right to know."

"I'm glad you think so," Meg said.

She didn't want to ask questions and betray that she had not been listening. Unfortunately, it seemed that she had heard the end of a discussion, not the beginning. Mrs. Adams smiled and fell silent.

"I am interested in genealogy," Meg said, hoping to prime the pump. "I found a book, written in the thirties, about the Emig family—"

"Oh, my dear, that is quite inaccurate. A frightful hodge-podge of fact and fantasy. I have a book I'd be delighted to lend you; unfortunately it is out on loan just now to another friend. She is a Gross; the Sadlers, Grosses, and Emigs are closely connected, you know. I will ask her for it and send it to you."

"I don't want to put you to so much trouble," Meg said. She wasn't interested in family history; she wanted to ask about the murders.

"It is no trouble at all, my dear. I hope your interest is—that is to say, I hope you have no reason for your interest beyond the general?"

"I'm afraid I don't understand."

Mrs. Adams looked distressed. There was a spot of color on each withered cheek.

"One hates even to mention such nonsense," she said, avoiding Meg's eyes. "But one has heard . . . you haven't had any unpleasant experiences in the house, have you, my dear?"

"Are you saying that the house is supposed to be haunted?"

Mrs. Adams started as if she had used an obscenity. "I don't credit such stories for a moment," she said.

"Then there have been stories?"

"Not in general circulation, my dear. Few people know the history of the place."

The room was getting darker. Mrs. Adams rose and turned on a lamp. Meg realized she ought to leave, but she didn't want to; this was getting close to home.

"The site was abandoned for almost a century," Mrs. Adams said. "Not surprisingly. When Benjamin Emig built there, some of those who remembered warned him against it. But it was a robustly rational age, and Benjamin was not a sensitive man. He certainly never experienced anything in the house. My father used to say that Mr. Emig would send a ghost packing in a hurry."

"But someone else did experience something?" Meg asked. Her hostess was beginning to glance at the clock. She knew she must leave soon; Andy would be foaming at the mouth.

"Matilda once mentioned . . ." Mrs. Adams shook her head. "No, I really shan't repeat such tales, it would not be fair to you. She was only a child, and children do imagine playmates and pretty ladies, don't they? She grew out of it, my dear. I am so glad to hear you have not had any trouble. I hope your home will be fortunate for you. You must come again, and let me hear how you're getting on."

It was a dismissal, long overdue; Meg could only rise and thank her hostess.

Once she was out of sight of the house she began to run. It wasn't dark yet, but the shadows of night were falling fast. Andy was parked around the corner. He had refused to come nearer the house for fear of being trapped. He was standing by the car, waiting for her. She slid under the wheel and sat with her shoulders hunched in anticipation of the lecture she expected.

Andy slammed the car into gear with the usual objections from the clutch, and they took off. Not until they were almost out of town did he speak.

"We may have to spend the night at a motel."

"Maybe we can get in the back door," Meg said.

"Maybe. Did you have a fun time? You must have, to stay so long."

His tone was milder than she had expected. Meg deduced that his inquiries had gone well. She decided it would be tactful to ask.

"Negative information only," Andy said, in answer. "The records are complete for those years and there is definitely no mention of a title transfer."

"What about the marriage certificate?"

"No luck. I checked Emigs—also Stoltzfusses and every other name I could think of, from 1837 to 1840. Even in that day and age girls didn't marry before they were fourteen, I assume."

"I wouldn't think so."

Andy switched on the headlights. Meg privately felt this was overdue; Andy wanted to put off the fact of night as long as possible. He was driving too fast.

"I gave your regards to Mrs. Adams," she said.

"That's nice. What did she have to say?"

"Plenty."

"Don't kid me. Little old ladies never say anything interesting."

Meg started to laugh, and then sobered. "Andy, we've been ignoring a valuable source of information. Little old ladies like Mrs. Adams have nothing to do but read and gossip and collect old things. She's an intelligent woman, and family is important to her. I'll bet if I could get her to sit down and answer questions, she could tell us a lot. Family legends, old stories. . . . Ow! Andy, watch out—"

The animal that had darted into the road—cat, rabbit, possum, she couldn't tell—saved itself by a mighty leap as Andy twisted the wheel. Meg fell against his shoulder and bounced back as he swerved back into his lane.

"You were saying?" he asked.

Meg gulped. "I don't remember. . . . Oh, yes. It may interest you to know that we are unofficially engaged and that we are fixing up your old ancestral mansion so we can live in it. With, presumably, ten or twelve children."

Andy hooted with laughter.

"Furthermore," Meg went on, in a smooth, silky voice, "I was unaware of the fact that you are a best-selling novelist. Who are you really? Norman Mailer? Philip Roth?"

The car swerved dangerously.

"Oh, hell," Andy muttered. "I thought I'd be safe out in the boondocks."

"That's where you aren't safe. I tell you, the espionage service out here is fantastic—like jungle drums. Mrs. Adams knows everything there is to know about you."

"Not everything," Andy muttered. Then he shrugged. Meg saw the movement in silhouette. It was almost fully dark outside. Only faint streaks of sunset lingered.

"I wrote one book," Andy said. "It was a lousy book, but it sold well. And don't think I'm going to tell you the name of it. I'm working on another one now, and I'm behind schedule, in case you want to know."

"And you let me make all those cracks about unpublished writers," Meg exclaimed. "You must have enjoyed yourself."

"I did. Continue; that isn't all you learned from Mrs. Adams, superspy."

"The house is haunted," Meg said.

"You're telling me!" The car leaped forward.

"I'd rather take a chance with the ghosts than become another highway fatality," Meg said, through clenched teeth. "Mrs. Adams wouldn't say much. She doesn't believe in ghosts and she hates to imply anything that reflects on the honor or the good sense of the old families. But I think your great-aunt saw Anna Maria. 'A pretty lady,' according to Mrs. Adams. The aberration passed away when she got older."

"Maybe we're emotionally retarded."

"The most puzzling thing, though, was the series of hints she threw out that there was some connection between your family and the Hubers. She's hard to pin down; that's why I said we wouldn't get anything out of her unless we could make her answer specific questions. But she doesn't answer them. She just sort of babbles on and edges around unpleasant subjects, like murder."

"What precisely did she say?"

"I missed part of it," Meg admitted. "She really stunned me with the story of your literary success, and then I lost track of what she was saying for a while. But she referred to murder, and then she said she wouldn't discuss such nasty things with strangers; but that I, as a potential member of the family, had a right to know."

"Know what?"

"That's what she didn't say."

"You overestimate her. I doubt if she knows anything."

They were silent for a time. Andy drove as if the fiends were on his trail; Meg sat with hands clenched on the edge of the seat and her feet braced. They were in the home stretch, with the gates only a mile away, when the inevitable happened. A car, waiting at a side road, emitted a long wail as they sped past. Looking back, Meg saw the ominous red flasher in hot pursuit.

"Pull over," she said resignedly. "You couldn't outrun a tricycle in this car."

"I never race police cars," Andy said virtuously. He put his foot on the brake and stopped on the shoulder of the road. The police car pulled up behind them. A man got out and walked toward them.

Andy leaned out the window. "Fred? That you?"

"Yep." In the glow of the headlights Meg saw that the officer was a tall, burly man of about Andy's age. He was grinning.

"Caught you this time, Andy. Evening, ma'am. Aren't you scared to ride with him?"

"Yes," Meg said truthfully.

"Fred Zook, Meg Rittenhouse. Sylvia's cousin. Fred and I went to school together," Andy added. "He's had it in for me ever since. Watch him; he's going to claim I was driving twenty miles over the speed limit."

"Twenty-five," Fred said. "I don't know whether to give you a ticket, or congratulate you; this heap doesn't look as if it could go that fast."

"Just give me the ticket and skip the wisecracks."

"Matter of fact, I was on my way to see you. You were supposed to stop by and sign a complaint against Culver."

"Oh, hell, I forgot."

"The town isn't going to let you forget. They want to nail Culver. Go ahead, I'll follow you home. Got the papers with me."

"Trusting soul," Andy said.

He drove the rest of the way at twenty miles an hour. Fred, behind them, kept the flasher going; occasionally he touched the siren. Andy was grinning idiotically as this childish game went on, but Meg had not forgotten what might be waiting for them at the house. She wondered what Fred would do if confronted by three menacing apparitions. Read them their rights before arresting them for trespassing? She suppressed a hysterical giggle, which Andy probably took to be shared amusement. He drove up to the front door and stopped the car.

The lawn lay dark and empty under starlight. The moon had not risen. If the shadows were there, they were invisible and unfelt. Meg probed, wincingly, as one touches a tender spot. Nothing.

"Dark as the inside of a cow out here," Fred's voice boomed. "Get on up there and turn on some lights, Andy."

In the hall Meg tried to catch Andy's eye. He avoided looking at her, but she saw that there were drops of sweat on his forehead. If he had felt anything, he had kept it under control.

Meg was baffled. Did the presence of an outsider, a nonsensitive, prevent the manifestation? Or was it too early in the evening? Some time they ought to stand at the window, watch in hand, and find out when the shadows took shape.

Fred accepted a cup of coffee and they sat down at the kitchen table while Andy signed the complaint—and received a whopping fine for speeding. Meg was unmoved by his howls of anguish. A rich author didn't deserve pity.

"You're lucky I don't lift your license for reckless driving," Fred said severely. "What was the big hurry?" He glanced betrayingly at Meg and then looked quickly away.

"I'm scared to be out in the dark," Andy said caustically. "Cut it out, Fred. Here's your complaint; what are you going to do with it?"

"Can't do much now. If you'd come in the same day. . . . Culver seems to've left town, unless he's hiding in the woods someplace. Anyhow, this'll give me an excuse to grab him if he shows up. I've been looking for a chance to get that guy for quite a while."

They talked about Culver's iniquities and exchanged gossip about former classmates, and then Fred rose to leave. He refused Meg's invitation to supper, but promised to take a rain check. She had started dinner when Andy returned from seeing his friend to the door.

"He's nice," she said.

"A fifty-buck ticket, and you say he's nice? How long till we eat?"

"Fifteen minutes, if you peel the potatoes, and chop 'em up small."

"Good. We've got a hard evening ahead of us."

They worked under the naked light bulbs in the attic until almost midnight. Andy refused to move any more furniture from the room that interested Meg until they had cleared space in the outer rooms. This necessitated carrying things downstairs; there was simply no room in the attic. Meg carried small tables and lamps and chairs; she helped Andy with sofas, chests, and dressers. By the time she made the last trip she was staggering with exhaustion and covered with a paste of dust and perspiration. It was not until she had tumbled into bed that she remembered she had meant to keep an eye on the front windows. If there were shadows outside, she couldn't care less. . . .

The next day was even worse. Andy showed unexpected Simon Legree traits; he drove her, and himself, like an overseer. They worked in the yard all morning; the sky was overcast, but no rain was predicted. The thick coating of dead leaves was a hopeless job; they didn't bother raking, but Andy trimmed the shrubs along the driveway and Meg weeded and gathered up dead branches. At noon Andy decreed that they had done, not enough, but all they could do. They started moving furniture again, and kept it up all afternoon. Meg headed for the library after supper;

but when she reached for her embroidery Andy shook his head.

"Time to clean house," he said cheerfully. "Come on, Meg, you can relax after tomorrow. Tonight we labor and suffer."

The phone rang while they were in the kitchen collecting rags and buckets and brooms. Andy went to answer it. He returned looking pleased.

"Georgia's coming out," he announced. "She said she called all morning, to see if we needed any help. Didn't get an answer."

"We were outside all morning. Why didn't she call this afternoon? It's too late for her to come now."

"She had a client, I guess. It's not too late; she can arrange furniture while we mop floors. I told her she might as well spend the night."

"For God's sake, Andy! That means we've got to make up a bed, clean the bathroom—"

"We're going to clean anyway. Come on, Meg, it makes sense; you said yourself Sylvia will be here at dawn, and she wants Georgia on hand. She can get a ride out from Harry Schlegel, he lives down the road a piece. Also," he added, with a grin, "she can assure Sylvia that we sleep chastely in separate bedrooms."

"Damn it! I wish you hadn't—"

"Why, darling, why this sudden desire to be alone with me? I didn't know you cared."

Meg knew why she was annoyed. Andy had outfoxed her the previous night; she was hoping to try for contact tonight. But there would be no psychic shenanigans with Georgia in the house, and Andy knew it.

She grabbed the vacuum cleaner and dragged it into the hall.

She had worked off some of her annoyance by the time Georgia arrived and announced her presence by pounding on the door and yelling. She had to admit Georgia was a help. She worked like a Trojan, and she had brought some of her own cleaning materials, waxes and polishes that were better than the commercial products for old furniture. It was after midnight when they stopped. Meg was sitting in a yellow brocade armchair, legs stuck straight out ahead of her; but Georgia, leaning on a dry mop as a medieval knight might have leaned on his lance, looked as fresh as Georgia could look.

"Not bad," she said, with a pleased glance around the room. "The carpets make quite a difference. That was a good job, Andy, finding that roll of rugs. Imagine putting Persian carpets away in the attic! This one is a Bokhara and the big one is a Kerman. They'll look even better after they've been cleaned."

"Somebody thought enough of them to pack them full of mothballs," Andy said, wrinkling his nose.

"They look lovely," Meg mumbled. Her eyes closed.

"Wake up, honey, and we'll have a nightcap," Georgia said cheerfully. "I've sure earned it tonight."

She insisted Meg join them in a drink. The alcohol finished the job. Meg was almost asleep as they helped her up the stairs.

The doorbell rang at six forty-five next morning. Meg opened one reluctant eye; then, realizing what was happening, she leaped out of bed with a speed that made her head swim. The bell rang again, impatiently, as she emerged from her room, tying her robe around her. In the hall she met Andy, fully dressed, on his way downstairs.

"Get some clothes on," he ordered. "Make it fast."

Meg fled back into her room, pausing only long enough to pound on Georgia's door. She put on jeans and a shirt and ran a comb through her hair; then she went down, to find Andy helping Sylvia take her coat off. It was a leopard this time; Sylvia looked like a tired old cat.

"You don't look well," Meg said impulsively, after the brief, formal embrace Sylvia permitted. "You didn't have to get here so early, Sylvia."

"I'm not tired. It seems I woke you, though."

"I was upstairs trying to waken Georgia," Meg said evasively.

"She must get up at once. I haven't much time."

"I'll go yell at her," Andy said. "You could probably use some coffee, Sylvia, even if you are twice as strong as we are. How about your chauffeur? What time did that poor guy have to get up?"

"We left Philadelphia at five thirty," Sylvia said in her precise voice. "Courtenay had breakfast before we started, naturally. I don't starve my employees. He'll come in if you want him to help you."

Meg never forgot that day. She had never worked so hard in all her life. She had thought Andy a hard taskmaster, but in comparison to Sylvia he was Little Eva. And Sylvia did it all without ever raising her voice. As Meg was to say later, she now understood how Sylvia had collected so much loot from her various husbands; she only wondered how they had kept so much as a pin for themselves. It was mesmerism, or magic, or something.

When Sylvia looked at you with those cool gray eyes and said, "Do this," you did it.

Sylvia worked as hard as the rest of them, Meg had to admit that. She had brought a surprisingly ordinary little cotton housedress, and as soon as she had had one cup of coffee she put it on. Georgia had stumbled downstairs by then, a gruesome sight in the cold gray dawn. She was swept into Sylvia's wake, and they moved through the house like an orderly hurricane.

At Sylvia's request Meg produced her inventory. Sylvia dismissed the scribbled unfinished pages with a sniff and proceeded to make her own list, in a leather-bound notebook she had brought for the purpose. She didn't argue, though. Meg said, "Keep this," or "We might as well sell that," and Sylvia simply made a note.

Meg had never seen Georgia so subdued. She produced estimates at Sylvia's demand, although once or twice she rolled bloodshot eyes eloquently at Meg when Sylvia insisted on a price for a questionable item. Andy was in a state of suppressed hilarity all morning; whenever Meg caught his eye, which wasn't often, she saw that he was bursting with laughter. He worked, though. So did the chauffeur, a grizzled black man whom Andy greeted like an old friend; apparently he had worked for Andy's father. Meg didn't think Courtenay ought to be doing such heavy work, but she could hardly raise an objection when Sylvia was at the other end of the highboy that was being carried.

Around noon Meg mentioned lunch.

Sylvia fixed her with a piercing stare. "We'll finish first. I never eat lunch when I'm in the middle of a job."

And that ended that. They continued for another hour.

Meg had taken refuge behind a sofa for a well-deserved breather when she saw Sylvia going by under the weight of a heavy carved chair; and the look on her cousin's face made her forget her fatigue and Sylvia's bossiness. She sprang up and took hold of the chair.

"Sylvia, you're positively gray! Andy and I will finish this. Come on—hand over that chair."

She was surprised at her own effrontery, and even more surprised when Sylvia yielded.

"I guess that's about all, really. We'll go into town for lunch—"

"No, we won't," Meg said firmly. "You're going to lie down while I get lunch. Really, Sylvia, you look exhausted."

She took Sylvia into her own room and made her lie down. Then she went to the kitchen and started opening cans. The released prisoners upstairs knocked off as soon as the overseer had left; Georgia came sneaking into the kitchen and collapsed into a chair.

"Damn that woman! She'll drive me into an early grave. Meg, darling, have you got a drink? Just a little, teeny sip of Scotch—or bourbon—or rubbing alcohol—"

"You'd better not risk it yet," Meg said, smiling. "I promise, Georgia, we'll all get drunk after she leaves. Where are Andy and Courtenay?"

"They've gone to the caretaker's cottage. Andy said to tell you they'd open a can of soup or something. Probably he means a bottle of gin. I should have gone with them."

"I'm getting lunch for all of us," Meg said. "Go tell them to come here."

"Uh-uh. Sylvia doesn't eat with the help, honey. Oh,

don't look so shocked. Courtenay is supporting six grand-children, and he wouldn't have a job if Sylvia hadn't kept him on."

"I don't understand people at all," Meg muttered.

"That's because you expect them to act like stock characters—all good or all bad."

"I know the rest of the lecture—I'm still young. I'll know better when I get older. What do you want, chicken noodle soup or cream of mushroom?"

"I don't care. My God, how that woman can work!"

They had no more time for gossip; Sylvia joined them sooner than Meg had expected. She decided she had exaggerated Sylvia's exhaustion. Sylvia looked fine; she ate her soup and cheese sandwich with the air of a prize Persian who has been offered scraps instead of his accustomed creamed liver. When she was finished she glanced at her watch.

"Goodness, it's almost three. I must be off. Where is Courtenay?"

"Waiting in the car," said Andy, making his entrance via the back door. "We've had lunch, Meg. Don't worry."

He winked at her. Meg suspected that Georgia's guess was accurate. They had probably been sitting around drinking beer.

"Well," said Sylvia. "Is there anything we haven't settled? The old place looks nice. I always hated this house," she added.

Meg and Andy exchanged startled looks.

"Why, Sylvia?" Meg asked. "I'm very fond of it."

"It's too isolated, for one thing. You'll be bored to death in six months."

"I don't think so," Meg said. "I can't imagine being bored. I certainly haven't been, so far. . . ." Andy emitted a choking sound, and Meg said hurriedly, "I want to tell you, Sylvia, how much I appreciate your letting me stay here. I really do love it."

"You do? Are you sure?"

"Yes," Meg said, wondering.

"Well, we'll see how you feel after a winter here. As for you, Andy, I spoke to Jack Gordon last week in New York. He's furious with you. Apparently you are already six weeks behind schedule, and he wants to know when the first half of the book will be finished. He has a big publicity campaign all set up."

"Oh, damn," Andy muttered. "Sylvia, I wish you wouldn't—"

"Someone has to keep after you," Sylvia said. "I think you need an agent, Andy. Or a wife." She giggled.

Meg looked at her in astonishment. Sylvia never giggled—or looked coy. She certainly had an odd expression on her face right now.

Andy looked peculiar too. "Hands off, Sylvia," he said. "I admit you're smarter than I am; if you hadn't approached your buddy Gordon, the big-time publisher, I wouldn't be where I am today. Wherever that is. . . . But I'll pick my own wife, thank you. If I ever decide to indulge in that aberration."

"I wouldn't dream of interfering," Sylvia said loftily. "I must go now. I don't like driving at night."

Andy went out for a last word with Courtenay. After Meg had helped Sylvia with her coat, Sylvia turned.

"Are you all right, Meg?"

"I'm fine. Really."

"And you really like it here?"

"I love it, Sylvia."

"How are you and Andy getting one?"

"Oh . . . fine."

"You used to fight," Sylvia said. "I thought at the time. . . . Well. Good-bye, Meg. I'll keep in touch."

She held out her hand; they exchanged the ritual embrace. Meg thought the older woman's arms clung rather more tightly than usual, but she decided she had been mistaken; when Sylvia stepped back her face wore its habitual expression of cool composure.

Sylvia didn't like long farewells, or nods and smiles from the doorway. Meg went back to the kitchen, where Georgia was slumped in her chair like a floppy rag doll. Neither of them spoke till Andy joined them a few minutes later. He leaned over the kitchen counter, looking from one of them to the other, and smiled.

"We can drink to celebrate, or drink to forget," he said. "Or we don't have to drink at all—"

"Not that." Georgia sat up straighter. Her lipstick was gone, except for a ragged pink rim on her lower lip, and the bags under her eyes looked like wrinkled tissue paper.

At six o'clock Andy and Meg hauled Georgia upstairs and Meg put her to bed. When she came out of the bedroom, from which snores already reverberated, Andy was waiting in the hall. His eyes were anxious.

"Is she—"

"Sleeping like a baby. She's just worn out."

They moved a few steps down the hall. Andy, who had matched Georgia drink for drink, showed no signs of intoxication. His eyes were brighter than usual, that was all.

"We shouldn't have let her work so hard," Meg said guiltily. "I keep forgetting she isn't so young."

"Neither is Sylvia," Andy said. "She doesn't look too good, does she?"

"No." Suddenly, to her surprise, Meg felt her eyes flooding with tears. She looked helplessly at Andy. He put out his hand as if to pat her shoulder and then pulled it back.

"It is sad to be old and worn out," he said gently. "But you do as much as you can for them, Meg. I never realized it before, but in her funny way Sylvia thinks a lot of you. Here, now, cheer up. I'll tell you something that will make you good and mad, and then you'll stop feeling sorry for Sylvia. You know what she's up to, don't you?"

"I never know what Sylvia is up to," Meg muttered, wiping her eyes with the back of her hand.

"She's matchmaking," Andy said calmly. "She more or less hinted to me that she'd do well by us if we decided to get married. Jim—Jim Courtenay, he and I were buddies when he worked for Dad—told me she made a new will recently. He drove her to the lawyer."

Andy had been right; this news made Meg forget her sympathy for her cousin.

"But that's—that's medieval," she exclaimed. "You mean she's got some kind of clause in her will, making your inheritance contingent on our getting married? You and your friend Jim are crazy, Andy. How could he know what Sylvia put in her will?"

"Sylvia *is* medieval, love; she thinks she can boss

everybody, and, by God, she's usually right. As for Jim's info, he's known Sylvia for years, and she's not what you would call subtle. She asked Jim a lot of questions about me and the house and so on—the gracious chatelaine chatting with the serf."

"It's the weirdest thing I ever heard of," Meg muttered. She was finding it difficult to meet Andy's eyes.

"The sad thing about Sylvia is that she's defeating her own purposes. If she hadn't tried to bribe me. . . . Look at me, Meg. Don't worry, I'm not going to crush you to me, à la the Sheikh." He laughed softly. "It's the damnedest situation, isn't it? I can't even make love to you; every time I touch you, a whole crowd of ghostly spectators pops into sight. Talk about chaperones!"

"We could try ignoring them," Meg suggested.

Andy stared at her. "I guess we could," he said, and took her in his arms.

The kiss was longer and more desperate than either of them had meant it to be. Meg's head spun; every nerve in her body leaped in response to his touch. And she knew, for there is no mistaking these things, that his response was equally strong. But after a while his arms loosened their hold and when he raised his head, freeing her lips, his eyes were dark with doubt.

Slowly he turned and stared down the length of the long, empty corridor.

"There's nothing there," Meg whispered.

"No. This is the wrong part of the house. But it's still waiting. What are we going to do about this, Meg? Hell's bells, we're too old to cut off our noses to spite Sylvia. I think maybe—just maybe—we could make it work. But not yet. Not while the other thing is hanging over our heads."

"Then we'll have to solve it," Meg said, wishing she could feel as certain as she sounded.

It was easier than she had expected to fall back into their old relationship. They had gone too far too fast, and the resumption of the former roles was a relief. The barrier could not be broken down, it had to be removed piece by piece, with knowledge and understanding.

"So," Andy said, as they were getting a light supper, "how do you feel about moving some more furniture?"

Meg moaned. "I don't ever want to touch another table."

"Neither do I. But we've almost cleared that room. When we shift the slate-topped stand, we can reach the door under the eaves."

"How odd," Meg said slowly. "I'd almost forgotten about that."

"We've had a lot of other things to do. When you read about cases like this, investigations of various kinds, they always read so smoothly. But that's just the author's arrangement of the facts; he leaves out the distractions and interruptions. Life isn't like that. The kids get measles, the puppy chews up the carpet, guests drop in, meals have to be prepared. . . . Don't forget, also, that we've been pursuing a dozen different avenues of research at the same time. Instead of driving straight down the road toward the goal, we've been distracted by side roads and detours. It's like a jigsaw puzzle. We have a lot of pieces in place, but there are still gaps."

"Okay, we'll look. But I don't really expect to find anything."

"It's a missing piece. It may be blank, but we've got to look at it."

Darkness had fallen by the time they went upstairs. Meg paused to look at Georgia. She hadn't stirred.

As soon as they entered the small attic room, Meg knew she had been wrong. There was something waiting for them in the space under the eaves. She felt it, as tangible as a gust of cold air.

Andy's face was sober. Neither of them spoke, except to exchange brief suggestions, as they shifted the few remaining pieces of furniture.

The door was still ajar, as Meg had left it. She looked at Andy.

"Give me the flashlight," he said.

Meg knelt down beside him as he opened the door all the way. He made no move to enter the dark space, but directed the flashlight beam inside.

"Boxes," he said. "Or chests. Something else. Jeez, it's filthy in there. Hold the light."

He had to crawl into the hole in order to reach the contents. He worked methodically, removing all the objects before making any attempt to look at them, and feeling around the dust-covered floor to make sure he hadn't missed anything.

"That's it," he announced, crawling out. His hair was festooned with cobwebs. It looked like an eccentric gray wig.

Meg brushed off encrusted dirt with a cloth. There were two fair-sized wooden boxes and another oblong container of wood bound with rusted metal, plus a roll of indescribably filthy, rotten fabric. This, upon examination, turned out to be draperies. The material had once been bright-green taffeta, as the patches of color in the folds showed.

"Somebody's old drawing-room curtains," Meg said. "Your ancestors were a saving lot."

"Not so saving, or they would have wrapped this up a little more securely." Andy sneezed. Dust billowed up from the fabric as he pushed it away.

The wooden boxes were filled with old clothes. Andy removed the garments one by one, his nose wrinkled fastidiously. A strong smell of camphor accompanied the withdrawal of the garments.

"Mid-nineteenth century," Meg said, as Andy held up a woman's gown. Black satin had turned brown with age, and the jet beads, their fastenings rotted, pattered down like particles of hail. "It's someone's formal mourning attire. They packed it away, for future use; then decided it was out of style when the next death occurred, I suppose. Even the children had to wear black. . . ."

Andy folded the child's black wool pinafore that had come last out of the box. He started replacing the clothes.

Then they both looked at the iron-bound chest. Both knew it was their last hope, and something about its looks of venerable antiquity told them it might be old enough to have something they wanted.

The box was locked. There was no key; Andy had to go all the way downstairs for a chisel and hammer. The blows of steel on steel echoed hollowly, followed by a sharp crack as the hasp gave. Andy wrenched the top back.

"You were right about my ancestors," he said. "They didn't throw anything away."

He began removing the contents of the box, piling them on one side after a cursory examination. Bundles of old letters; account books; diaries, with tarnished gilt clasps; ragged brown pages clipped from newspapers. . . .

They contemplated one another rather blankly across the little mountain of papers.

"That will keep us busy for a month," Andy said gloomily. "We can't even ignore diaries and letters from a later period; someone might have referred to the time we're interested in."

"Yes, we'll have to read every word," Meg agreed, picking up a bundle of letters. "Good God, look at these—crossed and recrossed, and the ink had faded out to nothing. I'll bet some of these stamps are worth money, Andy."

"Why the hell do you suppose anyone would save an ad for Jordan's Finest Horse Collars?" Andy demanded, holding up a crumbling piece of newspaper.

"Maybe it was a bargain. . . . Look at this—some-one's old recipe book. 'Take fourteen eggs and a pound of butter. . . .'"

"These look interesting." Andy had untied another bundle of letters. "The guy was in the army during the Civil War. 'Your affectionate husband, Captain Harold Emig; somewhere in Virginia.'"

Meg giggled. "Here are forty-five installments of a serial that was running in the local paper. 'The Desperate Heart: A Tale of Old Pennsylvania.' Listen to this Andy: 'Annabelle reeled. Kneeling at her feet, Sir Edward wrung his hands and cried, "Dearest lady. . . ."' You ought to learn to write like that, Andy."

She glanced up, and the amusement died on her lips.

Andy was holding a small leather-bound book. The crumbling calf left a dusty brown stain on his hands. Silently he held it out so that she could see the inside front cover.

The marbled paper bore a bookplate with a design Meg knew. The colors—blue and silver—were delicately hand-tinted, and the space under the design had a man's name, in a firm, ornate script. Christian Huber.

Meg's mind was a jumble. The first thing she said had the inanity of utter confusion.

"I didn't know they had bookplates then."

"I remember seeing one that belonged to George Washington. We've lucked out, Meg. This is his journal. And it looks as if your hunch about his name change was right on the mark. Listen. 'Entering upon a new life in a New World, with a new name, what could be more fitting time to begin a new volume of notes and meditations? I have abandoned title, family and home; I abandon my native tongue as well. This alone I retain, for the quest for Eternal Life and Wisdom cannot be abandoned. It has cost me all I possessed, but the price was not too high.' "

"I don't understand," Meg murmured. "What is he talking about?"

Andy was turning the pages. "My wild hunch was right. This confirms it. I know why Christian Huber was murdered."

# Chapter 12

They took their prize to the library, and Meg picked up her embroidery. Andy held the diary; but he was too full of his theory to do more than read isolated excerpts.

"Christian Huber was a Rosicrucian, Meg. Also a Swedenborgian, a Hermetic philosopher, a Gnostic, and probably an Ophite. Before I started reading up on the subject I hadn't heard of half those terms myself; but when you mentioned a cross with a flower as one of the symbols on the sampler, I was reminded of the rose and the cross which are the symbol of Rosicrucianism. Some of the other motifs on the sampler reminded me of things I had read, years ago, when I was a kid interested in the occult. I got a book from the library on magic, and sure enough, it was all there.

"The Ophites considered the serpent in the Garden of Eden to be a good guy, not an evil spirit; it had given man the gift of knowledge, which he was entitled to have. The tree and the serpent became favorite symbols of alchemy.

The Greek letters alpha and omega, which were also on the sampler, indicate eternity; they're the first and last letters of the Greek alphabet. The two in combination are a Christian symbol, but it was also used by various Gnostic sects. Gnosticism was regarded as a heresy by the early Church, and was vigorously persecuted. The Gnostics believed in the pursuit of wisdom. They dabbled in magic, which included a lot of things in those days that we wouldn't consider particularly mysterious. Alchemy was one of those pursuits. You could call it the great-grandfather of chemistry, although in the beginning it was based on mystical ideas that have no scientific value. Still, in their quest for the Philosopher's Stone, which could change base metals to gold and grant eternal life, the alchemists hit on a number of ideas which they handed on to modern chemists.

"I suspected Huber—I can't think of him by his real name yet—was an alchemist when we saw his study-bedroom. You remember the bottles and boxes and re-torts?"

"Well, at least I've a vague idea of what alchemy was," Meg said. "I've never heard of those other things. What was a Swedenborgian?"

"Present tense, not past. Some people still believe in the teachings of Emanual Swedenborg. He was a Swedish scholar, born in 1688; a brilliant mathematician and scientist. Later in his career he cracked up—or saw the light, however you look at it. He became a mystic and a clairvoyant. They say he saw the great Stockholm fire—from his home three hundred miles away. Huber may have corresponded with him while he was developing his theories; although, of course, the Swedenborgian church wasn't founded until long after Huber's death.

"All these mystical sects, or faiths, had certain ideas in common. Hermetic philosophy is based on the books of a mythical Egyptian character named Hermes Trismegistus. The secrets of the faith were expressed as allegories to keep the profane from understanding them. Here's an example, quoted by Christian Huber in his diary:

" 'That which is above is like that which is below, to perpetuate the miracles of One thing. And as all things have been derived from one, by the thought of one, so all things are born from this thing—' "

"Stop it, you're making my head ache. That's crazy!"

Andy shrugged. "Maybe. But I can't help admiring these men. They wanted to *know*. They couldn't accept the smug dogmas of the established Church, which demanded faith instead of understanding. They risked fire—hellfire in eternal damnation, and the fires of the Inquisition on earth—to find out. They were brilliant, imaginative thinkers, many of them; if they fell into error, at least the errors were original, not the complacent acceptance of doctrinal stupidities.

"Anyhow, that's what Christian Huber was—a philosopher, a mystic, an alchemist. It's all in here—quotes from Hermetic and Gnostic books, notes on his experiments. What a mind the man had! He was interested in everything—plants and their properties, the habits of animals and birds. . . ."

"But not people," Meg said.

"What?"

"He wasn't interested in people. At the beginning, when

he says he has given up everything, lost everything—he doesn't even mention Anna Maria. I don't think much of him if he forgets his grandchild in favor of some wild-eyed system of philosophy."

"This wasn't meant to be a diary," Andy protested. "He just jotted down his ideas as they came to him."

"Then I don't see how it can help us. Doesn't he say anything about his life here, or why he had to leave Europe?"

"I haven't read the whole thing yet. He has a few paragraphs of more or less mundane comment stuck in between experiments. Here's one: 'Pastor Klemm called on me today. A good man, but foolish. He cannot offer crumbs to one who has tasted the divine elixir.'"

"If that's the best he can do, we're out of luck."

"All right, if you're going to be so critical, I'll tell you what I think happened. Everything I've read confirms my theory, only you have to know how to interpret it."

"So interpret," Meg said grumpily. She was getting annoyed with Christian Huber.

"Huber—or von Friedland—was a fugitive. What from, I don't know, but I can guess. I think he was run out of some small German state because of his heretical ideas and practices. The Inquisition was dying, but some of the German areas were devoutly Catholic, and Huber was not mealymouthed. It's also possible that he was involved in a plot against the local ruler. The Rosicrucians of that time were regarded as a secret society, and they were not above dabbling in politics in order to promote the ideal world they believed in. Even the Masons were suspected of espionage in their early days. Remember one of the Three

Musketeers books, where the old schemer Aramis becomes the director general of a secret Masonic organization and tries to replace Louis the Fourteenth with his brother, the Man in the Iron Mask?

"Why Huber left doesn't matter. The important thing is that he didn't learn discretion from his experience in Europe. He continued his experiments in this country; he refused to go to the local church and he talked too freely of his wild ideas. The colony was supposed to be based on a concept of religious freedom, but that didn't give a man freedom to be an out-and-out atheist, or to dabble in Black Magic. Huber's honest, stupid neighbors thought he was a warlock. Oh, yes, it's all here—scattered but consistent. The pastor called on him several times. He must have been a good man and a little brighter than his flock. He warned Huber to shut up, if he couldn't conform:

"'Again the pastor. He took me from my search for the alkahest, and I was short with him. How anger clouds the mind! I must cultivate patience; but he maddens me, with his warnings and his threats. What have I to do with the superstitious fears of these poor deluded farmers? I was forced to agree with him concerning old Berthe, and I have forbidden her to continue with her vile practices. She deludes the peasants, promising them good fortune, wealth, love. . . . Nota bene: my amusement when the pastor said my neighbors equate my experiments with Berthe's petty tricks.'

"Old Berthe was practicing witchcraft," Andy went on. "Petty stuff, as Huber says—sticking pins in waxen images, mixing up love philters and curing the ague. Naturally the neighbors couldn't understand the difference between her games and his serious studies. The fact that she was a practicing witch confirmed their suspicions about Huber.

"You have a point when you accuse him of being disinterested in people. If he had been a little more concerned with human feelings and a little more tolerant of human stupidity, the tragedy might not have happened. They say the burned child shuns the fire, but that's a lie; some kids keep on burning themselves, not because they forget the pain but because they think maybe it won't happen the next time. Huber was like that. He couldn't believe people could act irrationally. He jeers at the pastor's warnings. Other people warned him too, including his granddaughter. Yes, he mentions her now and then. The longest reference is a paragraph where he says he will allow her to go to church, since she insists; it can't do any harm, and maybe it will keep the pastor off his back."

"What a selfish old man! She wasn't a—whatever he was, then? The symbols on the sampler—"

"She probably copied them from his books because she thought they were pretty, and she knew he had a high regard for them. No, she wasn't a convert. She didn't even assist him in his experiments.

"She's the really tragic figure. Huber and the old servant share the responsibility; their behavior led to their destruction. But the girl was wiped out, not for what she had done, but for what she was—Huber's granddaughter, tarred by association with his heresy. They were killed for the same reason Blymire's victim was killed in 1923, in that hex case I told you about—by ignorant men who thought they were witches and heretics. It wouldn't take much to convince the killers that they had been hexed—a few sick cows, the death of a child. People are always looking for scapegoats, and you could say Huber asked for it."

"It sounds convincing," Meg said slowly. "You can't prove it, though. I don't suppose the last entry—"

"There are no dates, so I can't be sure when it was written. It's all about the alkahest—the perfect solvent that would dissolve all matter. But I'm sure I'm right, Meg."

"Maybe you are. But it doesn't solve anything, really."

"No."

The next morning was mild and foggy. Meg decided that the humidity accounted for the feeling of oppression that surrounded her from the moment she awoke. She and Andy got Georgia up and more or less awake; then Andy took Georgia home. She gave Meg a feeble smile and a feebler handclasp when she left.

"Call you later. God, what a hangover!"

As soon as the car had pulled away, Meg went to the library and took up Huber's journal. She was still reading it when Andy came back.

"Anything new in town?" she asked.

"Rumors are flying. Four different dealers stopped me to ask when Sylvia's going to start selling. There is a distinct impression that we've found a treasure trove."

"Well, Georgia can handle them. Sylvia put her in charge of the selling end."

Meg returned to the book. Andy hovered, shifting from one foot to the other.

"What is it?" Meg demanded.

"Culver's back. Somebody saw him last night."

"Oh, Lord. I hoped we'd seen the last of him."

"So did I. Cherry wasn't with him."

"You don't suppose . . ." Meg began.

"No, if you mean do I suppose Culver has done her in and buried her in the woods." Andy fingered the healing scratches on his face. "I'd back Cherry against Culver any day. She's probably split."

"I never thought that relationship was permanent," Meg agreed. "Anything else?"

"Cold front coming in from Canada," Andy said brightly. "Better get your woollies out."

"Thanks. Now why don't *you* split and leave me alone?"

"I'm restless. What are you reading? Oh, the journal. Found anything I missed?"

"Not much. He lapses into German every now and then, did you notice? I guess when he got excited he forgot his resolution to stick to English."

"I noticed, but I couldn't do anything about it. I don't understand German. Hey . . . do you . . . ?"

"I took it in high school. I can't make much of this, though; it's scholarly German and it's all about Huber's experiments. That was what he got excited about, not his family. You know, I can understand why his neighbors thought he was a magician. He was trying to raise ghosts."

Andy looked interested.

"Not ghosts, Meg. Not if you mean the spirits of the dead. That would make him a necromancer, a black magician. He wasn't that. Maybe he was trying to summon spiritual entities that could help him in his alchemical studies. Or else—the alchemists believed that everything that had once lived could be re-created. Like the spirit of the rose."

"*La spectre de la rose?* You mentioned that the other night."

"Most people know the music and the ballet, but few music lovers realize that the plot is based on alchemy. What you do is you take a flask and put in it the ashes of a rose, mixed with morning dew. Seal the flask and put it on a pile of horse manure—no, I'm not kidding, that's what the recipe says—and leave it for a month. Expose it alternately to sunlight and moonlight. Eventually the specter of the rose will appear in all its original beauty— leaves, petals, all intact. It will disappear when the flask is cooled and reappear when it's heated."

"He wasn't re-creating plants," Meg said. "He talks about people; the spirits of human beings."

"He succeeded?"

"Well, he thought he did. There's one entry that's all scribbled, he got so excited; but it says something about the spirit of young Hermes, and the pentagram, and so on."

"Good Lord. That sounds like necromancy all right. No wonder he got in trouble if he bragged about that."

"There's one thing," Meg said, dismissing this piece of useless information. "Your ancestor, John Emig, did have a son who was in love with the girl. Christian mentions the fact; I'm surprised he considered it worth recording. He even shows a touch of human vanity; says a farmer's son shouldn't aspire to marry a von Friedland. Besides, the girl was only fifteen at the time."

"They married young," Andy said. "You want to take a walk or something?"

"Later, maybe. I want to read some more."

Andy wandered off. Meg went on reading, but found no more useful information. She was exasperated with Christian Huber, and she felt a profound pity for Anna Maria, shut up with a cold old man and a mumbling old servant.

At noon Andy returned and insisted that she come with him. He had packed a picnic. Meg yielded, recognizing his need to get away from the house for a while.

The force of the wind, as they left the house, took her breath away. It was noticeably cooler, despite the fact that the sun was fighting through scattered clouds.

It was warmer in the woods, where trees broke the force of the wind. They ate their lunch in the clearing they had found earlier, and then walked for several hours. Andy was not feeling chatty; he spoke seldom, and then only to comment on some feature of the woods. Meg was in no mood for trivial talk either, and a mounting sense of oppression kept her silent. She couldn't blame it on the weather, not with the keen wind blowing away clouds as it ought to have blown away mental cobwebs.

The sun was setting in brilliant angry streaks of color as they reached the front door. Andy opened it. To Meg, it was as if invisible hands were reaching out for her, so strong was the sense of anticipation. As soon as she was over the threshold, the feeling left her. The house waited, but not for her.

Andy didn't seem to notice anything, but he lingered in the doorway before coming in. "Want a drink?" he asked casually.

"After seeing Georgia, I'm beginning to think I should

go on the wagon. Oh, all right. I'll see what there is in the freezer. It's been a long time since lunch."

The bright, cheerful aspect of the yellow-painted kitchen restored some of her confidence. The setting sun, pouring in the western window, gave a brilliant theatrical glow to the countertops and chrome. After she had taken meat from the freezer she went upstairs to change clothes. The house was cool. Meg took out sweater and slacks; then she changed her mind and reached for her long blue robe. She heard Andy pass her door and then ascend the stairs to the attic. What was he doing up there?

She went back to the kitchen and started dinner. Andy joined her after a while. He was carrying a bundle of papers—one of the packets of letters they had found in the chest.

"Thought I'd look at the Civil War letters," he explained, sitting down at the kitchen table.

"Turn on the light, why don't you. It's getting dark."

Meg went to the sink to clean vegetables for a salad. There she noticed a small pile of letters on the countertop.

"What's this?"

"Oh, I forgot. I picked up the mail this morning. There isn't anything much, just catalogs and junk mail."

"Junk mail, indeed." Meg picked up a brown paper parcel. "This is for me from Mrs. Adams. It must be the book she promised to lend me."

Andy grunted. He was deep in the letters. Meg ripped the wrappings off the parcel and found what she had expected—the Sadler-Gross-Emig genealogy. It was a thick, scholarly-looking book bound in dark-green cloth, worn by much handling.

Meg put it aside until she had cleaned the lettuce and tomatoes. Then she wiped her hands carefully—it wouldn't do to damage one of Mrs. Adams' treasured books—and sat down across from Andy. The chicken was sizzling gently under the broiler.

"You ought to look at this, Andy," she said, after a while. "It puts your cousin Emig to shame. He wasn't very accurate."

"Anything I ought to know?"

"It's pretty dull," Meg admitted, turning pages. "Two Gross boys married Sadler girls, and a Sadler boy married an Emig; that's how the families are connected. Oh—here's your great—whatever he was—grandfather, Benjamin. It's the same portrait that was in the other book. Family resemblances are funny things. He looks a lot like his son and his grandson—that thick jaw and bulbous nose. You don't look like that."

"I resemble my father's family," Andy said, without looking up from his letters. "The handsome Brenners," he added.

Meg snorted. "Handsome is as handsome does—as Mrs. Adams might say. Your mother's ancestors were a pious crowd, even if they weren't pretty. John Emig sounds like a prize bigot. His daughter committed suicide. Hanged herself."

"What the hell—" Andy looked up.

"That's what it says here. She got herself pregnant by an infidel—a Lutheran. Emig belonged to a narrow, straitlaced sect that considered everybody else damned. He locked the girl up in the attic on bread and water and she—"

"My God," Andy muttered. "I thought things like that only happened in folk songs."

"He was married four times," Meg went on. "The first three wives died young. No wonder. Everybody had to work till midnight Saturday and start again at midnight Sunday, to make up for resting on the Sabbath."

"Don't tell me anything more about the old bastard," Andy begged.

"He didn't prosper, though. Not at first. Those feeble wives of his kept dying on him—inconsiderate women. . . . The infant-mortality rate in the family was even higher than the average—which wasn't low. The author says John was so parsimonious he wouldn't feed the cattle enough to keep them healthy. Imagine what he fed his kids."

"Enough," Andy said with a groan. "Please—"

"He figured God was chastising him," Meg went on remorselessly. "I would have, if I'd been God. . . . You'll be sorry to hear that in later life he became rich and respected throughout the colony."

Andy refused to comment. Meg took pity on him and turned the page.

"No Hubers," she announced, after an interval.

"What?"

"No Hubers in the family tree. That finishes your idea that Anna Maria married an Emig. I believe this man; nobody could write a book as dull as this and get his facts wrong."

"How do you know there aren't any Hubers?"

"There's an index." Meg demonstrated, lifting the book and riffling through the back pages. As she did so, a white rectangle slipped out of the book. It was a letter, addressed to Meg. Mrs. Adams had cheated the United States mails; the package had been sent at the lower rate appropriate to printed matter. Meg opened the letter.

"You've got to see this," she said. "She's underlined every other word. What an old darling she is. All these vague hints. . . . That's funny."

Altered by the change in her voice, Andy looked up.

"Here it is again," Meg said. "The suggestion that your family is related to the Hubers. She says, 'It is, of course, only a legend, part of the family tradition, that I pass on; perhaps I ought to have mentioned it when I saw you, but I hesitate, even now, to recall such a tragedy.' What do you suppose she means?"

"God only knows. Why don't you shut up and let me read these letters?"

Meg paid no attention; she was too absorbed in what she was reading. After the first few words she began to read aloud.

". . . the legend concerns the young soldier of militia, stationed in a nearby town, who was the girl's lover. Word reached the doomed family, early that evening, that danger threatened. The legend does not name the messenger; he was presumably a neighbor who suspected the assassins' intentions. He feared their vengeance too much to remain, but he consented to carry an appeal from the young woman to her betrothed, in the nearby town. She would not leave her grandfather, who refused to take the warning seriously. There was ample time, she declared, for help to reach them. And so there would have been, had the captain heeded the appeal. It was faithfully delivered, although it took the unknown messenger too long to find his quarry; and when he finally ran him to earth he found the young soldier drinking and dicing in a tavern. He laughed at the wild message, and the messenger dared not linger. Later, when the wine was gone,

the young man reconsidered. He set out for the lonely
farmhouse, though he thought the message foolish; and when
he arrived, he found—but you know what he found.

"There is an equally tragic sequel, according to the same
legend. For several days the neighbors searched the woods
for the missing girl, to no avail. On the third day a body
was found—not the body of the girl, but that of her lover.
He had been shot with his own pistol. Since the rites of his
faith condemned the suicide to unhallowed ground, his
family insisted that he had been the victim of an unfortunate accident. Their appeal was successful; but those who
knew felt that the young man had taken his own life,
overcome by his sense of guilt at having failed to—' "

Andy's chair went over with a splintering crash. When
Meg looked up she saw him leaning toward her, across the
table; his hands were pressed hard against its surface and
his eyes looked almost black.

"What is this?" he asked, in a queer, quiet voice. "Some
crazy idea of therapy? Sylvia told you, I suppose. What did
she tell you? That smug, sanctimonious. . . . She never
knew the half of it. Both of you, thinking you know what's
good for other people. . . . I was all right till you came
here. I had it under control. I stopped dreaming. It wasn't
my fault! How did I know she was really taking the
damned stuff? It wasn't the first time she called me. Five,
six times before. . . . False alarms, all of them. I'd go
tearing over to her place, scared out of my wits, stomach
pump in hand—and find her sitting there doing that
damned embroidery, grinning at me. How was I supposed
to know that the last time she really had taken an

overdose? I had an appointment that evening. With the publisher, about my book. If I had gone. . . ."

He stopped for breath. His voice had gradually risen, become shriller and quicker. Meg felt sick. The tumbling, incoherent words made terrible sense to her.

"If you had gone, you'd have been in time to save her life," she said, through stiff lips. "Who was she? Someone who loved you? Someone you loved—once? But you had stopped loving her. You must have, or you would have gone to her. She wouldn't have died."

"Love!" Andy laughed wildly. "What are you talking about? She was just a girl, a girl I . . . knew. One of those things. . . . But she wouldn't let go. She kept talking about love too. You women always do. She didn't love me. She used me—as an audience for her sick performances. The way you're using me now! You invented that bloody legend. You must have; it fits too damned well. You—always you! The catalyst, the focus— you and your obsession with a dead girl. I was all right, everything was all right, till you came!"

"No," Meg said. "Not me—you. Not my obsession with a dead girl—your guilt and your shame, the catalyst that invokes his guilt and his shame. That's what you feel, in the drawing room, out there under the tree—his horror, when he learned what had happened. She waited, and he didn't come. She's still waiting. I didn't make it up, Andy. Read the letter, if you don't believe me. No wonder he can't rest. He died in mortal sin, taking his own life; guilt and remorse had driven him mad. My God, if ever a house deserved to be haunted, this one does!"

Andy's body sagged until his whole weight rested on his hands, flat against the table. He began to shiver.

"The house isn't haunted," he said, trying to control his voice. "You're right. It's me, not the house. I try to justify myself, make excuses; but the hard fact remains, I failed another human being who needed help. It doesn't matter what she was, or how I felt about her. She needed help and I didn't give it. I'm doing it again now—trying to blame you for something I caused. You caught it from me, like a bad cold in the head. All my fault, always my fault. There's only one way of dealing with a spiritual leper. . . . Everything I touch. . . . I won't let it happen to you."

He turned and walked out of the room.

The movement was so sudden Meg didn't understand at first. When realization dawned she felt a stab of terror that made her former fears tolerable by comparison. She ran after him.

Gray moonlight filtered in through the curtained rect-angles of glass flanking the front door. The wind was rising, sweeping away the last of the clouds. Meg could hear it battering the trees and whistling around the eaves.

She paused long enough to turn on the lights. She craved light as a starving man craves food; there was too much darkness, all around. Andy stopped, putting his hand up to shield his eyes. As Meg ran to him he turned a blank face toward her and waited, with a dreadful remote courtesy, to hear what she had to say.

"That's not the way," Meg shouted, shaking him; she would have said anything, done anything, to bring some emotion into that white mask of a face. "We're both wrong, Andy. It isn't you or me alone; it's both of us. The thing is here, it's been here all along; we only gave it an opening, a way through. Feeling guilty doesn't help. It just makes things worse. Guilt is a cheap way of copping out. Andy, help me. I think I'm in love with you. Don't walk out on me."

A flicker of emotion marred the calm of Andy's face.

"I think I'm in love with you too. That's why I can't stay around you."

He shook Meg off with a dispassionate violence that sent her staggering back, and opened the front door.

From where she stood, flattened and breathless against the wall, she felt it like a wave of icy water. She saw, too—straight past Andy's motionless body, out across the lawn.

They were not shadows. They were men, or the exact similaera of what had once been human. Three of them. Tall, burly men, bearded; dressed in somber black, with broad-brimmed black hats pulled low over their foreheads. The moonlight was bright, but not bright enough to show them so distinctly, for they stood in the shadow of the oak tree. Another kind of light, faint yet sufficient, shone around them, so that Meg could make out even their features. But that wasn't the worst thing. The worst thing was that she knew one of them—recognized the heavy jutting jaw and the bulbous nose. He looked incredibly like his descendant, the Benjamin Emig who had built Trail's End, but he had never known this house. He and his companions were standing before another house. Trapped in a spiderweb of time, they eternally repeated the crime they had committed over two hundred years before. The murderer of Christian Huber was his neighbor, Andy's ancestor, John Emig.

# Chapter 13

Meg never remembered how she got the door closed. She crawled the last few feet; it was like making progress underwater, in freezing Arctic cold. But she did it, somehow, and when she stood gasping, her back against the wooden panel, she saw that something had happened to Andy. His face was not a pleasant sight; too many emotions warred for supremacy on his features.

"They moved," he said.

"I know." Meg's teeth were chattering. "None of them ever moved before. Andy, you were wrong about the date, you must have been. This is the night. This is what they've been working up to, all along."

"The date." Andy clutched his head in both hands. "My brain's all shook up, I can't think. . . . I've got to. What is it, about a date . . . ?"

Spinning around, he ran toward the drawing room.

Meg followed, the old fear revived, but when she saw what he was doing, fear yielded to relief and then to bewilderment. He was kneeling on the floor in front of the bookcase. Before him was an open volume of the encyclopedia.

When he looked up, his face was alight with an incredible amusement.

"October eleventh," he said. "That was the date of the murder, wasn't it? I wasn't wrong about that; you checked the newspapers, they agreed. But in 1752 England revised the old Gregorian calendar. It was based on a year of three hundred sixty-five and a quarter days. The astronomical year is longer than that by several minutes; in 1752 the calendar was more than a week off. So they fixed it, by adding ten days. Every date before 1752 is ten days off, according to our reckoning. Modern historians automatically correct for that. Apparently my source didn't, and the newspaper account naturally had the old date. The old October eleventh is our October twenty-first. Today."

Meg nodded dumbly. The news didn't reassure her. She couldn't understand why it had had such an electrifying effect on Andy. He saw her confusion; rising to his feet, he came toward her.

"Don't you see? If my confused subconscious made that complex calendrical adjustment when it invented a stable of ghosts, I take off my hat to it. I read something about the change in the calendar—somewhere, sometime—but I don't recall ever reading the precise number of days involved. The ghosts are real, Meg. I'm not—completely crazy."

Meg's knees gave way. She caught at the back of a chair for support.

"All right," she said. It was an inadequate response; but

at moments of extreme emotion the mind is often reduced to inconsequentialities. Meg's emotions were all at fever pitch; overriding the others was simple animal terror. "So do something. I can't stand much more. You saw—you recognized him, didn't you?"

"Yes. Ordinarily I'd be mildly distressed to find a murderer among my ancestors. Right now I can't seem to worry about it. Let's see. . . ." He went to the window and drew the draperies back. After a moment he turned to Meg. "They're moving, all right," he said flatly. "Slowly; but they are coming. I still say they can't hurt us, Meg. They aren't real. What can they do?"

"Do you want to stick around and find out?" Meg asked. Her teeth were still chattering.

"My poor love." He held out his arms. "Shall we risk it?"

Meg didn't hesitate. She stumbled across the space that separated them and fell into his embrace. She wanted to close her eyes, but they weren't working very well; they stared, wide, as the shadows shivered and the penultimate vision shaped itself.

It was night in the other room, which was lighted by firelight and the glow of candles. They were all there— Christian Huber, his granddaughter, and the old servant, who was huddled by the hearth in boneless, mindless terror. Huber stood by the table. The girl clung to his arm. She was no longer pretty; her open mouth was a black hole, and her face was witless with fear. Christian's other hand held his sword. He had been a fine figure of a man in youth, and he still looked magnificent—straight and slim as a boy one quarter of his age, his white hair rampant and his face flushed with defiance. In the last minutes before the end, the old man's philosophy had deserted him. He knew the truth and faced it like a soldier.

Meg blinked. When she opened her eyes, the room was back to normal.

"So long as that's over. . . ." said Andy, and kissed her.

For a few seconds Meg forgot ghosts, murders, and all minor details. Then memory returned; she pushed at Andy till he let her go.

"How can you do that at a time like this?" she demanded, outraged.

Andy laughed. His face was flushed; his hair, damp with perspiration, stuck up in absurd wisps. He looked drunk.

"I'm fey. How much can a poor worn-out brain stand before it cracks? Old Huber shaped up, didn't he, at the last minute? I wonder how much damage he inflicted before they got him. Clubs against a single blade—he couldn't last long. But I'll bet a few of the sanctimonious jurymen at the hearing had bandages under their black clothes."

"Andy . . ." Meg groaned.

"Okay, okay. Suppose we try to get out of here. Maybe the back door is unguarded. Unless you want to retreat to the attic? It's above the space occupied by the earlier house."

"I want out," said Meg emphatically. "No, don't look out the window. Let's go."

Hand in hand they ran through the hall and into the passage that led to the kitchen. Andy kept turning on lights as they went; he shared Meg's hatred of darkness. The final light, the one in the kitchen, brought an incongruous figure out of the darkness—a man who stood paralyzed by their sudden eruption into the room.

Culver was a pitiable sight. He was wearing a stained, torn jacket over his familiar T shirt. His eyes were rimmed with red. His mouth gaped open; a thin trickle of saliva oozed out of one corner. He looked sick, undernourished—and dangerous. The reddened eyes were as mad as those of a rabid fox.

"You're not supposed to be here," he said suddenly. "Why didn't you stay in the other room? I have a rope." He pulled his jacket aside and showed them; the rope was coiled around his meager waist. "I was gonna lower the stuff from the window and then get out the same way. You wouldn't ever know. Now you've loused it up! Why couldn't you stay where you belong?"

He put his hand in the pocket of his jacket. Meg gasped, and grabbed at Andy, who was making queer gurgling noises. He shook her off.

"First ghosts," said Andy, getting his voice under control with an effort. "Haunted houses, homicidal maniacs on the family tree, murderers besieging the house—and now this. A goddamned rotten little junky burglar! I tell you, I've had it. This is too damned much!"

Meg doubted whether he ever saw the gun, but he probably would have done the same thing even if he had seen it. He was literally beside himself.

The gun went off with a flash and a roar. Andy's body jerked back; he stood swaying by the counter, which had stopped his backward movement. An expression of intense surprise spread over his face; he looked down at his sleeve, where a trickle of blood had started to spread.

Culver looked just as surprised. The gun dangled loosely from his hand. Meg couldn't decide whether to jump at him or to help Andy. He did not appear to be in immediate danger of collapse. On the other hand, Meg was a self-confessed coward, and Culver's reactions, with or without a gun, were totally unpredictable.

Culver solved the problem for her. Waving the gun in all directions, he backed out of the room. His footsteps pounded along the hall and went up the stairs. A single-minded man, he was still after the antiques.

"He's flipped," she said, staring at Andy. "Does he really think we're going to let him—"

"I'm going to let him do any little thing he wants, as long as he has a gun," Andy said. "Damn. I didn't think he had the guts to use it."

He was clutching his upper arm, but the blood still spread. It was dripping from his fingertips now. Meg started toward him, but he shook his head.

"We've got to get to a phone. Come on, the extension in the library is the closest."

He was gone before she could say anything. Meg stared at the small red puddle on the floor by the counter. Jerking open one of the drawers, she grabbed a fistful of cloth— dishcloths, potholders, anything—and went after Andy.

She could hear Culver on the floor above. He was running back and forth like a mad thing; an occasional crash marked his progress. When Meg burst into the library, Andy was on the phone. His face was twisted with pain and anger.

"Goddamn it, I don't care if you are tied up with a car crash on 40-S. I've got a hopped-up maniac with a gun here! I'm wounded; I'm bleeding. . . ." He let out a convincing yell as Meg started winding dishcloths around his arm. "See? All right, for God's sake make it fast!"

He dropped the phone with a crash and caught at the desk.

"I can't do much except stop the bleeding," Meg muttered. "I'm sorry if it hurts. . . ."

"Okay." Andy sank his teeth into his lower lip. "Hurry up. We've got to get out of here before he—Oh, no. No, not now, this is no time for—"

His good arm went around Meg and they clung together. There was no way of stopping it once it began, and somehow they both knew that this vision would be different from all the others. The aura of breathless waiting, the supernatural horror blended into a single overpowering force, robbing them of the power of movement. When the shadow room took shape it had a reality it had never had before. The girl was solid and alive. Meg knew that if she reached out she would feel warm, living flesh.

Anna Maria was close enough to touch. She was in the act of whirling around; her skirts whipped out, her unbound hair was a veil of gold against the shadows of the night-dark kitchen. Her face was set in a glare of horror, and on the breast of her blue gown a dark stain glistened wetly. It was not her blood; Meg knew instinctively that her dying grandfather's head had rested there for a moment before Anna Maria fled from his killers.

Meg forgot Culver and his gun. The girl's plight was as real to her as her own. Once, when she had seen *Hamlet* superbly acted on the stage, she had found herself praying, absurdly, that the beleaguered Prince of Denmark would escape this time, and confound his enemies. This was the same irrational hope, intensified beyond endurance. She wanted to scream at the girl: "Run, hurry, get away!" Whatever fate she had met in 1740, Anna Maria was now dust; and yet Meg felt as if she saw a living, breathing girl who might be saved. There was no one in the firelit kitchen except Anna Maria, but she had turned to stare in terror at something, or someone. The murderers must be close on her heels.

Then Meg's heart gave a single, suffocating beat. The girl was breathing. She saw the small breasts rise and fall. For the first time, their vision was animated.

Anna Maria's head turned. Her eyes stared straight into Meg's, and widened until the whites showed all around the pupils. For a long moment the two girls, the living and the dead, looked into one another's eyes. Then Anna Maria's lids dropped. Her slender body crumpled. As she fell, the picture dimmed; it was gone before they saw her body strike the floor.

Andy's arm was like an iron bar around Meg's waist. She could hardly breathe; when she heard the screaming wail in the distance she thought at first it was the last faint echo of Anna Maria's terror.

"The police, God bless 'em," said Andy, in her ear.

"She saw me," Meg gasped. "Andy, she—"

"I know, I know, but there isn't time for that now. When Culver hears that siren he'll lose what few wits he's got left. I don't want to be in his way when he does. For Christ's sake, Meg . . ."

He dragged her toward the door. Meg tried to walk, but her knees felt disconnected. Then Andy stopped. The siren was coming closer, and Culver's feet were pounding down the stairs. He was screaming. Meg couldn't make out the words.

Andy pulled her back against the wall. It was too late to leave the room now, they would just have to hope Culver wouldn't come looking for them, in a final orgy of destruction.

Culver ran into the drawing room. A lamp went over with a crash. Then the running footsteps came back. Andy looked desperately around for something to use as a weapon; but the footsteps passed the door and went on. He was in the hall. Meg heard the front door open. The sound of the police siren burst in, it must be on the drive by now.

Then they heard a sound neither of them ever forgot. It was audible even over the mechanical scream of the siren, and it came from a human throat. Meg didn't know when it stopped. It blended with the noise of the siren, and when the latter cut off, a silence like death descended on the house.

Finally Andy stirred. "Shall we have hysterics now, or wait a while?"

"I'm all right," Meg whispered.

"Then let's go greet the calvary. Right on time."

But he hadn't taken two steps before he swayed and collapsed. Meg was kneeling beside him when Fred found them.

## II

"No," Fred said. "We never fired a shot. He took one look at us and keeled over. Must have been his heart. There wasn't a mark on him—except needle marks."

They were sitting in the kitchen. Fred had his notebook open. Andy was drinking coffee strongly sweet with sugar; he had requested brandy, but had been refused. His arm had been bandaged and was in a sling; he was full of penicillin and tetanus serum and pain killer, but the alert glitter in his eye told Meg he had no intention of obeying the doctor's order to go to bed until certain matters had been settled. Anyhow, as he pointed out, Fred had to write his report.

Fred had moved fast when the desk sergeant passed on Andy's call for help. He had even brought along a doctor from the scene of the auto crash, where the injured had been sent off to the hospital. The other officials had left now, taking Culver's body with them, and Fred was winding up the case, as he said with youthful satisfaction.

"Now then," he said, licking his pencil. "You say you found him in the kitchen when you came out—for a snack, or something?"

"Or something," Andy agreed.

"Then he shot you." Fred shook his head reproachfully. "Never jump a guy with a gun, Andy. Especially a junky."

"Belated, but useful, advice. I'll keep it in mind."

"From what he said, you figured he was planning on stealing some more stuff. The town's all excited since Sylvia was here; they figure you found something valuable or she wouldn't bother coming. I guess Culver heard the stories. He's been hiding out in the woods. I could almost feel sorry for the poor devil, now he's dead. Living like an animal out there."

"There never was any hope for him," Andy said. "I wonder what it was that drove him to kill himself."

"Naw, he didn't kill himself," Fred said. "Oh. Yeah, I see what you mean. Well, I'm glad I don't have the poor bastard's death on my conscience. We never touched him. I could see him plain in the headlights when we pulled up. He was on the porch steps. I thought for a minute he was going to go for his gun, but he just let it fall. God, I never saw such a look on a guy's face. I guess he knew he was caught. He just plain scared himself to death. You could call that suicide, I guess."

He closed his notebook.

"Well," he said, more cheerfully, "that about winds it up. You better go to bed, Andy. Want me to help you upstairs?"

"I didn't get a shot in the leg," said Andy coldly. "Run along, Fred; I'm sure the good citizens of Pennsylvania need you more than I do."

"Okay." Grinning, Fred slapped him on the back. Andy's eyes opened wide, and Meg said indignantly,

"Hey, that hurt!"

"Oh, I forgot. Well, good night, all."

They let him find his own way out. The front door slammed.

"Heart failure," Meg said.

"You're thinking what I'm thinking."

"Drugs can induce hallucinations. Or visions."

"And fear, sheer terror, can stop a man's heart. We know what it felt like—out there—and we felt it from a distance. Imagine running right into it, not even suspecting it was there until you were face to face with them. . . . I guess old John Emig can carve another notch on his gun."

Meg shivered. "Want some more coffee?" she asked.

"No, thanks."

"Want to go to bed?"

"Give me about twenty-four hours," said Andy. "I heal quick."

"I didn't mean that."

"I did." He put his hand over hers, which lay limply on the tabletop. "Meg, I'll risk it if you will. I have a feeling the worst is over—with me, and with the house. We don't have to stay here—"

"I want to stay. Maybe Sylvia will let us have the house. Maybe I can get a job in Wasserburg. I don't know whether the worst is over—and I don't care. Maybe the whole horrible business repeats itself every year, over and over, like a broken record. We'll get used to it, after ten or fifteen years."

Andy laughed.

"Nod politely to Anna Maria as we pass her in the hall, and say 'Excuse me' to my bloodthirsty old ancestor when we come home at night? I should have suspected John Emig as the murderer, after the passage in the book that mentioned his streak of bad luck."

"He blamed it on Huber, of course. Having the old man reject his son as a suitor for Anna Maria would intensify his hatred. But the cool effrontery of the man—to think of him sitting there pretending to deliberate about Huber's death. . . . I wonder if the other jurors suspected."

"No matter what they thought, they wouldn't betray him. There are still a clannish lot; back then, they would close ranks for one of their own against a stranger like Huber, especially since many of them shared John Emig's belief in witchcraft. To them he was an executioner, not a killer. He had rid the world of something evil."

"And then to take over Huber's farm the way he did. That's just plain stealing. Wouldn't you think his conscience would prevent him from profiting from his act?"

"I think I've got that figured out too." Andy freed her hand. "Give me that book, will you? The one Mrs. Adams sent."

Meg handed it to him, but after a one-handed struggle Andy gave it back.

"Look up the Emig genealogy for the mid-eighteenth century."

"Here it is. Old John; his wives. . . . Twenty-two children! Sixteen died young. . . . Eldest surviving son, Jacob, married Ann Friedland. . . . Oh, my God."

"Anna Maria von Friedland—Ann Friedland. The name Huber was too notorious. But she was the old man's heiress; that could be proved. What's the date of the marriage?"

"It's 1741. I don't understand. If she survived, how come they didn't find her? How could she marry the son of her grandfather's killer? Why do the books report her disappearance, but not the fact that she survived?"

"The last question is the easiest. Tragedies make sensational reading. The murders hit the newspapers, but the girl's reappearance was anti-climatic. And John Emig would make sure it wasn't publicized, or even known, outside this area. No one else was interested. She had no relatives to contest the disposal of her grandfather's property, and her lover was dead. Emig's neighbors would accept any story he told. Maybe they knew the truth; maybe they didn't want to know it. We'll never know for sure either, but I think it must have happened something like this.

"John Emig was a witch hunter, a wreaker of the Lord's vengeance. But he wasn't a cold-blooded killer. He had no reason to murder the girl. She had attended church; she was a brand that could be snatched from the burning. He had practical reasons for keeping her alive, too. His son wanted her and he wanted her farm. The night the others were killed, Anna Maria was abducted. They took her with them, kept her imprisoned in some isolated place—God knows, there were plenty such places. The whole family was in a conspiracy of silence. They worked on her for a whole year. Lecturing, reading from the Bible, thundering denunciations. . . . It would work eventually. We know how well it works; brainwashing is a modern word, but the process is as old as these hills. And I suspect she was not quite right in the head after what she had seen that night. She'd be easy prey. I'm surprised it took them that long."

"That's the most horrible thing I've ever heard," Meg said in a shaken voice. "It would have been better for her if she had been killed."

"You know what I find the most horrible part of the business? The things that were in the box with the sampler. The girl's entire former life, wrapped up and put away. Even the buttons off a murdered man's coat. They were silver, after all. Worth money. The necklace was vain adornment. Emig wouldn't want to see it on his daughter-in-law, but he was too thrifty to throw it away. That sickens me, somehow. The hypocrisy of the self-appointed saints of God. . . . But in a sense, Anna Maria Huber was dead when John Emig packed up her pitiful heirlooms. Maybe she found some pleasure in life afterward—bearing Jacob's children, tending his house. Jacob wouldn't care if his wife was a little feebleminded. It wasn't her mind he was interested in. Oh, Meg, don't agonize over her; don't cry. She's long dead."

"But not at peace," Meg muttered. "I know it's silly, but I can't help it. She was innocent. She never hurt anybody. And I feel so—guilty. There at the end, when we saw her, she was trying to get away. She was in the kitchen. If she hadn't seen me—if she hadn't fainted—she might have escaped. Her lover would have found her—"

"He might have found her anyway, if he'd kept his head and not copped out," Andy said. "Aren't we supposed to learn nice neat moral lessons from other people's miserable experiences? That anonymous soldier should be a lesson to me. He was her only hope. My God, she must have cowered in that room where they kept her, praying that somehow he'd find her and rescue her. Her romantic hero, the gallant soldier—who was too big a coward to live with his sense of failure. I'm sure the Emigs told her when he shot himself. That would have been the fatal blow for her. And I did the same thing, after I failed someone who asked for help. I tried to cop out too."

"If she hadn't seen me—"

"Damn it, Meg, haven't you been listening to me? Here I am baring my soul and making profound moral resolutions, and you keep harping about feeling guilty. That's a cop-out too—guilt. You can keep yourself so busy wallowing in self-disgust that you don't have the energy to act."

"She's not at rest," Meg said. "Her spirit—"

"There are no restless spirits here," Andy said. "There are no ghosts. There never were."

"You can't possibly believe these were hallucinations."

"No. Don't you understand what happened? We got a clue from Huber's journal, when he bragged about raising spirits. I wondered then; and at the last, when Anna Maria saw us, I knew. We were Huber's spirits, Meg. If you want to wallow in guilt, there's a good excuse. Indirectly, we were partially responsible for Huber's death. He saw us, just as we saw him—and boasted to his neighbors about his prowess in controlling the unknown. Want to shoot yourself now?"

Meg stared at him unbelievingly.

"I can't feel guilty about—are you serious, Andy? If you're right, then what happened was like a slip in time—"

"A fold in the fourth dimension," Andy said. "Two different centuries overlapped for a time—but I can't use that word. Time is meaningless. According to some theories, every event, every moment, coexists simultaneously. If we knew how to do it, we could plug in on any event in the past, because it's all out there—somewhen. I don't know what happens after death. I don't know about the soul. But I do know that what we saw was not Anna Maria's anguished ghost. It was the girl herself, as she was—experiencing pain and suffering that is done, over with, finished—a quarter of a millennium ago. Where she is now, I don't know. I prefer to think she's  .  .  .  all right. And I don't think she'll come back unless we let her."

"Then we won't. We're going to have enough problems."

"True. I'm broke, you know. Every cent I made on the last book went for medical expenses."

"Me, too."

"I'm not exactly a good risk emotionally. I might crack up again."

"I may not be finished with my old-type hallucinations."

A slow smile spread across Andy's face. "There's no use trying to get out of it, Meg. We're helpless. Sylvia's already made up her mind."